SEASON OF THE SICKNESS

SEASON OF THE SICKNESS

HARRY J VAUGHN

ISBN-13: 979-8-9872875-0-7 (paperback)
ISBN-13: 979-8-9872875-1-4 (hardback)
ISBN-13: 979-8-9872875-2-1 (ebook)

For information contact: www.harryjvaughn3.com

Printed in the United States of America

First printing edition 2022

10 9 8 7 6 5 4 3 2 1

SEASON OF THE SICKNESS

HARRY J VAUGHN

ISBN-13: 979-8-9872875-0-7 (paperback)
ISBN-13: 979-8-9872875-1-4 (hardback)
ISBN-13: 979-8-9872875-2-1 (ebook)

For information contact: www.harryjvaughn3.com

Printed in the United States of America

First printing edition 2022

10 9 8 7 6 5 4 3 2 1

Dedicated to my loved ones

Tick tack

Samuel Black is

Back

PROLOGUE

Summer of 1980

The deep August sun fell like a veil behind the line of southern oaks on the West end of Lost Lake. It was a temperate summer in Georgia that year, but this day particularly was unusually hot and humid. Too hot, James recalled as the group decided to head out of the city to cool off a few miles outside of town. An adventurous bike ride to the usual gathering place for kids to hang out until sunset while the teenagers stayed into the wee hours of the night drinking beer and losing their virginity under the moonlight.

All of thirteen years old, dark skin and oddly short for his age with knobby elbows and skinny calves, James Elba or 'Jimmy' as his friends called him, didn't get attention from the girls, or think much of them for that matter. When he did, it seemed he couldn't see them as more than just one of the guys. His friend Emma was the only one who ever really gave him the time of day. Somewhere deep down he knew he felt something for her beyond friends. But love or anything resembling it was something he didn't really believe in, as he watched a father whose abuse and alcoholism left his mother a shell of a person and their family in its wake.

Everyone else came from decent families, or so he thought, but no one really knows from the outside looking in. It's only when you bite into the apple that you see the fruit is truly rotten.

As James and his friends sat drying off along the lake shore on that hot late afternoon, Scotty was the first one to bring up the idea. He and Scotty had always been the closest out of the group. Scotty, the freckle-faced redhead who smashed an apple over his forehead once to prove he could make apple sauce. Scotty, who told the teacher he missed class because of an alien abduction. Scotty, who thought he could dig a hole to China until he broke a water line and flooded his parent's basement. The guy could make you laugh and question his sanity all at the same time.

Regardless of his escapades and infamous notoriety, all the others fell into place quickly and there was no turning back after that.

"Who wants to see the old Plantation?!" Scotty asked with fervor as James and the others all looked at each other with sudden nervous excitement. James knew of the legends which had inexplicably been at the forefront of his mind lately. Ghost stories really. A tale of a cruel slave master whose spirit remained upon the grounds after all these years. Stories upon stories had been told about people disappearing within the forest along the western edge of the old rice plantation outside of town. Even sightings of strange figures walking the grounds circulated in the web of local myth and legend. It was a place for the older teens to come and drink and make out or just cause

hell. For the younger kids, it was just a place of nightmares. A place James never wanted to see.

"I don't think so," James meekly chimed in, not being heard by the rest of the group who were already rising into an excited fury.

"They say he dug up something in the woods. Something that drove him mad," Scotty continued, building the energy into a concoction of terror and excitement.

"Those are just stories, the only thing he found in those woods is deer poop," Harold added, giving the group a little laugh. Always the overweight awkward kid trying to be funny and get attention. He was one of six children and seemed to find his uniqueness in making people laugh at his unusually bad jokes, but James knew it was more this time. He was scared. Just as scared as everyone else was and didn't want to admit it.

"Why don't you go see for yourself then if that's all he found," Scotty shot back.

"I don't gotta do nothin'," Harold replied, brushing off the challenge.

"It's okay if you're chicken," Scotty exclaimed as Harold now looked a bit cornered.

"I'll do it!" James shouted out, trying to impress Emma, the cute brunette with pigtails sitting across from him. The only girl of their group. A tomboy that loved to get dirty and ride bikes with the boys. Underneath the ripped coveralls and dirty fingernails there was something else though James could never stop thinking about. A spark his mom would call it. That's when you know you've found someone special, she would say.

He glanced over at Emma to see if she was impressed. Her eyes said she was, and that made James feel all the more like he was going to faint.

"What do I have to do?" he added, not understanding what he'd exactly gotten himself into.

"My brother told me. Okay first thing you have to do is stand at the window staring out over the western fields towards the forest," Scotty excitedly replied, throwing his hands in the air as if to emphasize the drama. "All alone in the upstairs bedroom where he died."

"Where who died?" Emma asked.

"Samuel Black," Scotty replied, "what are you, new?"

Emma rolled her eyes and tossed a rock into the lake. "You guys are crazy. We should just stay here."

"So, then what?" James asked ignoring Emma's advice, still trying to be the big man.

"You really want to know?" Scotty asked.

"I said I'd do it, didn't I?" James replied as Scotty looked back through his coke bottle glasses and a sly smirk exuding from the curl of his lip.

"Then...you have to say the words and tap your finger on the window." Scotty lowered his voice and seemed to extend the syllables like some scare fest host on late night cable television. "Tick tack...tick tack..."

He stared at James as he tapped his finger on the dock. "Tick tack tick tack Samuel black is coming back."

Scotty recited the phrase in a slow methodical rant. Then repeated it, the second time picking up the pace and volume a bit as he looked like a mad man.

"That's stupid," Harold interjected.

"Shut up, Harold. Scaredy cat," Scotty exclaimed. "Jimmy isn't scared like you, are ya, Jimmy?"

"Of course, I'm not," James answered but felt his throat almost close at the thought of standing alone in that house. "So, then what?" he added, feeling Emma's eyes upon him. He couldn't show he was scared like the others. Not now.

"Then Samuel Black will come back and show you what he found in those woods all those years ago," Scotty answered, wide-eyed with excitement as the moonwake cast its spotlight upon him.

"Yeah, your mom's underwear," Harold chimed in, laughing hysterically.

"You're not going to be laughing when you see what's really out there tonight," Scotty exclaimed, now more serious than before. "But don't forget to tap your finger on the window and stare towards the forest when you say the words. That's the most important part."

"What do you think is out there in those woods?" James asked as he could feel the hairs standing on the back of his neck.

Scotty just gave him a look as a sly grin grew on his face before taking off towards the trail. "Only one way to find out!"

***

The first sight of the plantation was one James would never forget. It was as if a mouth had sprung out of the ground and stood gaping, waiting for little children to walk inside. The teeth, of course, were only pillars on the dilapidated portico and the two windows curiously resembled eyes that seemed all too real as they peered down upon the group.

The grounds were severely overgrown as years of neglect had taken its toll. Strange paint laid around many of the windows and doors. A bluish green hue, one he knew from his mother. *Haint paint.* It was superstitious nonsense, supposed to protect one from evil spirits. Even as a young kid he was a pragmatist. A logical thinker who studied history and science and thought about things far beyond what his thirteen-year-old mind should have been thinking.

As he stared at the paint outline on the windows, he thought of the remnants of the old ways lingering in a modern world. James never put much stock into what he had heard about the old religions. Voodoo, hoodoo, or whatever you wanted to call it. To him it didn't make sense but right now he would take what he could get as he felt the finger of some ghost drawing itself down his spine.

"How am I supposed to know what room to go in?" James asked as Emma stood by his side, her arm nearly touching his. The tingle was almost electrifying as James stood in silent fright.

"Second floor, end of the hall, last door you see. You can't miss it," Scotty replied.

"How do you know?" Harold chimed in.

"My brother told me. They've all done it."

"Then why don't you do it?" Harold exclaimed.

"Yeah, why don't you do it?" Emma echoed Harold's sentiment, shooting Scotty a little glare.

"Who said I haven't," Scotty replied, practically puffing up his chest.

"Yeah, right," Harold said, waving a dismissive hand in the air.

"You don't believe me. Fine. I'll go next. Jimmy, you're up first though," Scotty said, while giving James a little pat on the back and handing him a flashlight out of his backpack. "Pretend it's a light saber."

James hesitantly grabbed the flashlight with a sweaty hand and held it out like a sword, feeling the beat of his pulse increase with each step closer to the front door. It was getting hard to swallow. The blackness within those windows seemed endless, like he was about to walk into some rip in time.

He went up the steps, hearing the boards creak beneath his feet, almost speaking to him as he walked across the front patio.

Looking back at the group, one person in particular caught his eye. Emma, stared back at him as if he were the bravest boy in the world. It was those eyes of hers and that smile he would take with him inside those dark hallways. It was the only way, he thought. He would do it for her.

Inside, the house seemed to awaken as he listened to the squeal of the large oak door closing behind him. He was alone now. More alone than he'd ever felt before in his life.

He turned and stood a moment in the large foyer. The moonlight illuminated the dusty marble floor and grand chandelier as it gently swayed overhead.

"Whoa," James uttered under his breath as he walked towards the large sweeping staircase. Even in this condition it was more amazing than anything he'd ever stepped foot in. His imagination turned back time as he pictured how beautiful this place once must have been.

"Come on, Jimmy!" Scotty's voice echoed from outside, followed by a couple pounds on the door. The sound startled him and snapped him out of his daydream, bringing him right back into a dark reality and the task at hand.

"I'm goin', I'm goin!" James yelled back, regaining his composure.

Heading upstairs, one cautious step at a time, he ran his hand up the dusty railing for balance as his knees felt a little weak. The red carpet-runner beneath his dirty Chuck Taylors looked almost like a river of blood, coming down from the top floor and flowing beneath him. He put the thought out of his mind as he stopped a moment and took a deep breath, reminding himself of Emma's eyes outside that front door watching him.

Upstairs, it was even darker as the light of the moon seemed to be swallowed up the farther down the hallway he went, past crumbling walls and torn red and gold wallpaper. Broken sconces intermixed with spray-painted graffiti made the place seem none too pleasant to say the least, as the door at the end now stared back at him.

It was just a room.

Nothing here was anything but what it seemed, he told himself over and over.

Just an old house. That's all it is.

Reaching out, James grabbed the small brass knob feeling as though he were about to step into another world. One where he might

not be able to come back from. He could feel the beads of sweat building on the back of his neck. They ran down and tickled his spine like a specter playing tricks on him. The air upstairs was stifling and had Emma not been outside, he would have probably turned around right there.

With a gentle twist of the knob, the door squealed open, and he peered inside the dimly lit room. A putrid moonlit space on the precipice of some other world. A space that many teenagers visited. Their mark forever seen as James stared at the graffiti scrolled across the walls, coupled with empty beer cans, broken bottles of liquor, and melted wax pooled in dark corners where the remnants of dozens of candles laid.

See, it's just a room, he told himself, as his eyes surveyed his surroundings. The small window ahead of him that faced the western field was just a few feet away. Below it, a chalk circle. Within it was the outline of some winged creature. Upon closer inspection, James deduced it was a cicada. The small-winged creatures that left their outer shell scattered over tree trunks after they shed it like a snake. Their sounds even at that very moment could be heard coming from the forest, penetrating the thin pane glass window, like a symphony of insects playing a fateful tune.

Around the outer perimeter of the circle were thirteen hieroglyphs which drew his curiosity, reminding him of something he saw in history class on ancient Egypt. But this wasn't class, and everything suddenly felt all too real as these were places and things his mother had taught him to stay away from.

The Devil feeds on your fear, James, she would tell him. Remember to never give into your fear. It is there and only there that the darkness can see you.

Stepping one foot into the circle James felt like a soldier preparing for battle. He wouldn't be afraid. He wasn't going to give in. He was better than that. He knew it. Even at the age of thirteen he felt somehow stronger than the others. Not just physically but mentally. If he could face his father in one of his drunken rages, he could face anything.

Standing within the circle, he placed his palm on the window trying to remember what Scotty had told him.

It's too late. Can't turn back now.

He stared out over the swaying field grass which once was the western rice fields. Just on the other side he could see the moonlit tree line, marking the edge of the forest over a hundred yards away. James imagined what it was like all those years ago. In the very place he was standing, a man of unspeakable horror stood and watched as people suffered in pain and torment. His own ancestors toiling away in the heat with breaking backs and blistered hands. But he felt beyond those fields something else laid. Something much worse than anything he could yet imagine.

Maybe sometimes death was better, he thought.

He took a deep breath and felt his throat close as he tried to swallow. His mouth felt like a desert. His tongue twisted within as the first syllables felt like he was swallowing glass.

"Tick tack...tick tack," he said, feeling his nerves pulse though his body as he began tapping his finger on the window, attempting to avoid the dead bugs and cobwebs. "Samuel Black is coming back," he whispered slowly and methodically as if reciting lines from a school play.

Only two more times.

"Tick tack, tick tack...Samuel Black is coming back," he repeated the second time quickly as if saying it fast enough would negate that it was ever said at all.

"Tick tack...tick tack…"

This is it.

He could barely speak, his throat dry as if he hadn't tasted water in days. He closed his eyes feeling the hardened callused hands of his father upon his neck. The smell of the liquor on his breath. The hatred in his eyes. Everything James was ever afraid of was standing before him. Opening his eyes, he said the final words.

"Samuel Black is…back."

CHAPTER 1

James Elba stood silently in front of the congregation, his hands clenched to the sides of the worn oak pulpit. The sweat beading on his brow dripped down his cheek as the sound of the little boy's toy tapping on the back of the pew rang through his head like a bell.

Tick Tack Tick Tack.

He hadn't thought about that night for a lifetime and yet here it was today, staring him in the face in the form of a little boy and his toy truck. A simple plastic truck. His mother unaware of what her son was actually doing as she hung on James' next words for this morning's sermon, oblivious to her child's actions beside her.

James straightened up and released his grip on the sides of the pulpit, his senses coming back as the room began to take its former shape and his mind turned back to the task at hand. He shot his white cuffs from beneath the dark navy-blue suit and loosened his black tie. His large stature always got attention as his broad shoulders and tall athletic build commanded respect, despite how he was now feeling on the inside.

"It is souls the Devil is after here. Not lives!" Pastor James cried out, shaking his head and hands as the neighborhood congregation bled sweat under the relic of an air conditioning unit struggling to cool the hot Los Angeles summer air.

The small Southern Baptist church sat quietly at the intersection of Crenshaw and Jefferson, just south of the ten in central Los Angeles. An area that had been in full recovery mode since the riots as the congregation did anything and everything they could to assist in the rebuilding of the neighborhood.

Charity fundraisers, neighborhood cleanup crews, free drug and alcohol counseling. It all was at the heart of the message of salvation. One for which their leader, a former medical doctor now pastor, James Elba, fought so boldly to maintain. He was a man that seemed unbreakable within the confines of the darker corners of the city of angels. A place and people at war with themselves seemed something he could understand. The inner struggle, like a virus eating away at the good that is left within the body.

It had been years since he had given up practicing medicine to follow the calling to serve his Lord. To heal the greater sickness, he would call it. The true virus at the heart of humanity. It was not with pills and surgery he would heal this plague, but with the word of God.

"What shall we find within our own hearts if we were to see its true nature?" Pastor James spoke out to the crowd packed tightly in the modest sanctuary. Each face gazed upon him with hope and desire as they hung on his every subtle inflection.

He looked out over the congregation as if waiting for an answer, allowing the question to sink into their minds. The Southern

Baptist church he had come to love with all his heart was everything and more to him, despite what his own atheist father would have thought. A veteran of the Vietnam war, James remembered all too clearly his father insisting that this world had no God.

A man whose horrors would haunt him until the day he died, would never let his own son accept any grand architect. The kaleidoscope of tragic events burned into his psyche left no room for any benevolent deity. 'God ain't here son' he would tell him as the whiskey wafted past the nose of his eight-year-old self. His father's breath was like a foundry of liquor and hardship and still to this very day he could not smell the sweet-honeyed scent of bourbon without being reminded of these trying moments so long ago.

Growing up in the South, James was no stranger to the plight of the times, and it was both outside and inside those walls situated on Waters Avenue in Savannah that a madness seemed to ensue, rising like some unseen force wrapping its hands around everything and everyone he loved. The area was a far cry from the large Victorian mansions that lined Victory Drive and he wished nearly every night that one day he'd be the one sitting out on the front porch of one of those architectural marvels. Until then he just put up with the violence that grew within his world as he sat up in bed listening to police sirens outside accented by the sound of broken dishes and screaming inside while his mother attempted to calm a husband resembling more a beast than a man.

She was the gentlest woman and was not prepared for the man that came back from the war. Each night James heard it all. Took it in like a sponge soaking up the last of life's breath not knowing that one day those very moments would define his own life in more ways than one.

As a boy he would wait until the chaos subsided then cautiously walk out of his room and tip toe softly down the long hallway. The floorboards creaking beneath his feet would stop him in his tracks, to keep from getting caught. But he never did.

Looking around the corner he would see his father standing alone staring at the wall. The rest of the room would be in chaos, his mother's tears still wet upon the floor as he watched the face of his father like a stone statue devoid of life staring into some black hole from which there seemed to be no return.

He would often stand for quite some time and imagine what his father was looking at. At first, he didn't understand. The war seemed too complex for an eight-year-old boy. But as he grew, he realized that a piece of his father never really came home and what was left standing there alone was not his father anymore. Instead, he had been replaced with something else altogether, some unknown darkness that grew darker with each passing day.

He wanted to love his father for the man he knew he was, but as the years grew and his mother's tears became something he could no longer bear to see, his own perception began to change. His love and forgiveness were replaced with his own special kind of hatred and animosity. But he would not allow his father to take him to that place. That dark place where nothing lives and memories turn to hate, sorrow and regret. The place where human souls go to die. Where a man no longer is a man but a shell devoid of things that once made him human.

The rot that ate away at the inside of their marriage was the same that ate away at his soul. Something that never really healed, even after his mother's passing.

His father would remember the woman he loved in a different way. People seem to see things differently after death he thought. As if a mirror was no longer held to his face and he was no longer forced to look at the tragic monster he had become. Instead, he would talk of things like the day they met. Their first dance at a little bar outside of Waco, Texas, where he was stationed after the war. The way she used to roll her eyes whenever he said something funny or the way she smiled when he held her in his arms. He did not remember the bruises, the screams, the tears. It was as if whatever evil held him within those moments had died with her and he was just a sad old man, attempting to put together memories of a life too far gone to make any sense of.

On the day of her funeral, James could still remember the color of the leaves on the southern sugar maple in Laurel Grove Cemetery as he sat quietly staring at the light brown oak casket being lowered into the hard Georgia clay. He wished he could somehow have given her some comfort before leaving this world. He did not understand where she was now, but he would always cherish the stories she would tell from her King James bible with the tattered and worn cover she kept in a dresser hidden from his father's eyes.

It wouldn't be until many years later that those words written in red would come back and remind him that there was something much bigger than himself transpiring underneath his very eyes and that thing was a seven-pound, five-ounce little angel.

Standing at the pulpit, James stared down at the worn pages of his mother's old King James bible, remembering the day his daughter was born and how his mother never got to meet her. She would have loved her so much. Her soft, precious skin and gentle smile is what told him that he was meant for a greater calling. That medicine alone wasn't the only answer to saving lives.

He looked up, staring out at the congregation as he clenched the bible feeling it in his hand as if it were about to fall and crack into a million pieces. His eyes began to water as a sudden and intense emotion of something he hadn't felt in quite some time rushed over him. Sadness and pain rose upward as if his very world had suddenly just shifted.

"I'm sorry," he said in a low sullen tone, "I wish you all a wonderful Sunday and God bless." He caught his wife's concerned eyes from across the room as he cut the morning's service short and slipped offstage, out the side door.

James headed for the bathroom feeling suddenly ill. He just needed to be alone and quickly closed the door behind him, but it was too late. Karen was already there, poking her nose in, staring into his bloodshot eyes with nervous worry.

"Honey?" she said, drawing a hand across his back as the sweat poured down off his neck.

He did not say a word but merely grasped the side of the sink as if he were about to rip it off the wall.

"James, you're worrying me. Did you take your pill?" Karen asked as he looked up, seeing her in his smudged reflection, her blonde hair and blue eyes staring back at him with anxious concern.

He was deadly silent, staring back down at his trembling hands, one of which clenched a pill bottle.

"I'm out...but I'll be fine," he replied, dropping the small plastic container on the floor.

"Then we need to get that refilled. I thought it had been years since you needed one of those. You should have plenty."

"I flushed them."

"You what?" Karen gasped.

"I just held onto the bottle to remind me I have the strength. I don't need the pills anymore."

"You can't let these panic attacks control you like this and it's not weakness to admit you need help. Those pills help."

"They mess with my head," James replied, taking a deep breath, going through his silent routine of counting his breaths. *One, two, three, four...*

"You need to go back to the doctor," Karen insisted.

James swallowed hard as he held on for dear life, feeling as if his heart were going to pound out of his chest. "Where's Elizabeth?" he asked, feeling the concern for his daughter rise within.

"She's with Tiffany. They went to the mall."

He stood silently a moment, not sure what he was really thinking. Thoughts spun out of control as he found himself tapping his finger on the side of the sink.

Tick tack tick tack...

James quickly turned around as if running away from whatever thought had just crept up. "I'm gonna lay down. I just need to rest a minute, I think," he said, then kissed his wife on the forehead and slipped past her into his office.

He laid down and could only stare back in silence as she stood helpless in the doorway with growing concern. He did not know what to say to make it all better as a fear rose within that he hadn't felt in a very long time.

***

James lay alone on the worn black leather sofa he had been toting along through the years, something Karen didn't want in the house. It had been relegated to his office, as it was there that he spent many late nights anyway.

The door was slightly ajar as a warm breeze brushed past his face feeling like fingers drawing themselves upon his skin. His heart had slowed, which calmed him, but the feeling of electricity that ran over his body forced him to get up and shake off the moment before it drove him into madness.

"Get it together," James whispered under his breath as he headed to his desk and sat staring down at the scribbled notes for next Sunday's service. He tapped his pen on the table.

Tick tack, tick tack.

The sound was unbearable, and he threw the pen across the room and pushed himself away from the desk.

He hadn't had a panic attack in years, so why now? He had forgotten something. Moments, hid within his past causing such terror and pain that he had to bury them so deep as to never let them see the light of day again. But suddenly something peeked out of that darkness. And it was as simple as a child tapping his toy truck on the back of the pew during this morning's service that opened the door.

Tick tack, tick tack.

He hadn't thought of that night in so long; he didn't know if it were even real. That's when the panic attacks had started, but he still couldn't understand why. He only saw the faintest image of a moment standing at an upstairs window in that old plantation by the lake with Scotty, Harold and Emma outside, waiting for him. God, how could he have forgotten about Emma?

Those green eyes.

He didn't remember much else, only that his life was somehow never the same after that night. How had he forgotten until today? He laid there quietly, trying to put the pieces together, as he continued his breathing exercises, but nothing else came of it. The memory was as black as a starless night sky. But something else was in that darkness calling him and wouldn't let him go so easy.

Then he heard it! Just a note at first. Then two, three, and the first phrase completed. The song slowly unfolded within his mind.

Moonlight sonata.

The same song his mother used to frequently play on the old upright piano in their living room. He was remembering more. Hidden for years, now here it was. Notes of an old piano whispering forgotten memories within. Phrases of music guiding him down a path he wasn't sure he really wanted to go. You can't unsee what you have seen...but what did he really see? It was all just a blur.

Suddenly the sound of piano keys turned into the steady ring of a black rotary phone. The thought that he'd been there his whole life waiting for this call shot through his mind and by the time he picked up the receiver his hand was already shaking. His own breath felt heavy and the air thick. He was having trouble breathing and he could barely speak. The world around him, a distant echo. His voice trembled as he attempted to reply.

"I'll be right there."

***

Pulling up to a chaotic scene in front of the mall entrance, James stopped his car in the middle of the road and got out, making his way through the crowd.

The scene was surreal as the disillusion and pain boiled to the surface, accented by the red and blue lights passing rhythmically over his eyes. He felt his heart slow down as if the blood no longer ran through his veins and his body was just an empty void.

"James!" a woman's voice rang out.

He turned to see Rosemary; the mother of his daughter's friend Tiffany, whom Elizabeth was supposed to be with. She was standing in tears, sobbing uncontrollably at the edge of yellow police tape, her arms wrapped tightly around her daughter.

James attempted to push his way through the crowd before being pushed back by a rather large officer at the edge of the yellow tape.

"He's, her father!" Rosemary screamed in tears as the officer stood back seeming unsure of what to do next.

"Sir, you don't have to be here," the officer exclaimed as James glanced over his shoulder, seeing his reality rip apart before his very eyes.

Hi Daddy...

He could still hear his daughter's voice as the last breath upon his lips hung onto her name.

"Lizzy?" he whispered softly as he stared down at a child's hand protruding from the plastic sheet, they had laid across the pavement to hide the body beneath. Upon the wrist, the familiar silver charm bracelet his daughter wore every day. Each birthday a new charm would be added. Now it was complete, he thought not fully comprehending what he was really seeing.

"It was a drive by shooting," Rosemary forced out the words still unable to look him in the eye as she held her daughter pressed to her side. "Stray bullet. It was just a stray bullet."

His legs nearly buckled as he watched detectives examine the crime scene. The movement of it all seemed slow as if time seeped out of an old grandfather clock ticking away the final hours of his life.

He clutched his mother's bible in his left hand. His fingers felt numb, the book heavy. He wanted to drop it and let the moment pass him by like a cargo train carrying its load to some unknown destination never to return. But whatever this was, it was his to bear.

"She was only twelve," he whispered under his breath.

"Sir," the officer's voice passed by him like an echo within a fishbowl. The syllables warbled inside with no recognition of the meaning.

His stare remained vacant looking right past the officer's shoulder and into the eyes of Tiffany standing with her mother. The scene was now drawing quite a crowd as the many afternoon shoppers stopped to gaze upon the dead girl before they went home to their families and thanked God it wasn't their child.

"Sir! Can you hear me?" the officer's voice rang like a bell finally catching his attention. He looked back into the officer's eyes with no acknowledgement of any kind. He did not hear a word, only a sound. A sharp piercing sound suddenly ringing inside his head.

"Sir! I need you to please step away, you don't need to see this," the officer stated as James stood frozen against the edge of the yellow tape.

The pool of blood looked almost surreal, like a canvas forming abstract images within a cloud. He could swear he could see the shape of a wavering palmetto. The tall ones that lined the streets of his hometown of Savannah. Their leaves fanned out, blocking streaks of sunlight passing by corners of old brick buildings.

The sounds of the city muffled his thoughts as he heard his daughter's voice calling to him from some dark place, he couldn't see...

Daddy?

"Sir, please. I need you to come with me," the officer took him by the arm and walked him slowly away from the scene to the patrol car.

"James!" Karen's voice rang out through the crowd. "James!"

Karen ran to her husband, wrapping her arms around his neck. Her tears exuded more madness than sorrow.

"Where is she, James? Where is she?!"

He couldn't answer, staring his wife in the eye; he could not say a word. Something before this moment he had never really felt before. Since he was a boy, his mother had always told him of his gift of speaking to people. A calmness that ran through his soul. As a doctor, he gave his patients hope and comforted those that needed it the most. As a man of God, he did the same but in the light of different sun. One that burned brighter than he had ever seen before. But now it was dim and so was his gift to comfort the one that needed him most.

Karen turned to the officer; her eyes lit with fire.

"What happened to my baby?!" she screamed as James held her back from getting any closer to the scene.

He held her tight against his chest. She tried to move, to run, but could not break past his strength, all two hundred pounds of him holding her back from something she should not ever see. The image was his to bear and he alone would be the one to carry it with him. She would share the pain, but she would not bear witness to the blood.

She shook in his arms, shivering uncontrollably. He raised her head. Their lips, only inches apart. Her lips quivered and her skin felt ice cold. She was pale, as if a sickness had descended upon her. The blood was wanting to leave her body. The pain, rotting her from the inside out.

It moves quickly, he thought.

He did not see nor feel God within that moment, nor would he ever be the same man again. A pastor whose light would forever be dimmed upon this earth. The heart of his faith now held within some distant void watched over by a caretaker whose presence felt all too sinister.

Years of faith gave no reprieve to the madness growing inside him. There was no voice telling him she was in a better place. There was nothing but the silent echo of his wife's cry and the feeling of her wet cheek pressed against his.

The summer sun shone, but he did not feel its warmth. The world spoke but he did not hear its echo. So, it was there at that moment Pastor James R. Elba stood silent under an overcast Los Angeles sky holding his wife in his arms and with a single thought denounced God and everything he once held sacred.

CHAPTER 2

The sweat poured down James' face as the humid air gave him no reprieve from this night's unexpected escape into the woods.

Visibility was like a maze of shadows as the clouds passed by the waning yellow moon, giving a sickly light to his path. He felt himself push harder, faster; his legs ached, and his mind spun so fast it was almost as if he weren't thinking at all.

Why? was the only thing running through his mind now.

Why me, why us?

The pain and suffering reminiscent of Job's hardship as God and the Devil played a supernatural game of thrones. Testing one's power over a mortal's life. A life that he once loved. He once had it all. But nothing was the same now. Nothing was what he expected it to be. Not anymore. He had seen too much and could no longer turn back to the life that once was.

As he passed through the outer forest of oaks, the moonlight seemed to open up the shadows and give way to a different forest altogether. The thicker oaks and sycamores changed into tall thin trunks covered in knots reminiscent of eyes. *Birchwood.*

Its knotted pupils followed his every move, asking him why he had come so far. He slowed down as if knowing he was close. Close to what he did not know until he suddenly emerged into the clearing, he never wanted to believe was real.

The circle itself was unnatural. Just dull chalk with a reddish hue as if a hint of blood was added to its mix. It was out of place here. It didn't belong in this world, and neither did he.

The clearing was no more than fifty feet in diameter and the inner chalk circle half that. The light seemed dimmer here. The air, colder. A scent of rotted meat wavered in the air.

James leaned over feeling queasy as the taste of vomit stung the back of his throat. The taste of bile and acid made him nauseous and dizzy. He had run for what felt like hours to get here. An unholy place he never thought was real. But here it was, drawing him back like a bad tarot card. The demons now at his back were nothing compared to what lay before him, buried deep within the sour Georgia clay. A place where the moon could not shine, and the darkness was thick as oil. You could feel it on your skin here. Feel the pain and suffering that had taken place hundreds of years before.

It was nothing more than a large circular clearing in a forest. A place where life could not grow; the soil no longer capable of carrying the formula. But it held something else now; a secret, buried deep within the earth itself. He had heard rumors that whatever lay here had been here long before the twisted soul of a man who ran this plantation had unburied it on that hot Georgia night so long ago.

Unfortunately, what he had discovered should have stayed buried. It should have been left within the earth to rot and never see the light of day. But it was hungry, and it had to feed.

As James stood wide eyed, dripping in sweat, he stared down at the ground before him and could almost hear its thoughts within his mind. Not the mind of the man he was, but of the boy who had been here all those years ago. A boy who had seen things he never should have seen.

This place wasn't supposed to be here. It wasn't supposed to be real. It was just a child's nightmare. But he was a man now and he had returned. Back to the place where it all began. Back to where the Devil knew his name.

***

James awoke in a cold sweat staring out the smudged, cracked, paned glass window overlooking Gaston Street as the nightmare and its memory drew back to the darkness from which it came. The tall palmettos stood still in the early morning light. The sway of the Spanish moss on the ancient southern oaks were all but silenced in their dance as the morning unfolded to a new day.

It had been a month since they had buried Elizabeth next to James' mother in that small white casket in Laurel Grove Cemetery here in Savannah. A place which his mother would often brag about housed some of Savannah's most prominent residents and one day would house her, too. It was always a morbid thing to say, James thought, but he remembered how fondly his mother would talk about it as if it were the only thing she had to look forward to.

He and Karen were staying in a quaint sixteen-room mansion in the heart of the city. The Inn at the Dresser Palmer House was in and of itself the essence of everything James had missed about the south and why they chose to spend the extra money on staying there while they looked for a home in the very place where he grew up.

Tucked away in the historic district, it was only a few miles away from a clinic in which James would be working part-time as one of the local physicians. The old-world charm and history in the area seemed to be locked in time and preserved like a ghost trapped in a mirror, staring back reminding him of how elegant and how dark life once was.

Back to his roots, he thought. Back to something that made sense. Something he could control. Science and medicine. He was looking forward to the normalcy of the job and he needed to get back into a daily routine.

***

James could have driven to work but he enjoyed the fresh air as he strolled through the town square almost like a tourist. Things weren't the same anymore with Karen and a morning walk helped him focus and clear his mind.

There was something growing between them. A dark void that had opened and with every moment, felt her slip further away, but didn't have the strength to save her. Just like he didn't have the strength to save anyone anymore. The congregation he had left behind felt like a group of children he had abandoned. The thought of God and everything that had transpired since the day he saw his little girl's lifeless body laying beneath that plastic sheet on dirty concrete made him question a heaven that in his heart, now felt did not exist. He attempted to move on and live as if a piece of him wasn't missing, but every day, felt that emptiness inside his heart.

They had been in Savannah only a month and already a subtle peace rose within as he strolled past the large sun filtered oaks hanging with Spanish moss in the adjacent cemetery on Abercorn Street. Cracked and weathered statues basking in the morning light, watched closely as he passed. Their eyes lifeless yet somehow a spirit still lay buried deep within them. Something James felt since he was a boy.

The large arched gateway of Colonial Park Cemetery reminded him of taking shortcuts as a boy, through the quiet empty grounds. His heart, racing as he hurried home late for dinner, feeling like at any moment a hand was going to reach up from a grave and pull him under. The dates of many of the deceased going back hundreds of years. Headstones, mausoleums, and statues of the forgotten ones. He recalled the thousands of souls stricken with yellow fever. Some were even buried alive. Nails found broken off and driven into the underside of the pine tops. A thought he could almost empathize with as he often felt just the same. Trapped in a nightmare, scratching, and clawing to get out.

James had wandered a bit off his normal path this morning. His mind, getting the better of him. The rumination not giving way. Thoughts of what he could have done. What he should have done to keep his Elizabeth safe.

As he passed a massive angelic statue covered in layers of time sitting on the outer edge of the cemetery, he thought about that place…that other place in which his little girl now lay. Like a prison for souls frozen in time, it was something he realized surprisingly that he did not understand and didn't even want to anymore.

He stopped a moment and stared through the space in the iron fence. As he stared into that place where the dead lay, it gave him no feeling of peace but rather an emptiness which continued to grow. Suddenly what was once looked at as a place of rest now seemed like a sour plot of earth where bodies lay to rot.

There was nothing beautiful about it. Put up all the statues and elaborate stone monuments you wanted but still underneath it all was just death.

He could feel the panic within begin to rise as he gripped the hot iron gates. The cold sweat. The heavy beat of his heart. Sweaty palms and a dizziness swelling within. His mother always did a good job at calming down the panic attacks, but she had long since passed.

He began the ritual of counting his breaths as the panic was just a splinter for now. But it was enough to be afraid of the large crack it could turn into and without his pills he was on his own.

Nothing to worry about. Nothing at all.

Continuing down Abercorn he let the dark thoughts drift away as he remembered what he loved so much about this place. The uneven ballast stone streets down by the Riverwalk. The way the late summer sun shown off the old brick buildings, the streetlamps, and sidewalks lined with live oaks draped with Spanish moss coupled with rows of palmettos interspersed along the sidewalk. A place where the past seemed to never die and the spirit of the human soul could walk for eternity.

Mostly keeping to himself and no longer in the business of God, he found himself almost back where he started as a young man out of med school wondering what the future might hold.

He stopped a moment staring up at the tall bronze statue of James Oglethorpe guarded by the shielded lions. The squares of the city all had their unique appeal but this one he especially liked. Everything was familiar yet new, like his eyes were adjusting to a dark room slowly coming back into focus.

He felt the past today more than others. *Thinner.* That's what his mother would have said. When two worlds exist side by side, sometimes it's only a thin sheet that separates them. Despite his mother's outwardly Christian presence later in her life, deep within still lay the local ways she was raised in. The stories of Baron Samedi and the voodoo culture brought in from the old country. She never talked about those stories much, but James knew of their presence. He could feel them in the air when he walked by the local shops with windows full of powders, potions, and elixirs or passing an alley marked with the symbols he had recognized from his youth. None of it really made any sense to him and even as a boy felt it all something he didn't care for. But as dark as the history that rested beneath these Southern Oaks was, it was still good to be home.

Passing by an old corner grocery store, James paused a moment as if something suddenly told him to do so. Dozens of colorful flyers pinned to a reader board beside the door fluttered in a light breeze. He stood and stared at the collage filled with local listings of real estate, autos, babysitting, and any other service one could possibly want. An old world mixed with the new as lost religions seemed to still hold their grips within a community on the edge of strife. A flyer for drug and alcohol counseling, A psychic promising fortunes untold, adds for voodoo elixirs to heal a broken heart or a broken wallet along with dozens of other odds and ends. A mix of strife and struggle, magic and mystery, voodoo and hoodoo that made this area what it was.

Suddenly the bell on the front door broke his gaze. Looking over, he gave a little nod to an old lady with a head of curly white hair who was walking out with a small handbag. She looked up and smiled with a large mouth of crooked yellowed teeth.

"Welcome home, Jimmy. You look more and more like your father every day," she said in a low raspy tone.

"Excuse me," James replied feeling his stomach suddenly sink wondering if he heard her right. "Do you know me?"

The little old lady just shook her head and gave him a smile. Her mouth was now completely normal. Just a line of straight dentures.

He stood there dumbfounded noticing a small silver brooch upon her blouse. A cicada...

He leaned in to look closer as she nervously turned away and continued down the sidewalk as if he were the odd stranger.

"Hey!" he yelled again, feeling a sudden dread rise up inside of him.

He could only watch as she disappeared around the corner. His thoughts ruminated on the encounter.

Jimmy.

Yes, that's what she said. He could have sworn it. Then just as he was about to turn and continue on his day, there within the collage of flyers was a picture. A familiar picture. One that he swore wasn't there before. But here it was as if it were taken out of a dream...or maybe a nightmare. A piece of his past back to welcome him home.

Looking closer, he gazed upon a wrinkled flyer emblazoned with a heading for the deal of a lifetime. Below it a photograph of an old run down, boarded up plantation. A sales listing claiming the price was too good to be true. **CALL NOW!**

He recognized the place all too well. The old plantation on the outskirts of town. Wrapped within its own dark lore James remembered the stories as a boy. There were things that happened at that house. *Bad things*. But it was just a house, and he wasn't a boy anymore. Taking a closer look at the picture it looked like it could barely stand let alone terrorize a whole generation of children. Whatever it was, it was old and on its last leg. Even as a boy it had been abandoned for as long as he could remember. There was talk of renovations by different parties but for some reason it always stayed empty. Uncared for and unkempt after all these years.

The work was sure to take years he surmised as he looked closer at the recent photograph. The structure looked like bones draped with a layer of cracking flesh ready to peel off. The once elegant antebellum architecture withering away as a world that had all but left it behind sat aside to watch it decompose into the bloodied soil from whence it came.

Six enormous front columns, cracked and worn like elder statesmen dead upon their once regal throne, stood as watchman upon the front stoop. Their bases were overgrown with ivy like tentacles from some mythic Lovecraftian tale. The dirty smudged windows were broken out and the rest of the property looked just as disheveled. The ad had only a single front exterior picture, almost like a self-portrait. A rotted corpse that had been picked over by centuries of neglect and was coming back from the dead calling his name.

Welcome home, Jimmy.

Unusually excited, James let the moment sweep him up like an easterly wind carrying a new day upon its back.

He would face his fears and immerse himself in something real and tangible. Nothing to lose and nothing to bring him down except his own will. Certainly, Karen would feel the joy of getting her hands within the soil and making it her own. He convinced himself it was just what she needed, too. A big project to take her mind off things. A place they could make their own and call home while staying busy, rebuilding more than the house but their own lives alongside it.

He was surprised at himself by the sudden desire but the overlapping thought of a black man owning an old rice plantation seemed fitting enough to give him some sense of transformation already. A piece of the South's dark past once draped in the blood of his ancestors reminding him every day how far society had come since those distant days. He would bleed himself next to their memory. He would put his life's blood into that house and make it a home. A place where Karen could feel safe, out in the country where new life could flourish.

But somewhere within that picture he could see the scared boy staring out that upstairs window. More pieces of the memory were coming back, and he remembered the night he and his friends ran for their lives. A memory he had buried so deep that he had forgotten that it was even real. He really didn't know anymore. Whatever happened in those woods behind the old plantation he had left there that night unable to carry such a burden upon his back. But here it was, staring him in the face, welcoming him home. A home where the dying happened, and the dead called his name.

CHAPTER 3

They drove together in silence. James glanced over at Karen with anxious concern as if he were a child needing his mother's acceptance. Deep down he knew this was his fate and Karen, whether she saw it or not, would have to accept they both needed this in their lives to heal. He could already feel the hammer in his hands, the sweat on his brow, day after day forgetting what they lost and rebuilding something they could see and feel. Something they could truly call home. Their healing was locked up within the old bones of the plantation and somewhere inside that front door they would find their salvation. Perhaps he might even find his faith once again.

He watched her eyes grow more vacant with every mile, wondering where she was behind that distant stare. If she was anywhere at all or perhaps just drifting in some void, ripped ever wider with each passing moment.

He hoped she would use this change to mark a new beginning as he had gotten all too used to finding her alone in a dark bedroom lost within some novel attempting to escape to another world as this one seemed all but vanquished before her. A translucent fog now shadowing her once vibrant glow, but despite how long this dark shroud seemed to linger, he could still see the girl he fell in love with all those years ago.

James quickly slowed down the car, almost flying right by the two cracked stone cherubim still standing resolute upon their posts at the head of the long gravel driveway. His heartbeat was very noticeable as he turned off the main highway passing through a broken wrought-iron gate where a crooked 'For Sale' sign slanted to the side like an old scarecrow left alone in the fields.

The driveway ran for a couple hundred yards flanked by majestic southern oaks dripping with beautiful Spanish moss. The sun glistened through its tendrils as the plantation stood astute off in the distance just as he remembered it. A once vibrant estate left to die, withering away with each passing day leaving only the shell of a place that once was. Obviously why the price was too good to be true. After all these years the stigma of the old mansion still left a bad taste in folks' mouths like a rotting carcass left in the summer sun.

The large columns came into view as James saw them with new eyes. He remembered them as foreboding but today they just seemed sad. The tall, massive pillars caught the late afternoon Georgia sun, looking as if they were struggling just to stand. The front portico was covered in dirt and debris and the cracked and faded front door waited for its much-anticipated guests to arrive.

Standing beside a blue Cadillac was a middle-aged woman with a leather folder held by her side. James recognized her picture from the flyer. Her serious yet inviting nature gave rise to a certain level of comfort in such a big life decision. Greeting them with a smile, she leaned over, giving them a little wave as the car came to a halt just behind hers.

Looking over at Karen, James waited a moment as she didn't seem to want to get out. Her eyes scanned the front of the house, avoiding the real estate agent eyeing her from only a few feet away.

"Just take a look. Please," James pleaded, watching his wife struggle to cope with the current situation.

She turned to him, staring with the same eyes he had gotten all too used to. He could only look back with subtle trepidation rising within as if the entire decision weighed heavy on his mind. The cost of it all. The move. The numbness that was a whisper upon his back. Was he ready to take on something like this? Could he even? *Could she?*

The answer lay deep within Karen's bloodshot eyes as she stared back at her husband in silent response. He could see she needed him more than ever and he would walk her every step of the way if he had to. He would because she was all he had left in this world. The last piece of his soul staring back at him, asking for one good reason to go on another day.

Taking her hand in his, he felt her soft pale skin. The contrast held within his dark palm made her look all the more vulnerable as if she were only air cupped within. The most subtle movement and she would be gone. Closing her hand in his, James smiled and leaned forward. His mouth gently pressed against her soft pink lips.

She closed her eyes as they held that moment. His thoughts drifted back to days when a kiss was only routine. Now it felt like at any moment it could be their last. Her skin was soft as silk, coupled with a wafting aroma of lavender that made him remember how much he loved the woman still by his side. As they drew apart, he could see she remembered too. Even if just for a moment.

James got out first and walked around and helped his wife out of the car.

"Well, if chivalry ain't dead! James and Karen...Ain't it just a peach to meet you both," Richelle Merryweather, the local realtor with big blond hair and long red nails, held out her hand with a smile and spoke boldly in a heavy southern accent. James quickly shook her hand while Karen seemed pre-occupied staring up at the large columns before her.

"Quite a sight, ain't she?" Richelle boasted. "Isn't it just lovely? Don't make em' like they used to," she added with an almost fake grin, yet James felt her salesmanship harmless. "So, where'd you folks move from?" she continued, looking as if she sensed the sudden stale silence.

"Los Angeles," James replied, catching his eyes wandering off inside the dirty broken windows.

"City of Angels! Ain't that just a kick in the pants. What brings ya to our lovely state?"

James took a moment, glancing at Karen still staring off at the house.

"Just wanted a little change that's all," he replied sensing the half-truth mixed with a hidden pain that he wasn't yet ready to share with a complete stranger.

"Oh, I can imagine! Never been to L.A. myself, just seen all the stuff on television, ya know? Love Young and the Restless, I just can't get enough. How exciting to live right there in Hollywood," she rambled on, as if the enthusiasm would somehow translate into a sale.

James just smiled, his look exuding a certain reluctance to continue the small talk.

"Well…why don't we head on in so you can see her for yourself."

Karen lingered behind a moment as Richelle fumbled with the lock box.

"These things can be a real pain sometimes. Gotta get em' just right."

A sudden click and the key popped from the bottom. Turning back, she shot James and Karen a quick smile before she unlocked the door releasing the smell of dust and stale air.

James hesitated a moment then stepped inside before realizing his wife was still standing outside staring at the perimeter of the front door.

"Honey?" James called out as he looked back with sudden concern. "You coming?"

She didn't answer, but only stared. Her eyes lost within some vision beyond his own line of sight.

Stepping back outside, he followed her gaze seeing the source of her interest. A chalky bluish green paint around the perimeter of the front door.

James looked closely at the peculiar substance circling the doorway then glanced up at Richelle with a curious gaze.

"Ah yes...old superstitions die hard I'm afraid," she nonchalantly exclaimed.

"What is it?" Karen asked, suddenly seeming all too pre-occupied with the strange matter.

"Haint paint," James chimed in as if seeing a ghost from the past.

"A bit of nonsense I'm afraid," Richelle added, looking around at the doorway. "Well...if you believe in that sort of thing. Then I guess not. Personally, I never gave much stock to the superstitions of religions that cut the heads off chickens and read old bones as if they were the nightly news." Richelle gave out a little laugh as James and Karen didn't seem to be at all amused.

Karen stepped up silently running her hand over its surface as James watched her with particular interest.

"It's put there for protection. It's said that evil spirits can't travel over water and that color is meant to symbolize just that." James spoke quietly next to Karen's ear.

"Protection from who?" she replied, as James seemed a bit caught off guard with the question.

"Well..." Richelle looked as though she were thinking about how to answer a question such as this when James interrupted.

"Haints' are restless spirits of the dead who have not moved on from the physical world and exist in an...in-between space you might say. Haint blue is meant to keep those spirits from entering."

"Or leaving," Karen added, seeing the paint was also on the inside of the door, now seeming disturbed by the idea and took a step back.

"That's strange," James whispered, running his fingers over the paint.

"This place is as quiet as a church mouse on Sunday. No ghosts here," Richelle replied with a little forced grin as she welcomed her guests into the house with a grand gesture.

The cracked marble flooring was covered in a layer of heavy dust as they stepped inside, leaving footprints behind them.

"Place just went up on the market, so still need to get a cleaning crew to spruce it up a bit," Richelle commented in her most salesman-like voice. "You two are the first lucky ones to see her in all her fallen glory."

Up ahead a grand staircase swept to the right and wound up and around, disappearing to the second floor. Overhead an elegant chandelier glistened in the late afternoon sun as teardrop crystal prisms reflected tiny shards of light across the balcony and walls.

"Ya just need a little imagination to see its amazing potential but unfortunately the light reveals all," Richelle exclaimed, while running a finger across a dusty table.

"Excuse me?" James asked. His interest suddenly peaked, staring her in the eye.

"The light." She pointed up. "You can't hide anything from the light. No matter what, when that sun shines through that upper window, every spec of dust is front and center. I swear it looks like heavens on fire raining down ashes upon us. Place needs a woman's touch, though," she added, glancing at Karen. "Come on, you two, follow me."

The echoes of their footsteps sounded distant as they walked through the grand foyer. The cracked black and white marble flooring reminded James of a large chess game. He found himself wondering what piece he might be.

The king always falls.

"On your left, you'll see what once was a simply breathtaking library that just needs a little TLC to be brought back to life…do ya'll read much?" Richelle asked, as they walked into the big empty room.

Dusty built-ins lined the walls and torn pages, covered in layers of dust, laid scattered about.

Karen looked around as James leaned down and picked up a page torn out of some forgotten manuscript.

Lost but not forgotten, he thought and laid the page down on a shelf before heading off into the next room.

A small office rested adjacent to the library and contained nothing but what appeared to be a large desk draped in a sheet. The walls were covered in torn wallpaper and the corners filled with cobwebs and dusty shadows.

"A little home office, Doctor Elba. Could be quite quaint, I would say," Richelle said, giving James a big smile.

"Across the hallway is the kitchen," she continued, while moving the party along seeming to try not to spend too much time in the darker and dingier parts of the house.

"Needs a lot of work, of course, but she's got good bones. Plumbing is in working order and the electricity, although installed back in the late thirties, is functioning just fine. Although I'd probably have that on your list to upgrade in the future. This old knob and tube wiring, ya know."

Karen looked around as they walked into the kitchen area. Running her finger over the dusty countertop she seemed to be almost lost.

"I don't know, James. Seems to be in pretty bad shape," she quietly uttered.

"Nothing that a little elbow grease can't fix," Richelle quickly replied, giving her biggest smile as Karen turned on the faucet. "Well water," Richelle added.

A brown liquid spat out, causing Karen to jump, but was followed by a gush of fresh running water.

"See just a little warm up that's all," Richelle chimed in, expanding her ever constant grin as Karen seemed to grow more and more apprehensive by the minute.

"It was built just before the civil war. Eighteen fifty-one. The plumbing was upgraded in the twenties so still has some years on her since the renovations."

"Why now?" James asked, seeming to catch Richelle off guard.

"I'm sorry," she replied, looking as if she was playing dumb.

"The house. Why is it for sale now? This place has been sitting here since I was a kid. Probably a lot longer, I'm sure."

"Well, some estate settlements with the previous owners have finally unlocked this diamond in the rough. Yes, it's a shame such a gorgeous home has been allowed to sit and rot like this."

Rot...the word echoed in James's mind as he thought of the cemetery and his Elizabeth resting silently in the ground. A deep sigh and he quickly swallowed the urge to break something.

"And off the kitchen we have an entertainer's dream," Richelle exclaimed, seeing James's mind spinning and quickly led them into the dining room area filled with a table looking fit for a large banquet. It's surface and center piece were covered in a dusty white sheet. Above it a beautiful chandelier hung a bit off, swaying gently from some draft circling the room like a restless spirit.

"Imagine the parties you could have here," Richelle said, continuing to put on her best salesmanship hat as James looked around, realizing he was watching Karen more than the house.

"What do ya think?" Richelle added as James just nodded in quiet dismay, trying to catch up to Karen, who had already disappeared out of the room and up the staircase.

"The upstairs view is just lovely!" Richelle exclaimed, attempting to regain some control over her sale.

"I'm sure it's quite nice," James added, heading off on his own up the main staircase until halfway up, stopping mid-step in sudden hesitation.

He remembered nervously walking up these steps while his friends waited outside. It was dark then. So much darker. He could sense a dread rise within his gut as he felt himself drawn back into the past.

The house was waking up.

And so were his memories. With each step he felt the hairs on his arms stand on end. Dark secrets that wanted to be told.

"Would you just look over there," Richelle called out directing James' attention towards the view out the window above the front door. The driveway coupled with a dozen southern oaks and Spanish moss leading out towards the road where the horizon seemed to go on forever.

"Can you imagine the folks that once came down that driveway? The elegant affairs that must have lit this place up. Oh, how beautiful!"

James fell back into the present as he looked out the window through a thin layer of dust.

"Yes...yes I can. It's quite magnificent," James replied in a somewhat sullen tone.

"I, ah...I don't mean to offend you," Richelle nervously added.

James turned and gave her a curious look.

"And why would you be offending me?"

"Well, I'm just saying…" she seemed to be stumbling upon her words as she met James at the top of the staircase. "It's just such a beautiful manor but I'm not unaware of the plight of your people."

"My people?" he added with a slight grin.

"Yes, well, you know because you're…"

"Because I'm black," he finished her sentence with a little half grin.

“Well, yes," she replied.

"I think it's quite fitting I'm standing here now, don't you?" he replied with a smirk and, turning, headed off towards the bedroom. "Karen?!" he called out as he peeked his head into what appeared to be the master bedroom.

"This room here was renovated by the previous owners in the thirties. Not actually the original master bedroom," Richelle said, trying to reconnect with her client. "The original master is at the end of the hall."

"I know," he replied as pieces of the past rose within like a woken spirit from its grave. "Excuse me," James said, as he exited the room. "Karen?!" he yelled out again.

"I'm sure she's just getting a feel for the place," Richelle exclaimed, attempting to console her client as she hurried after him.

"Karen, baby!" he called out as he headed past the other rooms, knowing somehow, she was in the last one on the end.

The one she shouldn't be in...

But it was just a house. He shook off the thoughts as the little boy inside him felt as if he were walking back into a nightmare. All these years he pushed this place out of his mind, never thinking he'd ever be back. But he was a man now and didn't believe in ghosts anymore…nor anything else of the sorts.

"Karen, honey, are you in there?!" he blurted out, barging into the room and seeing her standing silently, looking out the window overlooking the western fields. He quickly glanced around, taken aback by the graffiti and putrid smell that filled the air.

"Oh god," James exclaimed, covering his nose and mouth.

"Tick tack, Samuel Black is back," Karen exclaimed in a strange unfamiliar tone causing James to stumble backwards a bit as if the room just started to spin.

"I see you found the master bedroom," Richelle chimed in, catching up from behind. "Oh Lord!" she gasped as she now saw the depravity of the room in its entirety.

Melted candles scattered about. A pool of vomit teaming with flies in the corner. Strange symbols and phrases painted in white on the floor and walls.

"These kids and this nonsense! Oh, I'm sorry. I know how this looks. Of course, I'll make sure all this gets cleaned up. All of it will be gone and like new, rest assured."

James momentarily forgot about his wife or anything else for that matter as he stared at the words painted across the wall. His heart raced, wanting his pills now more than ever.

TICK TACK SAMUEL BLACK IS BACK

Streaked in red spray paint across the entirety of the wall. The sentence was crudely scribed. His eyes continued to scan the room, seeing the faint outline of a chalk circle on the floor by the window in which Karen was standing.

James' head began to feel funny as a long-forgotten memory flooded back into his mind before quickly pushing it back into the darkness from which it came.

"Karen, honey! Please don't stand there," James exclaimed grabbing her shoulder and breaking her gaze out the window.

She just looked up with a strange stare and stepped to the side.

"Thank you," James replied feeling very uncomfortable standing so close to that window.

"Karen, I see you're already appreciating the view. Fifty acres," Richelle chimed in, trying to move everyone's attention to the stunning views out the window. Acre upon acre of waist-high grass fluttering in the breeze ending at the forest's edge. "That's yours, too, yes indeed!

Or it could be," Richelle said, still putting on her best show. "A sprawling forest of sycamores and southern red oaks. Quite a gem for any land developer I would say. Or just your own personal oasis."

"Birchwood," James whispered under his breath.

"What was that?" Richelle asked as James looked up with a peculiar gaze as if suddenly remembering something.

"Birchwood…There's also birch trees."

"Oh, I don't think so, it's oak and sycamores as far as the eye can see." Richelle replied while double checking the paperwork she was carrying. "Yeah, I don't see anything of that sort listed," she added.

James paused a moment as the three stood in an awkward silence.

"So, you've been here before then?" Richelle asked, but James did not reply. Only seemed more and more concerned with each passing second.

"May we have a moment, please?" he asked.

"Of course, you two just take all the time you need. I'll be right downstairs if you need me," she confidently replied and backed out of the room with a big fake grin.

"Baby, you okay?" James asked, feeling his wife's tense body press against his.

"I just need you to promise me everything is going to be okay here…promise me, James," Karen said with large, worried eyes.

"Of course, you know I'll never let anything happen to you," he replied feeling his own words already deceive him. The room was listening, he thought. Standing there holding Karen in his arms he could almost feel its breath upon his back.

"Who's Samuel Black?" Karen asked.

"No one baby, just a boogeyman to scare kids," he replied in a low reserved tone as if trying to convince himself.

"Then what does that mean?" she asked, pointing towards the sentence on the wall.

James hesitated but saw he needed to quell any fear within her, regardless of how he himself felt.

"It's just a game kids would play. Like bloody Mary. You're supposed to repeat that phrase alone in this room and…" James' voice trailed off.

"And what James?" she asked.

"And nothing," he replied. "Nothing, Karen. It's just a stupid game to scare your friends," he said feeling the past's cold hand upon his shoulder.

***

Back downstairs Richelle waited in the foyer holding her leather portfolio folder to her chest. She greeted them with an overly eager smile.

"So, I know it's a bit of a fixer upper but I'm tellin' you at this price the place will…"

"We'll take it," Karen blurted out, cutting her off mid-sentence.

Richelle clapped her hands sending an echo across the expanse of vaulted ceilings and dark dusty corners.

"Oh, you won't regret it!"

James glanced down at Karen with a bit of surprise.

"How about we meet back at my office, and we'll get an offer drawn up. I'll give you two a minute. Welcome home!" Richelle turned to leave as James and Karen stood in the middle of the grand entryway taking in their new world.

"Don't do this just for me, baby," he said softly, looking down at Karen, whose eyes seemed to sparkle once again as a glimmer of light flickered onto her face off the crystal chandelier swaying above.

"Just don't leave me alone in the dark," she stated in a strangely sullen yet desperate tone. "Promise me that."

"I promise, baby," James replied, giving her a big kiss, and squeezing her tightly against his chest. "You know how much I love you. We're going to be happy here. I can feel it."

Karen just looked up and nodded. At five-foot one she was significantly shorter than James with his six-foot tall stature. Quietly turning away, she seemed reluctant still as she headed outside but turned back one last time, giving James a rather unsettled glance.

"I love you baby," James whispered, blowing her a kiss, trying to unsee the fear he felt building in her eyes.

James stood alone in the grand foyer looking around, feeling something anew rise. Kneeling, he rested a hand upon the dusty checkered floor. His eyes already piecing together the first renovations as a curiosity suddenly cast itself upon his face. Standing back up, he followed a set of very small footprints in the dust. Bare feet no bigger than the size of a child leading off into a shadowed corner of the room where a small rag doll sat silently staring at him with cold, vacant eyes.

He cautiously knelt and held it by its worn burlap skin and crude black stitching. It looked as if it were a hundred years old. There was no mouth and no nose, only eyes. Two black beads staring back at him. And there, somewhere within that endless void, he could see his own darkness waiting to greet him.

Welcome home, Jimmy.

CHAPTER 4

Summer of 1980

"Tick tack, Samuel Black is back," young James repeated the final phrase as he stared out the window overlooking the western fields. Just beyond the sea of wavering field grass, the moon shimmered off the edge of southern oaks; looking like guardians of the dark forest that lay beyond. The syllables electrified his tongue as he felt his heart beating out of his chest.

But as he stared out at those woods, he saw nothing to signify the words actually did anything at all. The same within the old decaying room. There was no change or dark magic released. Only the putrid smell of dried vomit and mold, churning his stomach into knots. It was all just a kid's prank. A myth to make the night a little more exciting. He felt relieved. There was nothing out there. Nothing but his friends waiting outside and the sound of cicadas to sooth his nerves.

"Jimmy!" the voice of Scotty suddenly echoed from outside the door. "Hide!" he yelled, bursting into the room.

James screamed as he dropped the flashlight on the floor. The moonlight, now the only light within the dark room.

"No, no, no!" James repeated as he reached down and flipped the switch back and forth giving it a few taps on the side of his hand.

"Come on! We have to get out of here!" Scotty yelled, pulling James up by the shirt sleeve.

"Geeze Scotty! What's the deal?" James anxiously asked, gathering his wits about him.

"No time, just come on. Let's go!"

They both ran out of the room and down the hallway to the top of the stairs. Even from this distance, James could hear the familiar sound of the rusted-out Chevy pickup screaming down the long gravel driveway like a shark to its prey.

He knew right away who it was. Tommy Clayton and Daniel Buckard. They weren't just bullies, they were dangerous. Two teenagers who would torment him to no end. He could already hear their voices emanating out of their tobacco laden mouths. Something terrifyingly real in their hatred towards him. Towards them all, for that matter.

Just a few days earlier Tommy held a switchblade to his throat, reminding him that his color was not the preferred skin tone in town, to say it eloquently, and he'd better think twice about sticking around. James knew very little about the source of their hatred, but the lessons were hard learned when they came in the form of these two.

James and Scotty stood frozen in fear listening to the truck getting closer, when the front door flung open, and Harold and Emma ran inside.

"They're almost here!" Harold yelled.

"Up here! Quick!" Scotty yelled.

James watched in disbelief as his friends ran faster than he'd ever seen them run before. They all were afraid of Tommy and Daniel. Whatever horror lay inside the house somehow was better than the horror that was driving to its doorstep.

James grabbed Emma by the hand when she got to the top of the stairs and led her down the hallway.

"This way, guys! We can crawl out the back window and jump."

"Jump? Are you crazy?" Harold yelled out.

"Better to jump than see the end of Tommy's switchblade," Scotty anxiously chimed in, out of breath.

The four went into the bedroom and quickly slammed the door shut.

"Whooa!" Emma exclaimed as her eyes scanned the room.

"Creepy," Harold nervously added.

"It's just a room guys," James exclaimed.

"So, you said the words?" Harold asked.

"Yeah, I said em'," James confidently replied, glancing over at Emma.

"And what happened?" Emma asked.

He could feel her hand squeezing him tight.

"Not a thing, just…" James began, but was quickly interrupted.

"Tick Tack Samuel Black is back little piggies!" Daniel's gut-wrenching voice echoed from downstairs. "Come out and playeee!" he yelled out, which was followed by the high-pitched sound of Tommy's insidious laughter.

"Oh my god, they're inside!" Harold exclaimed in a tense whisper.

"Quick, the window!" Scotty yelled, as they all peered out, seeing that it was a lot higher than they had anticipated.

"I'm not jumping out of that!" Emma nervously said, looking as though she were staring into the abyss.

"No choice," James said as he squeezed her hand.

The voices were closer now, echoed by crashes of empty beer bottles smashing against the walls.

"Tick tack, tick tack, tick taaaaaak," Tommy's voice slithered out in a drunken slur as he tapped the wall with what sounded like an empty beer bottle.

James prayed to God to please save him, to save them all. That if somehow, he could get them out of this situation, he'd go to church every Sunday and do every nice thing he could possibly think of. *Anything,* he thought.

"Gonna gut you like a pig boy. We don't like your kind in these parts," Tommy yelled out.

"Oink oink little piggy," Daniel's raspy voice echoed behind him, their presence deathly close.

James' heartbeat rose as the thought of Tommy's knife plunging into his side gave him sudden cause for extreme concern. The reality of the situation made him feel like an animal trapped in a cage.

"We gotta go now!" James yelled at the group. "Okay, Scotty you first."

"I'm not going first!" Scotty snapped back as the footsteps could be heard almost at the top of the staircase.

"Just do it!" James shot back.

"Damn!" Scotty exclaimed, putting one leg over the windowsill and then the other.

"Here, I'll hold you steady" James said, as Scotty rocked back and forth. The sound of the footsteps grew closer.

"Now!" James yelled as Scotty made the fateful leap falling two stories below onto the hard, dusty ground.

"Ouch!" Scotty screamed as he rolled onto his side.

"You alright?" James yelled, poking his head out the window.

"Fine, I'm fine. Come on, hurry up!"

"Harold, you're next," James urgently called, ushering Harold to the windowsill.

"I don't wanna do this," he pleaded.

"No choice. Go!" James said, pushing Harold out as he screamed all the way down, tumbling besides Scotty.

"Okay, now your turn," he said staring into Emma's luminescent green eyes. She looked up and didn't say a word. She didn't need to. He knew what she was thinking.

Helping her to the window, he held her hand giving it a big squeeze. She turned just before she jumped and gave him a peck on the cheek. He felt like he could have done anything after that moment, faced any demon. He could still feel the warmth of her lips on his cheek as he watched her land and tumble near the group below.

"You okay?" he yelled out.

"I'm fine," she yelled back. "Hurry up! Come on!"

James straddled the windowsill just as a large blow struck the door. Another, then another.

"Tick tack little boys and girls. Come out and playeeee," Tommy's voice rang out as the violent blows began splintering the old door.

James stared down at the ground below, seeing his friends huddled around waiting for him. They looked as though they were yelling but he suddenly couldn't hear a thing. It was as if he was in a fishbowl. The world became silent. The door breaking behind him. The screams of his friends. Even the thoughts in his own head. Everything slowed down as the room seemed to warp in and out of reality. He felt faint. Dizzy. Steadying himself he looked around trying to get his bearings and there standing in the corner was something he didn't believe was real. The shadow of a tall gaunt man that wasn't supposed to be, the shadow of death itself dressed in a black suit, tattered, and worn as if dug up from the grave.

James couldn't move as he stared into the man's sunken yellowed eyes, half covered by the white greasy hairs protruding from his dark wide brimmed hat. His shirt collar was dirty and stained in blood. The figure was as still as a statue, it only watched silently as James sat frozen straddling the windowsill.

He could suddenly hear the man's thoughts. See the violent death that happened in this very room. The screams of the souls that came before him trapped within his timeless gaze. The ones that died. They were all here now. All their eyes upon him. Then a voice rose within the madness whispering into his ear, telling him something sinister. Something he couldn't believe, something he had to do.

He tried to push the thoughts out of his mind as the figure wavered in the humid summer air like heat waves over a hot desert highway. James felt ill as the thoughts grew darker. Violent, horrible images of utter torture and pain. He could see the slaves that disappeared into those woods. Their bodies dissected and dismembered. Screaming tongues cut out of their mouths. Still beating hearts dug from their chests. The more he tried to resist the further he was drawn into the nightmare. Just as he felt he could take no more the figure opened its mouth and out came a single cicada.

James stood frozen in horror unable to move a muscle as he watched the small, winged creatures multiply into the hundreds, then thousands. Before he knew it, the walls and air itself were nothing but a swarm of insects. The sound of wings; a symphony of madness. Their legs against his skin felt like pins and needles as he flailed his arms until he lost control of his balance and fell out of the window, screaming into the darkness below.

CHAPTER 5

The sun beat down upon James' back as he replaced the old, rotted boards on the back veranda. He could feel the day's work in his bones, and it felt good. With each nail, he sensed a piece of himself healing. Forgetting almost. Silenced by the task at hand. It had been over three months since they began the renovations and things were coming along nicely. Karen even appeared to be finding little pieces of herself once again.

The house still needed a lot of work but, regardless of its rather run-down facade, James felt the work itself was the reward rather than the finished piece. If it took him the rest of his life to fix this old place up it would be just fine.

Anything to not give himself enough time to think too deeply about anything.

He had a lot of plans for the house. Restoring the front staircase to its former elegance was something he caught himself daydreaming about often. He pictured Karen walking down, in a beautiful evening gown, running her perfectly manicured nails along the railing, staring down at him while their other guests admired her from afar. Friends and colleagues coming in from the city to attend a distinguished evening of cocktails and delight. Feet shuffling along the black and white marble floors, no longer cracked and dusty but polished to a mirror finish, catching the light of the chandelier overhead. Each face smiling as they gazed upon his wife and their beautiful home. Cars up and down the front driveway lined by the subtle glow of candlelight alongside the majestic oaks. The moon casting its silver rays upon the fresh white paint while more guests entered, admiring the grandeur of the Corinthian columns. Then, later in the evening, talking stocks and politics with a few friends and colleagues over cigars and brandy in the library. The smoke rising past perfectly kept volumes of history and philosophy lining the dark mahogany shelves. Lastly after all the guests had left, he would take a moment in the office finishing his drink before meeting Karen upstairs and gently sliding her gown off her soft supple skin while kissing her neck. The spot just below her ear. The soft hairs tickling his nose. The smell of her perfume intoxicating as they made love in a sliver of moonlight passing through the slatted white venetian blinds.

He thought about all these things, and it made him smile as he stared down at that rotted board on the back veranda. Even if deep down he knew it would be just the two of them sharing quiet simple evenings together, he found the grandeur of the house would sometimes get the best of his imagination.

Setting his hammer down, James took a moment and looked out across the land. It seemed like nothing else, but the big house had survived the years. About a hundred feet to the east, he could see what he was told was at one time the overseer's cottage. To the right of that, a blacksmith shop and then the kitchen. Beyond that, the housing where the poor souls that tilled this land slept. All leveled to the ground and overgrown. Just remnants of boards and rusty nails. Every memory of what once was forgotten except the big house staring out over it all. Like a giant of the land slumbering in the wake of some great calamity.

James closed his eyes and took a deep breath, feeling the past whispering around him. But the weight of it all was nothing compared to losing his little girl. Everywhere he turned there was pain and his only salvation seemed to be in restoring this old house.

How odd, he thought. Here he was sweating under the same sun that beat down upon his ancestors. What a different world he lived in and guiltily could almost feel some semblance of peace wash over him.

Yes, everything seemed to be coming together except for the one room. The upstairs bedroom at the end of the hall. The old master bedroom with the window that overlooked the western fields. James hadn't gone in there since the graffiti had been painted over and the cleaning crew had spit shined and disinfected those floors. He didn't like that room. There was a coldness to it like a bad memory was trapped inside. So, he stayed out and asked Karen to do the same.

Getting back to work, James ripped out another rotted board and replaced it with a fresh piece of pine. The veranda was now nearly halfway complete. The moment gave him peace knowing Karen was safe and his world was starting to resemble something normal once again. But he couldn't help but think as he stared down at that hammer, with every sound of those nails maybe something that shouldn't be awoken was.

What else was listening, he thought. Maybe best to not be too loud. Maybe he should just take Karen and go…*run was more like it.* But he pushed those thoughts aside and quickly dismissed such childish notions.

He sat back, resting his hands on his knees quietly taking in the day's work as the late afternoon sun shined upon his sweaty brow. The buzz of cicadas soothed his every thought as he looked out past the overgrown field grass to the forest of Sycamores and Southern red Oaks that seemed to go on forever like a wall of shadows guarding the unknown.

That forest…

The thought made him uneasy as the trees seemed to whisper in his ear.

"Brought you some tea," Karen's voice rang out from behind as the creak of the screen door opened and slammed shut behind her. Her light blue eyes caught in the sun, glimmered in an almost translucent glow. Hair up in a bun and an oversized ripped Tom Petty t-shirt and overalls covered her paint splattered arms. She smiled, setting down some glasses and a pitcher of iced tea.

"Thought you might be thirsty," she said as James reached out and grabbed the glass with a smile.

He leaned forward, giving her a kiss as she poured.

"This is what I missed about the south. Sweet tea just doesn't taste the same in Los Angeles," he said wiping the sweat off his forehead.

"Porch looks good," Karen exclaimed, looking around at the new pine boards.

James nodded, taking in his handy work.

"Gettin' there. How's the guest room coming?"

"Gettin' there," she replied with a bit of a forced grin. Even despite the lack of sincerity James was happy to see her smile.

"You okay?" he asked, staring up at his wife, who seemed to be keeping herself and her thoughts occupied rather well lately.

"I'm fine, babe," she replied and took a seat beside him before taking a long pause as if arranging her thoughts.

"I think about her everyday still…every minute of every hour," Karen said while her endless gaze stared off into the distance.

"Me, too, baby…" James replied but didn't know what else to say. He missed Elizabeth just as much but guiltily hadn't been thinking about her today or most days lately, for that matter. He was getting caught up in the work just as he had planned. For him, it was easier. Karen seemed to struggle a lot more. He didn't love his daughter any less it was just a way of coping. A way of moving on. He had to…they both did.

***

The moon hung like an orb in the warm night air, casting strange shadows across the property as the distant past slumbered silently below.

Having woken suddenly James sat up, grabbing his chest. His heartbeat pounded harder than he liked. It was an uncomfortable feeling to say the least. One that made him more nervous than just about anything else.

"You're gonna be fine," he whispered to himself and began the routine of deep breathing and counting each breath, wishing he had not chosen to stop taking his pills.

"You don't need em'," he whispered as he drew another deep breath. Leaning over to put his arm around Karen, he suddenly realized she was gone. Alarmed, he got out of bed and gave the room a quick once over. No bathroom lights. No light at all besides the moon's silver rays spilling in through the open window.

He quickly forgot about his own momentary panic attack and headed out of the room; James stared silently at the door at the end of the hall which was slightly ajar. He knew he hadn't left that door open and always made sure that it stayed shut.

No draft could have done that.

"Karen?" James called out. The night swallowed his words and almost spoke back. He could hear so much at this time. More than he wanted to.

"Babe! It's me. Why don't you come back to bed now?" he asked, feeling his nerves heighten with each step.

Now at the doorway, he gave it a little push and leaned inside the room.

"Karen?"

He could see his wife standing by the window staring out across the western fields towards the forest.

"Time for bed, baby."

But she did not answer.

Taking a step closer, he got the chills as he walked farther into the room. The night he was just a scared little boy ran through his head like a broken projector spitting out bits and pieces of memories he wanted to forget.

He watched, only half awake himself, wondering what unseen images were haunting her. Sometimes she would stay up and read for hours until he had to suggest she get some rest, lest she stay up until dawn. Recently, she'd been reading a classic Stephen King yarn. One that he felt she shouldn't be reading under the circumstances but whatever took her mind off the evil in this life was fine for him. But never this. Never sleepwalking.

Then, just as he placed a hand on her shoulder to guide her back to bed she spoke.

"I seeeeee," she whispered in a low raspy tone.

James positioned himself closer, attempting to listen to what she was saying. He could see her eyes were wide open.

"Babe, are you awake?" he whispered, but did not get a reply nor even a subtle acknowledgment.

"I see," she said again, only this time the inflection was short, almost painful as if the words hurt to leave her lips.

"I'm going to take you back to bed now. If you can hear me just follow my voice and take my hand," he said, seeing her line of sight staring towards the forest. Her eyes were blank yet mesmerized by whatever dream state she stood awake in. Then suddenly, something caught his eye.

"What the hell?" James whispered under his breath, taking a step closer to the window.

A greenish hue emanated from deep within the forest. Like a pulse or a heartbeat, it briefly rose and fell until it faded to nothing. He stared a moment longer and rubbed his eyes, wondering if he had seen anything at all. He knew what the mind could do at this hour. Strange things. Things he didn't want to think about. But nonetheless whatever it was it was gone, and he was half asleep anyway.

Not the time for this nonsense.

"Okay, babe, let's go to bed." He turned and reached out to grab her hand but quickly retracted as if touching a hot stove when he saw the small rag doll she was holding. He hadn't noticed it until now, even forgetting that he had found the little doll in the first place. The worn rags that made up the body gave the figure a patchwork-like pattern. Its black beady eyes were like polished onyx and the longer he stared the more he realized there was a little life left in them after all these years sitting in a dusty corner of a forgotten mansion. But how did she find it? He had just tossed it aside in a pile of garbage…or maybe he hadn't. He thought back trying to remember. The moment inescapable as he felt some presence looming beneath the moonlight looking back at him.

Gently drawing the back of his hand across her forehead, he brushed the hair out of her face and kissed her before walking her back to the bedroom and laying her down.

Looking over he smiled as he saw her eyes gently close. He pretended that somehow this place was healing her. Healing both of them. He pushed aside that strange feeling in the pit of his stomach as he watched the moon glisten off her hair, and he remembered for a moment the way things were. The way they could be once again. Looking down at her hands he could see how she held the doll. Perhaps it was what she needed. A little piece of a child's life.

Something to hang onto and remember. Obviously, it made her happy and that made the moment seem all the more normal.

CHAPTER 6

James, now out of his tattered jeans and white tees from endless home renovations, was dressed casually in khaki pants and a dark button up, headed inside the small clinic off of Gaston Street. The feeling of an almost normal daily routine calmed his nerves while masking the anxiety that still plagued his mind when he thought about Karen alone in the house.

One by one he flipped on the bright fluorescent overhead lights. The small waiting room sat with its copies of Southern Living and two little palms by the window overlooking the outside cobblestone pathways.

"Morning ladies," he leaned over whispering to the plants. "Oh, Henrietta, not looking so hot I see," he said, taking a closer look at the one palm that seemed to be in need of some care. "Let's get you a drink," he whispered as he grabbed a small watering container under the end table in the waiting room and headed back to the kitchen.

"Morning, Margery," James exclaimed, seeing his rather stout and round secretary, hobbling in with her handbag the size of a Cadillac.

"Morning, Doc!" she replied, "here early I see." She continued getting herself situated behind the front desk, then headed back to the kitchen.

"Ya just wanted to get an early start on the day. Been havin' trouble sleeping anyway."

"I'll tell you what you need…tart cherry juice."

"What?" he asked with a sour grin.

"Yes, sir, tart cherry juice. If you'd like, add a little touch of honey and a pinch of salt. That'll do ya right up. I'm tellin' ya, Doc. You'll be sleepin' through the night like a baby," she said as he began to fill the watering jug.

"Maybe you should be the doctor today, Marge," he replied with a smile.

"Well, I'll tell ya, Doc, my family does have a history of healers," she said in a peculiar tone while putting her lunch in the fridge.

"You never mentioned that," he replied curiously. "Ya know we never really talked about these things I guess, have we?"

"You're always so busy, I don't want to bother you with my little ol' life now."

"Not at all, I think it's important that we get to know each other better. An office should be like family," James replied, suddenly forgetting his recent troubles back home, feeling like it was just another day at the office. "So is your family from here?"

"Well, yes, depending on how far back ya go. We all from somewhere else I suppose now, aren't we?"

"I suppose you're right," James replied.

"I grew up here, yes. My mother, she was a great woman. A wise woman. Grandmama, too. Generations go back til those boats dropped us off here, ya heard. Grandmama knows a lot about the old country…and the old ways. We've got a little shop over by the Davenport House on East Saint Julian."

"What kind of shop?" James asked.

"Oh, you know. Natural healing stuff, candles, incense, powders, and potions," she added with a bit of a humorous tone. "Things tourists just love to come see when they in town. They'll never know the real side of our religion though."

"You know about that sort of stuff, Marge?"

"I grew up with it, if that's what ya askin'. Other than that, I pretty much keep to myself. Don't have no need for no magic love potions for these tired old bones."

"Maybe I could stop by sometime and see for myself."

"Called The Black Palmetto. Grandmama runs the place. Deep thoughts that one. Knows more than you or I could ever imagine. I think you'll get a kick out of the place. I usually help out on Saturdays. Kinda my two lives I lead."

"I know what you mean…" he hesitated as his past crept to the tip of his tongue. "I used to be a pastor," he blurted out surprising himself.

"Well, powder my butt and turn me sideways," Margery replied, setting her coffee down and putting two firm hands on her rather large hips.

"You've got quite a way with words there. I had no idea," he said chuckling, nearly spilling his coffee.

"Well, Doc, sometimes life just never ceases to surprise you. But how come you ain't a Godly man no more?"

James gave a forced grin as if he didn't even know the answer himself and was trying to pretend he had never mentioned it in the first place.

"Ain't going to let ya off that easy, Doc. Come out with it now!" Margery exclaimed.

James hesitated a moment then spoke as if he were looking back in time. Like an old photograph was lying before him. "Sometimes we lose a piece of ourselves, and we know we aren't ever getting it back…I lost that piece," James said, as the room now felt awkwardly silent.

"Got a lot of pain going on in there. Be vigilant, Doc. Be vigilant."

"What do you know about it?" he replied curiously.

"I know when someone's carrying things they ought not to be. Can read it in your aura."

"You believe in that stuff?"

"Like I said, I grew up around it. Hard not to where I come from…where we come from, I should say," she corrected herself with a smile. "You's a local boy, I hear."

"That I am," he replied taking a big sip of coffee, feeling the warmth of Margery's smile. He could almost taste a normal life.

***

Later on that day after a few colds, coughs, and various minor ailments, James sat out back in the shade of an acacia with his sandwich looking at the old trees and buildings as if they were friends from the past. The air was hot and humid yet comforting.

"Daddy misses you Lizzy," he said under his breath while staring out into a cloudless sky beyond the building tops. "I need to know you're okay, if you could just let me know you're okay, that'd sure make me feel a whole lot better."

His own words surprised him. The moment feeling surreal as he imagined Elizabeth sitting there, sharing lunch together.

Wiping his tears, he shook it off, feeling silly, and took a bite of his sandwich. The taste was off. It was sour. *Rotten.* He spit it out and looked inside, seeing mold and maggots as if it had been sitting outside for weeks.

He threw the sandwich onto the ground as a smell rose, stinging his nostrils, coupled by a sickened feeling growing inside his stomach.

"Doctor Elba! Gonna need you inside right away," Margery's voice rang out as she stood in the back doorway calling him with a sense of urgency.

James got up and quickly hurried in.

Inside the waiting room, a vagrant lay on the floor shaking violently. His mouth was foaming, and his hands were clenched in tight fists.

"What happened?" he asked, kneeling beside the man.

"Nothin,' he just walked in, askin' for you, and when I asked what he needed he just glossed over and fell to the ground. Those eyes rolled back in his head like marbles on a table."

"Okay, roll him on his side," James ordered as Margery kneeled beside him and assisted.

James leaned over the man grabbing his shoulder, but as he began to turn him a hand shot up and clenched his shirt collar.

"Doctor!" Margery yelled out as the man pulled James near his heavily lined face. The smell emanating from his breath was sickening.

James tried to pull away, but the man's grip was too strong. Then suddenly his eyes changed. He could see it as clear as day. The once brown pupils were black as night. The reflection of James' own face appeared before him within the dark, insidious orbs.

"Little Jimmy. Have you found your faith today?"

The voice, a sharp raspy tone that sent chills throughout his body as he was suspended over the man's face like a victim meant to witness his own death.

"Tick tack, tick tack," the man's voice rang out like a nightmare risen from the grave, "Samuel Black is back."

Upon the last syllable he began to gasp as if the air had suddenly been taken from the room and with a sudden burst of energy spat blood over James' face, sending Margery backwards in horror.

James watched as a single cicada emerged from the man's blood-soaked mouth. He sat completely frozen as the violent spasms turned to stillness. The cicada stood upon the man's lips as if born unto this world from the death of its host.

It was then a song rose within James' mind. He didn't understand why but the subtle sounds of his mother playing Moonlight Sonata began to play within his head. The eerie somber tones drawing him into a distant memory. A place he wanted to forget. A place where life no longer existed.

James sat there in disbelief, his face dripping with blood, staring at the cicada. The urge to vomit rose within him as his saliva moistened the inside of his mouth. He hadn't even bothered to wipe the blood from his own face. It was just there as if it were a part of him, too. His own death within the man's last words and the elegant opening phrase of Moonlight Sonata ringing in his ear.

CHAPTER 7

James, found himself parked in front of the old public library just off Main street in the historical district, needing more answers than he wondered if he could handle. The worn brick exterior with the front awning and steps was just as he remembered it. He used to sit out there and read for hours on end. His mother always wondered why he didn't just read inside but he liked it out front best, sitting on those short steps feeling the breeze on his face and basking in the natural light.

He could still remember the smell of the musty old books and the way the lighting came in from the high rectangular windows as if they were in some large daylight basement. There was a quiet stillness in the air as everyone moved about in ways unlike the rest of the world. "Twelve-inch voices," he remembered the librarian Miss Ratcliff saying. A term he felt sometimes should have been adopted in the rest of the city as well.

Heading to the front desk he wasn't even sure he knew what he was looking for and perhaps should have just gone home. The homeless man's blood still felt fresh, and the lingering smell of his rotted breath made the day more unsettling than ever. But it was the words from a dead man's decayed lips that really haunted him.

Have you found your faith today little Jimmy? Tick tack tick tack.

Perhaps he didn't hear anything at all. He had just heard what his mind manifested among the chaos. The scared little boy. *Jimmy.* That's what his friends used to call him. The group of friends he thought he'd have forever. The memories he had pushed into some black void began to spring up and he remembered how much he missed them all. Especially Emma. How had he forgotten so much? Yet, he felt it all connected back to his returning to Savannah and buying some forsaken piece of real estate that opened a floodgate to his past.

He needed to see the history of that house like some patients x-ray, to analyze and perhaps get a grip on some semblance of what lay slumbering within his new home and even his mind. Things were becoming undone. His grip on reality loosening. Visions that he knew were not real, seeped into reality like a mist drifting in from a blackened sea. Deep down he had a gut feeling that it was all connected and that Karen was somehow in danger. He could not shake the thought no matter how hard he tried.

"Hello, how can I help you?" the young lady, no more than eighteen, said with a smile.

He paused a moment somewhat dumbfounded as she looked like his Elizabeth. A bit older he thought but this is what she might have looked like had she been able to reach that age. He imagined her standing there staring back at him. Eighteen and going off to college.

He thought of it all in that split second. Her graduation, packing for college, boyfriends, career, marriage, grandchildren…

"Sir?" she said again giving him a bit of a look, this time seeming to wonder if he was okay.

"Yes, sorry, you just reminded me of someone," he replied.

"Well, what can I do for you?"

"I'm looking for some information on an old house."

"How far back are you looking?"

"How far back do you got?" he replied with a smirk.

"Well…Tell me what you're looking for and maybe I can help ya."

"The old rice plantation outside of town. I have the address if you need it," James replied.

She already had punched up a few items on the computer and took a moment as her eyes ran over the screen.

"That place huh?" she looked down and began typing again. "Heard someone bought it, although I can't imagine why. Place gives me the creeps." She looked up with a little cringe as James just nodded his head.

"Yeah, can't imagine who would do something like that," he added feeling the tragic humor in his own words.

"Okay here we go…Here's a few articles. Looks like we have some things on microfiche dating back as far as eighteen fifty. Come on back and we'll get you all set up."

The back room seemed a little dimmer than the rest of the library as if the farther back you went the less people and the less light there was. The small back room had a few televisions, VCRs and headsets as well as a couple microfiche machines lined up against the far wall.

"I remember my mother telling me stories about that place. My friends used to go there and drink, but I never did. My mom's stories always scared me too much."

"What kind of stories?" James asked as he too remembered the stories when he was a kid. Horrible stories he seemed to have pushed out of his mind after all these years but were now getting the better of him.

"All sorts of things. She said that place was cursed. Terrible things happened there, and it was like they stuck." She stopped as if thinking back a moment. "Like whatever happened left some imprint that never went away. Kinda how peanut butter gets stuck on the roof of your mouth ya know." The girl snapped out of it as if lost within the memory. "Anyway, I was not one of the brave ones that would go to party there."

"Do any of your friends still try to go out there?" James asked, "maybe when the owners are away."

"Not that I know of but ya never know. Always some crazy things us kids are up to, aren't we," she replied with a smile.

James just gave her a little nod imagining how crazy this whole thing seemed to be.

"Anyway, here's the machine," she said loading up the microfiche. "Any questions just let me know."

"Thank you," James replied as she walked away leaving him alone in the back room feeling the anxiety continue to rise within him.

Taking a seat, he flipped on the machine and pulled up the first of the three old newsprint articles.

THE SUNDOWN GAZETTE

Oct 6th, 1895

There was no photograph only a small article titled with the heading:

SAMUEL BLACK PLANTATION

SLAVE AUCTION

TWENTY-THREE FINE NEGRO SPECIMAN. COOKS, CLEANS, FIELD HANDS. READY TO WORK. COME DOWN OCTOBER 13th 8:00AM TO BE THE FIRST TO CLAIM THIS FINE LOT.

The reality of seeing an advertisement like this firsthand was unsettling to say the least but why not turn the past into something beautiful. Why not make it good? Not forget the past but honor it by restoring and educating. Maybe he would even give tours one day to folks wanting a little history lesson. But that was for another day.

Flipping to the next article James found himself staring at a picture of his house looking as pristine as ever. There was no overgrowth on the siding or porch, the front pillars looked to be without a single crack and the grounds immaculately manicured. He was amazed. Even in an old black and white print it seemed this place had a beauty to it that he had not seen before, yet he knew it was locked beneath the grime and years of neglect.

A family portrait accompanied the picture. Standing on the front steps, an astute man dressed in a white suit, and his beautiful wife and daughter, both elegantly draped in what appeared to be the best fashion of the times. Below it the caption read:

Samuel L. Black and family 1851

And there, resting within the daughter's arms, was the rag doll. He knew it like he knew himself. He couldn't believe it. Suddenly it all seemed too real.

James stared at the family for a moment. He could almost feel himself within the portrait as if it were him, Karen and Elizabeth standing there. Scanning the article, the heading read:

PLANTER, SAMUEL L BLACK'S WIFE AND DAUGHTER MISSING

After an extensive search, the wife and daughter of planter and affluent landowner Samuel L. Black have been declared officially missing as the cause of their disappearance remains a mystery.

James stared with a rising consternation as he felt as lost as the man standing in the picture, staring blankly ahead into a void from which he somehow knew he could never escape.

Putting in another spool of film James made a quick scan through the articles until coming to…

SAMUEL BLACK SUSPECTED
IN SLAYING OF WIFE

An investigation has begun into the disappearance and alleged slaying of the wife of landowner Samuel L Black. There has been no body yet found, but authorities are believed to have evidence linking Mr. Black to the crime.

The plantation has been the sight of strange happenings and rumors of anti-Christian occult practices have made it a source of discontent for much of the town and its Christian citizens. One townsperson claimed that Black was resurrecting the

Devil himself to bring his daughter back who he lost to smallpox just last fall. Other theories have alluded to the use of black magic to bring back the dead and even claims that Mr. Black himself was possessed by other worldly spirits, but authorities recognize no such claims.

James stared into the black and white photograph. Samuel Black's eyes watching him from across time. His thoughts were brought to the surface as he stared into the face of his own nightmare. The wispy white tendrils of greasy hair strung to the side of his gaunt face and hollowed eyes. He had often wondered if the man ever even existed or was just a nightmare. A tale to scare children into behaving. *Best behave or Samuel Black will take you away.* He turned off the machine, not able to look at the image another second. The air was completely still. The silence almost deafening as James sat alone in the back room staring at a blank screen. He could feel his own heart beating almost too fast now as he took a few deep breaths and closed his eyes. The voices whispering within his head.

Tick Tack Samuel Black is coming back, Tick tack Samuel Black coming back, Tick tack Samuel Black is back...

He remembered it now, like it was yesterday. The rising of his friend's voices outside the house. The sound of Tommy's truck roaring down the gravel driveway. The syllables of the chant scratching the inside of his head like a rat trying to claw its way out of a cage.

"How are you sir?" the young assistant librarian spoke from behind, nearly startling him out of his chair.

"Oh my. I'm so sorry," she said, resting a hand upon his shoulder. "I didn't mean to scare you, was just checking up on you making sure you were finding everything you needed.

"Yes," he said catching his breath. "As soon as I'm done having a heart attack I'll be just fine."

The young woman smiled and turned to leave.

"Wait," James said grasping her wrist then quickly drawing back as she gave him an odd yet affirming glare.

"I'm sorry, I just..." he didn't know what to say, his thoughts still materializing as he attempted to piece together what he had just read.

"Do you believe in Samuel Black?" he asked suddenly, feeling like a scared thirteen-year-old boy again.

She stared down at him for a moment not saying a word as if she were analyzing what else was in his head.

"Tick Tack," she said in an odd tone.

"What did you just say?"

"I didn't say anything," the girl nervously replied.

"I think it's time I go," James said and got up and left the room.

Back out in the sunlight, he could feel something anew. A lingering feeling of dread mixed with the afternoon sun as if Samuel Black was still watching him from that old black and white photograph. The Boogeyman was real. The breeze was now his breath. The mind, his sanctuary. He knew these stories were better off buried and dead where they belonged. But things didn't seem to stay dead around here.

CHAPTER 8

James stood silently at the front door before entering. Closing his eyes, he tried to clear his mind of the image of Samuel Black and his family. Just like himself, he too had lost his daughter and a connection was growing he wasn't all too comfortable with.

Funny things can manifest when you've lost a child. Your mind is never the same. Today was just one of those moments. His subconscious, playing tricks on him. But now he knew the man in the black hat was real.

Tick tack Jimmy.

Inside, the house was still. The late afternoon sun shone upon the dusty chandelier. He took a moment to appreciate what was before him and imagined what it could be one day. What it had to be. He had invested everything, including his soul, into this place. There was too much to lose now, even though he felt like grabbing Karen and just running away.

"Karen, honey?!" he called out as he walked to the kitchen and set his worn leather satchel down. The one she had gotten him all those years ago. The deeply oiled sides looked about as tired as his own face after these last few months.

Drawing a glass of water, James stared out the window towards the western side of the property. The grounds seemed endless. An expanse of tall wavering field grass that would be quite the task to cut but wasn't sure he even wanted to. He liked the way it swayed in the wind, like waves lapping upon a shoreline. The thought of what went on in those fields eluded him most of the time but sometimes he would think about it, almost seeing the hands out there tilling the soil until they bled.

The water was cool to his lips and calmed his nerves. He watched the field grass sway in the breeze and the day began to fall away. His mind returning to some sense of normalcy as he saw his wife appear off in the distance.

She looks so beautiful, he thought. *But lost. Like a flower standing alone amongst a field of weeds.*

The back door creaked on its rusty hinges as James stepped out onto the back veranda. Karen was already making her way farther away from the house towards the forest's edge. He shielded his eyes from the sun to get a better look at her while listening to the gentle song of the cicadas. Each note seeming to calm his nerves as he watched the sunlight flow through the tendrils of her long blonde hair wavering in the warm late afternoon breeze.

He just stood and watched while she walked farther away. The field grass at her knees, the sun upon her face. He remembered all the beautiful things they had created together and hoped and prayed they would get back to that place. But something dark rested out there.

Something untoward grew within his heart and he couldn't quite place it. The closer she got to the forest the more nervous he became.

"Karen?!" James called out, running after her, but she did not turn. As he got closer, he could feel his muscles begin to tighten. He hadn't been this close to the forest since they had moved in, and he didn't intend to ever step foot in that place again. There were memories trapped within those shadows and he knew if he looked hard enough, he would see something he didn't want to see staring back. He didn't want to remember everything. He couldn't handle it. Not now. But he also couldn't stop the feeling from rising in his chest that something was still out there, like a pulse of electricity becoming stronger each day.

"Karen, can you hear me?" he called out again as he approached her, now just feet away.

She slowly turned and looked into his eyes. He stopped and stared as if trying to read her mind then looked down seeing the doll clutched in her hands.

"What are you doing way out here?" James asked, reaching for her hand. Her palm felt cold and clammy. "You, okay?" he asked, taking a step closer.

"I'm fine. I just felt like taking a walk," she replied seeming to not want to talk.

"I see you found the doll."

He reached out to touch it as she quickly pulled it away. James suddenly grew more concerned. She looked at him almost as if he were a stranger.

"It was on my nightstand last night. Didn't you put it there?" she asked as James felt a flutter in his chest.

"No, no I didn't," he nervously replied, even second guessing himself if he had done it.

"Well, someone did," she said, clutching it tightly to her chest. "It reminds me of her…I can almost smell her James," she said, holding out the doll towards his nose.

James leaned forward and sniffed. "I don't smell anything."

She pulled the doll back and shook her head as if angry. "Well, it does. It smells like Elizabeth. I can't believe you don't smell her."

"I'm sorry, I don't. But as long as you love it, I'm happy," James said, having a hard time taking his eyes off the doll which seemed to stare right back at him.

"Don't ever try to take it from me," she stated in a strange shift of emotion and turned back, staring out at the forest. She did not speak again. Only stared out at those woods which made everything all the more unsettling.

***

That evening, as the waning crescent moon rose into the starry southern sky, James finished up a little work on the back veranda while Karen prepared dinner. His thoughts were clear out here. The sound of cicadas comforted him. The humid air was like a blanket upon his shoulders. This is all he wanted. This was why he had bought this place, hoping that one day it would be a home.

He and Karen hadn't said much to one another all day, but it was fine, he told himself. As long as he stayed busy it was fine, he just needed to give her time. Time to heal.

Inside, James wiped the sweat off his brow and took off his dirty white tee, tossing it in the laundry basket.

"I'm gonna go take a shower," he said.

"Okay, dinner's almost ready," Karen replied.

"I'll be quick!" he yelled back, halfway up the stairs.

The quiet contemplation that fell upon him as he felt the hot water hit the back of his neck was something he treasured each day. He had put so much upon his shoulders and kept himself so busy he had to remind himself to take a breath and relax sometimes.

After his shower James toweled off and wiped the condensation from the steamy bathroom mirror. Looking at his face he began to wonder if he could handle all of this. Had he taken on too much? Was it the right choice to come here? He didn't know anymore.

***

After a rather quiet dinner and a quick clean up, James laid in bed beside Karen feeling a strange veil upon them. The unsettled thoughts ruminated into a frenzy as he tossed and turned trying to go to sleep. Looking over, he surprisingly saw his wife staring back at him with passion in her eyes. They hadn't made love since their daughter's death.

"I want you," Karen spoke calmly yet seductively, catching him off guard. The look in her eye. The touch of her hand. The vacant yet ravenous smirk that crept up, curling the corner of her lip as she dug her hands into his shoulders and wrapped her legs around him, forcing him inside of her. She clawed at his back digging her nails deep into his skin. Blood began to trickle down his side, dripping on the white sheets as she begged for more. Her voice, ravenous and nearly animalistic as her screams, echoed throughout the house. It wasn't like her. None of this was.

"Harder," she whispered forcefully into his ear as he drew himself deeper within her. His breath was fast and heavy as he could feel himself about to climax.

"Harder!" she yelled now as James attempted to keep up.

"Harder!" she yelled again, this time much louder and more aggressively. Her screams overtook him as she thrust herself against him, again and again until she climaxed. Her legs quivered, locking around him until he slowly pulled away. The moment lingered as he looked down upon her body shimmering in soaked white linens cast in splinters of moonlight.

He watched her in stunned silence. She had never acted like that before. Like an animal. *Violent.* He reached across his chest feeling the blood upon his shoulder blade and could see more blood on the sheets.

"What was that?" he asked but she did not answer. Her chest rose and fell as if she had already fallen asleep. Or perhaps never even awakened, he thought.

Reaching down he began to draw up the linens to cover her when suddenly he stopped. Scanning her abdomen, he blinked and rubbed his eyes as if he wasn't about to believe what he was seeing. It was shadows of moonlight. Just the darkness playing tricks on him.

Gently running a hand down her belly, he could feel the rise of her skin. Small, distended mounds formed a shape upon the center of her stomach. The faint outline of something; a small oval body. *Wings.*

He quickly pulled his hand back as something moved inside of her. The form pressed against the inside of her stomach.

He reached over and turned on the lamp but when he turned his eyes back to her it was gone. Her stomach was perfectly still. He reached over nervously, running his hand across the soft peach fuzz around her naval. Her body moved in rhythm, a deep sleep cast upon her. Something he, too, needed now more than ever. Maybe he was asleep, and this was all a dream. Maybe in his real life everything was normal; Elizabeth was alive, and the world was as it should be. But in this one, children died, and souls turned to ash.

He turned over to go back to sleep and could see on the bedside nightstand leaning against the lamp was the small rag doll staring back at him. Its eyes were black as the night, watching him like a silent voyeur.

CHAPTER 9

James poured himself a cup of coffee as Karen sat at the small breakfast nook looking through a copy of Southern Living.

"I have an idea," James said, suddenly feeling enthusiastic. "Why don't we get outta here?"

Karen looked confused. "What'd you mean?" she replied, setting the magazine down.

"I mean, let's get outta here. Head into the city tonight for a proper date. It's been so long since I've seen you wear that black dress."

"Not tonight," Karen replied looking back down at her magazine.

He remembered how things used to be. How they could be again. Even if it was just the two of them now. They used to all have so much fun together at the kitchen table playing games on Friday night. She was always the one to make him and Lizzy laugh, whether one of her endless bad jokes or impressions of some random character. She had this charisma that could charm anyone she met. It was a gift. A presence when she walked into the room. Now that person seemed a million miles away. But maybe she could find her way home...whatever home was.

Reaching behind his back James pulled out a small blue flower he had picked from the backyard and got down on one knee.

With that, a smirk rose from her tightly pursed lips and her eyes brightened for a moment. It was the old Karen locked inside and he was sure somehow, he could get her out. Even if it was with the help of a little blue flower.

***

The night was serene as James and Karen strolled River Street hand in hand. The cobblestone path clicked beneath Karen's heels; the ones he hadn't seen her wear in quite some time. Her dress was stunning; cut just above the knees with single spaghetti straps and a shimmer that caught glints of moonlight pouring over the Savannah River.

It was a rather quiet night as there were no crowds, rather just a few groups of folks mingling about, headed from one bar to another or seated out on a terrace enjoying food and drinks. A gentleman and his lady friend smoking a cigarette talked of the band they had just seen. A group of friends laughed and carried on as they talked of men like they were animals, making Karen laugh as they passed.

"Quite the conversation," James added, as Karen looked back to see if the ladies noticed her laugh.

"They're so drunk you could probably lick their faces and they'd just thank you for it," she said with a little giggle.

Karen turned and shook her head as James smiled, seeing the girl he remembered suddenly back by his side.

"I miss you, ya know," James said.

"What do you mean?"

"It's just nice to see you like this."

"Yeah well…" she replied, and he could see she didn't know how to even respond.

"You don't have to say anything," James cut in putting his arm around her. He knew nothing would ever be the same after losing Elizabeth. But still, sometimes he wanted to pretend it was all normal and they were just like any other couple. Especially tonight. Just another date night.

"How about tonight we just enjoy the moment. Not think about anything, okay?"

Karen nodded and gave a smile as they continued down the walkway passing a little French bistro. Its smell was intoxicating as they stopped for a moment to look in the window.

"Still hungry?" James asked, as she turned away and continued to walk.

"Let's just say you might have to roll me the rest of the way home," she replied strolling up ahead a bit.

James smiled as he watched her eyes stare off into the night. Her attention, caught by something.

He followed her gaze seeing an old man covered in his own filth lying next to a streetlamp. The amber glow shined down upon him like a spotlight upon a stage. James watched as Karen grabbed their leftovers out of his hand and quickly headed over.

She knelt and handed the man the bag of food. His face was unshaven. A heavy beard covered the deep lines of his dark complexion.

"This is for you," Karen said, as the man looked up with a peculiar stare. James was close by and could see the man appeared almost as if he recognized her. But he didn't take the food. He just sat silently and stared without saying a word.

"I'll just leave it here for you. How about that?" she asked as she placed the food down beside him.

"I know you," the man suddenly spoke up. His voice, raspy and low as he seemed lost in Karen's eyes.

"I'm sorry but I think you have me mistaken for someone else."

As she left the food and stood the man reached out and grabbed her wrist tightly, clenching it in his large, callused hand.

James instinctively lunged forward to grab the man.

"No!" Karen exclaimed as she held him back.

James paused, watching as the old man gently turned her palm over and began to read the lines.

"You've been here before," he said staring deeper into her palm, moving her wrist ever so slightly to the left and right trying to get the light cast just right.

"We were here a few months ago, yes," Karen replied.

"No, you were here when the slave masters called…when the sting of the cat o' nine tails flayed the backs of those that came before."

"Excuse me?" she replied.

"It's upon you. I can smell its blood still soaked into the ballast stones that pave these forsaken streets. But you're not like the others, noooo. They're afraid of you, aren't they? They've always been afraid," he said as if speaking right through her.

Karen withdrew her hand, sliding it from his grasp, and stood up, slowly backing away. The man's eyes fluttered in and out of consciousness as he leaned back against the lamp post and fell back into his former state.

"Come on, let's go," James said, grabbing her hand.

"What did he mean, James? What was he talking about?"

"I don't know, he's drunk I think."

Karen turned to look back as James held her hand tight and pressed on, feeling the need to get as far away from him as possible. There was something in the air. Mixed with the humidity and smells of the city. The food, the garbage…the rot. He could feel it wherever they went. Something watched them, but more importantly, it watched her.

***

A near full moon cast a beautiful glow across the property as James and Karen turned down the driveway and headed underneath the majestic oaks.

What a place this must have been a century ago.

James' thoughts always got the best of him, especially after a few drinks. He could see the horse and buggy pulling up to attend some affluent affair where, had the color of his skin not been what it was, he was sure he would have quite enjoyed it. He could almost feel a life waiting for him. A real life where he and Karen actually had a chance to be happy again.

Pulling up in front of the house, the thoughts of elegant parties and happily-ever-afters, suddenly vanquished as he stared up at a flickering glow from an upstairs window. But not just any window. The last bedroom at the end of the hallway facing the western fields.

"James?" Karen called out, squeezing his leg.

The car came to a halt as he turned the engine off and just stared for a moment without giving any semblance to what he was actually feeling. He absolutely didn't want Karen to see the terror that just shot through his blood stream. The hairs on the back of his neck standing on end.

"Did we leave a light on?" Karen asked.

"Those aren't lights…those are candles," James replied, as he could have sworn a shadowed figure had just moved across the room. He attempted to get out of the car, but Karen grabbed his hand and pulled him back.

"It'll be fine, just give me a minute. I'll be right back," he said, looking into her eyes. They were scared. But there was something else. Something he couldn't quite place. He gave her a kiss on the cheek and headed out.

Inside, the house felt colder than usual. Each step up the old staircase creaked beneath his feet. The moonlight cast shadows across the floor like watchers in the night.

Upstairs he could see the flickering glow from the bedroom at the end of the hall. The door was slightly ajar.

Taking a quick detour into his bedroom, he grabbed his .45 from the shoe box in the closet. Something Karen never liked but he always felt like sometimes God needed a little help, and now felt it his only protection as he believed God had all but abandoned him.

Checking the chamber, he headed back into the hallway and slowly crept down the long dark corridor.

"Whoever is in there better head out that window unless you're ready to meet whatever God you find fit to save your soul!" James yelled out.

There was no sound.

He stepped closer, growing angrier and more nervous by the second. He thought back to when he was a boy heading down this very hallway. That dark night when he found himself staring into his own nightmare and the nightmare just stared right back.

Now standing right outside the door all these years later he didn’t feel much different, only this time he had a gun in his hand. But a gun doesn’t kill the boogeyman, he thought.

James took a deep breath. Then in a sudden burst, he spun around the corner into the room like a cop busting into a drug house, the pistol held out before him.

The glow of candlelight illuminated the fresh chalk circle by the window. The same one he had seen the first night he came here. The outline of the familiar cicada within was surrounded by strange hieroglyphs and dozens of candles melted down to the floor. They pooled like blood as James' vision became a blur, staring upon the spot where he had stood as a boy with his hand pressed to the window. *Tick tack, tick tack.* Each tap awakening something he didn’t want to ever come back.

The room looked almost the same as it had all those years ago. At this time of night, it felt all too real as the glow of candles and the fresh chalk circle by the window called him to step inside and finish what he had started. A feeling, like he'd just walked back in time. The nightmare stirring within as if his eyes were getting accustomed to the darkness.

TICK TACK SAMUEL BLACK IS BACK

The graffiti just stared back at him like a bully taunting him to come play. Suddenly the voices of Tommy Clayton and Daniel Buckard rang in his head.

Oink oink little piggy. Come here darky. Come and playeeee.

The high-pitched laughter of Tommy was like a hammer pounding his head, and the memory of the rancid smell of his breath when he had him pinned up against a wall, running his switchblade across his cheek, made him want to vomit.

James leaned over, taking a breath as the saliva built within his mouth. Even the thought of their names caused the hair on the back of his neck to rise. He had forgotten about them for so long and the hell they brought to him as a boy.

"Oh my God," Karen's voice suddenly spoke up from behind. He turned to see her standing in the doorway.

"Call 911," he said urgently.

"Are we in danger?" she asked, her fear making her voice tremble.

"Just call 911!" he shouted, suddenly unable to contain it anymore, letting out the most blood curdling scream. His fists flew into the walls until blood poured from his hands onto the floor.

Karen drew back down the hallway crying hysterically as she watched her husband lose every ounce of self-control. His eyes were bloodshot, and veins pulsed from his forehead. The anger suddenly rising inside was uncontrollable. His hands ripped the room to pieces, tossing candles and punching holes. He didn't care. He didn't care about anything at that moment. He wanted blood. He wanted to find whoever did this.

"James!" Karen screamed, but he did not hear her. He heard nothing but the demons awakening inside his head.

CHAPTER 10

The lights of the police cruiser headed down the long gravel driveway as James and Karen sat beside each other on the front porch.

A tall man in his late forties with short dark hair and a rather pronounced jaw stepped out of the vehicle and stood a moment, taking in the sight of the grand columns.

"Mister Elba?" he asked, as he approached the front steps.

James stood up and extended a hand, noticing the badge read Sheriff Davidson.

"Thank you for coming, Sheriff," he said, as he watched the sheriff take in the house and all its grandeur.

"Some house ya got here. My grandmama used to tell me stories about this place."

"Yes, well…it's got a lot of history, I guess you could say."

"That's one way to put it," the sheriff replied, "you doin' all this work yourself?"

"I am, my wife and I," James replied, somewhat irritated as the Sheriff reached out and patted a hand on the column leading up the front steps.

"Some places just want to scare ya off," the sheriff said as his eyes continued to wander over the house. "They have this…" He stopped a moment searching for the word. "They have this soul about them, almost like they're alive inside and don't want anyone changing anything. It resists like some animal being put in a cage."

James didn't respond as the thought felt all too real.

"Look at me, just rambling on while your wife is sitting here practically scared to death. Apologies ma'am," he said to Karen, giving her a little tip of his hat. "Now you reported a break in. Is that correct?"

"Yes," James replied, as Karen stood up and stepped beside him, curling her arm around his waist. "We went into the city. Got back about eleven."

"And what did you find missing so far?" the sheriff asked, taking out a pad and pen.

"Nothing actually," James replied, seeing the sudden confused look on the Sheriff's face.

"Nothing?"

"No, Sheriff. As far as I can see they were just in an upstairs spare bedroom. A bunch of kids maybe. The same room was vandalized before we had moved in. They left graffiti all over the walls and some other things."

"What other things?" the sheriff asked as James stood silently, unable to speak.

The sheriff stood a moment looking up at the house as if he were trying to read its mind. "Show me."

***

Upstairs, James reached down and was about to open the door when he stopped for a moment. His hand was shaking. Even now, this room still bothered him, like the Devil lay on the other side. His nerves were getting the best of him as he felt his heart rate rise.

"Mister Elba, you alright?" the sheriff asked.

"I'm fine," James quickly replied as he looked up and nodded, pushing away the thoughts in his head. Taking a deep breath, he then turned back towards the door and twisted the nob, gently pushing it open.

The sheriff stepped past James, giving him a second glance as if making sure he was okay, then went inside the room.

"I'll be god damned," the sheriff said, taking it all in a moment as he stood shaking his head before getting out his camera and snapping pictures of the scene.

James just stood there watching. Each flash seemed to pierce his skull and send his nerves into a shock. His head pounded as if the room was getting the best of him.

"Someone really did a number on these walls."

"Well, sheriff. That was me," James reluctantly replied.

"You? Anger problem, have we?"

"No, I just…after everything we've been through, I just lost it when I saw what they did here to this room. It's a violation of our sanctity. Kids I assume. I just…"

"Yeah well, you do have quite a famous house here. As I'm sure you know. Kids been coming here since as long as I can remember," the sheriff said as he went about his investigation.

"It's our home now. Not some haunted amusement park," Karen replied, squeezing James' hand tightly.

"I hear ya, ma'am. I really do and I'm sorry that you had to experience this," the sheriff replied as he continued looking around the room.

"A cicada?" the Sheriff whispered under his breath as he knelt, touching the white chalk with the tip of his finger.

“You familiar with this sort of thing, Sheriff?" James asked, attempting to break the silence, more for his own sanity than anything else.

Another flash and a few more pictures.

"I am, grew up here myself. Moved out of the city many years ago but still seen my fair share of voodoo, hoodoo and all other sorts that have kept me up at night on many occasions."

He stood up taking a closer look around the room then glanced out the window before turning his attention back to the scene.

"This was the original master bedroom, am I correct?" the sheriff asked.

"Yes, how did you know that?" James questioned in a sudden curious tone.

"Well, like I said, my Grandmama told me a lot about this house. Might have even been here myself once or twice as a boy if I do recall," he said with a little grin. "I remember the stories. The plantation's original owner was an unusually cruel man. Samuel Black, if I'm not mistaken," The sheriff spoke like it was story time around a campfire, as he pointed to the name spray painted on the wall.

"His bedroom overlooked the western fields and the infamous forest where he took his slaves, they said." The Sheriff seemed to be lost in his memories, staring out the window.

"Yes, I've heard the stories. I grew up in these parts myself. But I'd like to please not talk about the past. Why don't we talk about what happened tonight if you don't mind." James replied in a curt tone.

"No, I want to hear this," Karen quickly chimed in and stepped forward into the center of the room, making James feel even more uneasy.

"Karen, it's..." James tried to speak but couldn't as she already had a hand up dismissing him.

"Well, Mr.Elba, if you grew up here then you know what I'm talking about," the sheriff exclaimed. "I take it your wife isn't privy to this house's history?"

"And there's no reason she needs to have that crap fill her head. It's all a bunch of stories to scare kids."

"Yes, indeed. I was one of those kids...and if you're from here, I imagine you were, too."

"James, please. Let him talk," Karen chimed in. Her eyes were drawn to the sheriff, seeming to hang on his every word.

"Please, tell me," she begged.

"Well, Samuel Black was the man that built this very planation which you now call home, back before the civil war. They say his cruelty knew no bounds as this place was the one place you absolutely didn't want to end up if you were one of the unfortunate souls getting off those boats."

The Sheriff gazed listlessly about the room as if imagining its former stature. "He also had a wife and daughter. As the story goes his little girl passed away when she was quite young. It was then the true nature of his cruelty began to manifest as he blamed the slaves for her death."

"That's so sad," Karen said, placing a hand on her heart.

"Well, to feel empathy for a man such as this is misplaced emotion, I'm afraid." The sheriff moved towards the window staring out towards the forest. "And it was out in those woods, clearing land for the expansion of his rice fields that the slaves came upon something buried. Something that would give him both hope and madness. Something that they said could bring his daughter back to him."

"What did he find?" Karen asked, looking as if she were on the edge of her seat.

"No one knows. But they say he killed his own wife out in those woods soon thereafter as if somehow her sacrifice could save his child."

"That's just a story, no one really knows what happened," James added.

"Well, whatever it was, it was enough to drive a man beyond madness. To do unspeakable acts," the sheriff stopped, seeing James' glare. He looked like he had gotten carried away and gathered his more sensible nature. "Seems there are still some believers out there, though. Ghost stories never die, I suppose," he said, pointing to the writing on the wall and looking around the room at all the candles and bottles of liquor.

"Sheriff, I appreciate the historical and philosophical lessons here but with all due respect, this was a break-in. Nothing more. So, if you could just find the people that did this, I'd be very grateful."

"You say nothing was taken?"

"As far as we can tell. No, Sheriff."

"And the damage to the walls was your own hand?"

James hesitated, making quick eyes with Karen before answering with a silent nod of the head.

"And did you see anyone or can think of anything else that might help me?"

James remembered the shadow moving across the room, but it was just a trick of light. He told himself over and over it was nothing and now almost believed it. "I'm sorry, Sheriff, but no."

"I'm afraid there's not much I can do then. This house has a history and kids been coming here for as long as I can remember thinking they're gonna see the boogeyman or somethin'."

"Then what? We're supposed to just wait around until whoever comes back and does it again. Maybe it's not just a bunch of harmless kids! Maybe next time my wife will be home alone and…"

"Slow down," the Sheriff said raising a hand. "I understand your concern, trust me, I do. But with this sort of thing our hands are just tied. My suggestion is put in a security system. I'd start there."

James stood quietly now, rather infuriated with the situation.

The sheriff made a few more notes in his pad and stepped up to James.

"I know this is hard. And I want you to know I empathize with your situation, I really do."

"Thank you, Sheriff, I think we can handle it from here," James replied, giving him a cold glare.

"In the meantime, keep the windows and doors locked. I know you don't think about locking your doors living out here like this, but times have changed. The world's gone sour, it seems," he said, giving the two a little tip of the hat. "Goodnight, folks…I'll see myself out."

"I'll walk you, Sheriff," Karen spoke up, giving James a concerned look.

The sheriff turned to head out but stopped as if something had just come into his head. He turned back, looking at James.

"Do you believe in God, Mr. Elba?" he asked, sending a strange feeling through James' chest.

"Karen, please see the Sheriff out," James bluntly replied as the Sheriff got the point and turned and left, leaving James alone in the room.

James' thoughts boiled. He wasn't about to indulge the Sheriff's question nor his tales, not in front of Karen anyway. He didn't want to believe the nightmare growing within his own home. His own dreams and visions told him something that deep down he already knew. A little piece he had carried with him since he was a boy. A piece that he had thought he had all but buried. But here it was dug up and laid out before him, welcoming him home and reminding him that nothing really dies.

He just stared at the words upon the wall. The cryptic phrase stared back at him as if eyes watched him from another world. A darker world.

Do you believe in God, Mr. Elba?

He tried to answer but realized that he didn't really know anymore. He had never really thought about it until now. He had forsaken something that summer's day he saw his daughter dead on the hot concrete. Not just his faith but his compass…his light within the darkness.

Tick tack, tick tack, Samuel Black is Back.

He stared up at the writing on the wall and suddenly as if a switch was just flipped on a loudspeaker could hear the voices of Tommy Clayton and Daniel Buckard in his head. This time chanting the forsaken rhyme as their heavy footsteps headed up the staircase. Each board creaking beneath their feet. Bottles breaking against the walls. Their voices echoing down the hall.

Like a veil being lifted, he remembered more of that night from so long ago. The night he met the boogeyman; something far worse than either of those two bullies could even fathom in their own sick minds. Something that he never really understood. Something that he pushed so far down into his psyche that he had convinced himself it never even happened. But it did happen…and people disappeared. His friends. Gone forever somewhere. Their souls, still lost in those woods.

CHAPTER 11

Summer of 1980

"You first," James exclaimed as Scotty, Emma, and Harold stood in a nervous panic beside him at the edge of the forest.

"You're crazy! I'm not going in there!" Scotty exclaimed.

"Hold on, I'm out of breath," Harold wheezed with his hands on his knees.

"Yeah, Jimmy. That's way creepy. We can just go around," Emma nervously chimed in.

"There's no time. We have to go through the forest," James said trying to convince his friends as he felt the shadowed hand of the boogeyman upon his back.

"I think I hurt my knee jumping out of that window," Harold said, rubbing his legs.

"You're fine. Don't think about it," James replied, giving him a little pat on the back.

Looking back at the house, James stared at the window they had all just jumped out of. He had seen something up there. Something he hadn't told the others about. He looked harder to see if anything else was there when suddenly there was Tommy and Daniel looking out at them.

"You're dead!" Tommy yelled. His voice echoing across the field. "You're all dead!"

"Guys! We gotta go now!" James yelled.

"Gonna gut you all like pigs!" Tommy screamed as Daniel echoed the sentiment with loud squealing noises. The two were now on the ground, having just jumped from the window.

"They're coming!" Harold yelled out as he pressed up against James' side, still catching his breath.

"Okay. We stick together in here, but we have to move fast," James exclaimed.

"Jimmy, you know what they say about these woods. How can we go in there?" Harold nervously asked, looking like he wanted to puke.

"Because we have no choice. It's all just stories to scare kids. None of it's real."

"My brother says that it's filled with dead slaves wanting their revenge," Harold added.

"I didn't do anything to them," Scotty exclaimed in a panic.

"There ain't nothin' in there, that's just a bunch of malarky," James said, but deep down he knew there was. He had seen it up in that bedroom. A dark vision he could feel spiraling deep inside his mind.

"Come on, we can't stay here!" Emma yelled, grabbing James' hand, pulling him into the forest.

"Run!" Scotty yelled as they all looked back and saw that Tommy and Daniel were already halfway to the forest's edge.

"Squeak squeak squeak!" Daniel screamed out, making pig noises.

"Ya'll are dead!" Tommy yelled, "all of you's dead!"

James and the group headed deeper into the cover of the forest's canopy. Shadows created a maze of light and dark as they dodged and weaved their way through. Branches brushed against their shoulders and snagged their shirts as if there were hands attempting to grab them.

"This way!" James called out as the group began to fall further apart. Harold, the slowest one, was now significantly back from the others.

"Wait up!" Harold called out.

James could feel his heart pounding as the distant sounds of Tommy and Daniel drew closer upon their backs. He ran as fast as he could. As fast as he'd ever imagined possible. Almost like he was floating on air. Except there was something else in the air. Something that couldn't be ignored. A feeling of danger, not so much behind them but ahead. A darkness wrapping its arms around him and pulling him into some void from which there was no return.

"Guys, look!" Scotty yelled out.

James looked over and wasn't sure if the green glow from up ahead had always been there or if it had just appeared.

"What is it?" Harold asked frantically.

"Get it together, wheezy" Scotty exclaimed, giving him a pat on the back.

"I've got a condition. My mom…" Harold tried to explain when he was cut off.

"Guys, not the time!" Emma yelled, "just go!"

"But what is that?" James asked, pointing up ahead to the green glow pulsating through the trees.

"Whatever it is, it's better than what's back there." She turned and pointed behind them as they could hear the branches and twigs being broken from Tommy and Daniel's heavy bumbling footsteps running towards them.

They quickly picked up the pace, heading towards the greenish glow. Within a minute, James noticed, the trees began to change. The large oaks and sycamores replaced with nearly evenly spaced tall thin trunks, knotted with what he could only describe as eyes watching them.

"This is creepy," Scotty exclaimed staring at the strange change in the forest.

"Guys! What are these?" James asked.

Emma placed a hand on one of the trees giving it a quick once over. "Birch trees…these are birchwood."

"How do you know that?" Scotty asked.

"My dad showed me once, on a hike," she replied.

James seemed mesmerized, looking all around him. "My mother told me about these. They're meant for protection."

"Protection from what?" Harold asked.

"From evil spirits," James whispered as if not wanting to disturb whatever was around them.

"Well, if they don't protect us from crazy lunatics then I really don't think it matters right now," Scotty replied.

"He's right, come on guys!" Emma exclaimed and continued running.

Before they knew it, they had all run into a large circular clearing. The sky hung over them like a blackened sea as the moonlight and stars were hidden by some strange change in the weather. Looking up James felt as if he could almost see his reflection in some wavering veil cast over them. The hairs on his arms and the back of his neck stood on end. His legs felt weak as if he were walking through quicksand. His heart rate slowed. His chest was heavy. It was as if time suddenly slowed down to a near stop. He looked around and could see the green glow emanating from the ground itself.

"Jimmy!" Emma called out as she stumbled into him.

"Just wait," James replied as he cautiously looked around. "Do you see that?"

Emma paused a moment as she too scanned the area. "What is it?"

"I don't know," James replied.

"Guys!" Scotty yelled. "Come on, let's…whoa," he stopped mid-sentence now staring at the strange glow pulsing from the ground. The perimeter of the clearing, marked with a chalk circle. Around its outer edge, strange hieroglyphic symbols.

"What is this place?" Scotty asked, looking more terrified than ever.

"Those look like hieroglyphs. I studied them when we did a chapter on ancient Egypt in Mrs. Thompson's history class," Emma answered.

"Those look just like the ones in the bedroom by the window," James added.

Harold suddenly charged through behind them as they grabbed his arm stopping him from crossing into the circle.

"Stop!" James yelled as Harold nearly fell to the ground. "Don't go any further."

Harold stood motionless catching his breath as he stared ahead into the green glow emanating from the ground within the circle.

"Wait a second!" James exclaimed, taking a step back and climbing up a bordering tree.

"What'r you doin'? Are you Crazy!?" Harold yelled out.

"I need to get a better look, there's a shape of something inside that circle!" James yelled back.

“Not time for picture pages Jimmy!” Scotty exclaimed.

"It's a cicada! Guys, it's just like the one in the bedroom. By the window! This whole thing is exactly the same."

"What does it mean?" Emma called out.

"I don't know," James replied, heading back down to the ground.

"We have to go. They're almost here!" Scotty yelled as James shimmied down to the ground.

"Wait!" James yelled, stopping the group before they ran any further.

"You wait. I'm outta here," Scotty replied.

"Stop! Everyone just stop!" James yelled out, "would you all just Listen."

The group stood motionless as the night sounds shifted to a hollow ambience. Even their own voices sounded distant, like they weren't even standing near one another.

"I feel funny," Scotty exclaimed looking down at his arm, "they tingle like pins and needles."

"Do you hear that?" James asked.

"Hear what?" Emma replied, standing shoulder to shoulder.

"Voices," James exclaimed looking down at his feet, "down there."

"Oh my god," Emma looked up wide eyed and afraid.

"I hear it too," Scotty added.

"Screams. Somebody's screaming," Emma's voice trembled in fear as she looked around with terrified eyes.

"What is this place?" Harold asked, looking like he was ready to run.

James' eyes were lost within the green glow and by the time the group noticed, he was already halfway to the center of the circle.

"Jimmy no!" Emma yelled out. "Stay outta there!"

"There's people down there," James' voice trailed off as he stood silently within the center of the circle. The glow rising from the ground, surrounding him on all sides.

He knelt, placing his ear to the ground. He could hear the voices beneath the surface. There were so many, he thought. *How could it be?*

"What do you hear?" Emma asked.

"People. I can hear them. I can hear them all," James said as his voice began to tremble.

"Jimmy get out of there, now!" Scotty yelled.

But James could not move. His body was stricken with something deeper than fear as he pressed his ear to the cold Georgia clay. There was something else down there. Something that moved in between the voices. It spoke to him, welcoming him home.

CHAPTER 12

"They don't make em' like this anymore," the scruffy headed security tech exclaimed as he stood on a rickety looking ladder fastening a small camera by the front door.

"She's got old bones alright," James replied attempting to make small talk as his mind spun at the reality of the situation.

Karen entered with arms folded, seeming both relieved and disturbed.

"Smile you're on tv," the tech said jokingly as he finished adjusting the angle before hopping down.

Karen didn't smile or seem to find anything funny about the rather light-hearted security technician in their home.

"So, you two ready for a quick rundown of the system?"

James seemed rather distracted still watching Karen more than the task at hand.

"Sir?" the tech repeated, seeming to notice the awkwardness.

"We're ready," James replied, snapping out of it.

"Alright well…the system is real easy to operate and everything can be controlled right here at the keypad at the entryway.

"How many cameras are there?" Karen asked, still staring into the one looking down at her from above.

"We got you fully covered ma'am. Two wide angle perimeter cams, one located on the back porch and one on the front. These two will give ya a range within a fifty-yard radius. Now coming inside, we've got your main entrance here…or 'foyer' as the fancy folks like to call it," he added with a smile, making quotation marks with his hands. Again, Karen was not amused. He quickly continued, "one in the upstairs hallway, one in the master bedroom, one in each spare room, kitchen and dining room."

"You really think we need one in our bedroom?" Karen asked, looking over at James with quiet concern.

"I think so. We need everything covered," James replied.

"I just don't like the idea of a camera on me when I'm sleeping or when we're…" her voice trailed off with a little embarrassment.

"Better safe than sorry," the tech chimed in with a smirk.

Karen retracted, as her eyes looked back up into the camera with resentment.

"Honey, we talked about this," James added.

"Well, you two have nothing to worry about because you're as secure as Fort Knox. Anyone comes in or around this place, you'll have them on camera. And should they break in, this alarm will let you and anyone around know."

Quickly covering their ears, James and Karen held their hands over the sides of their heads cringing at the loud siren like alarm.

"Yes, thank you, that's good!" James yelled over the screeching pulse before it all went silent again.

"Like I said, you'll know if someone breaks in," the technician said proudly with a big smile.

"Thank you, so where can we see the security footage if we need to?" James asked.

"Yes, was just getting to that. Follow me."

A moment later the three were standing in James' office looking at six small, interconnected television monitors on the wall beside the bookshelf.

"Looks like it should be in a James Bond movie," Karen said running her hand over the screen.

"You wanted the best and you got it! They all sync up remotely and you can flip back and forth between any camera in the house."

"What about at night?" Karen asked as her eyes glanced across the monitors.

"The system has automatic night vision so there ain't nothin' you won't see rest assured ma'am," the tech said with rather joyous excitement as he then noticed James staring at one of the monitors in the lower right corner. *The upstairs bedroom at the end of the hall.* Its walls looked strange in the small black and white image, James thought. But as he stared into that monitor, he could swear there was something staring right back.

"What is it, hon?" Karen asked with a soft concern.

"Nothing, guess I've gotta get used to these things," he said snapping out of it.

"Yeah, takes a bit. You'd be surprised what shadows and dust can do. Make you see things that aren't there. One client even said they caught a ghost in one."

"Really?" Karen replied looking very curious.

"Turned out it was just her husband sneaking out to meet up with another woman, but thought it was a ghost at first nonetheless."

Once again, Karen appeared not to be amused.

"Well, I'll be heading out now. You two seem to have things under control here. Eight hundred number on the desk there if you ever have any issues," the tech said with a smile and picked up a few things then awkwardly shuffled out of the room.

"Here, I'll see you out," Karen exclaimed, pasting a fake grin on her face.

"Thank you, ma'am," he replied giving them both a little nod of the head. "Sir, have a nice day."

James acknowledged the young man's manners then stood quietly staring into the monitors. Each one lifeless and alone. The image, like another reality laid over this one. One that he couldn't see but he knew all too well was there.

***

Dinner that evening was quiet. Even more so than usual. James kept staring up at the small red blinking light in the corner looking down at them. It felt strange to always be watched and have his office turned into what now looked more like a security room at a prison.

"How do you like it?" Karen asked as James quickly brought his eyes back to the table staring down at the plate of meatloaf and mashed potatoes.

"Baby it's wonderful. Just like your Grammy used to make on Tuesday night dinners," he replied, remembering the good old days when he and Karen first met.

The two ate in silence for another moment. Nothing but the sound of forks clinking and mouths chewing.

"I think things are coming along nicely, don't you?" James commented, forcing himself to break the intolerable silence.

"Excuse me," Karen exclaimed as she stood up to leave the room.

"You alright?" James asked.

"Are you?" she asked back. Her eyes lost in some distant torment, not letting her go.

"Yeah, I'm fine," James replied.

"Then, so am I," she said with a forced grin and disappeared with her plate to the kitchen.

James sat alone a moment wondering what had just happened to upset her.

In the kitchen he stood in the doorway a moment watching her stand at the sink aggressively scraping food in the garbage and rinsing off her plate.

Walking closer he could feel the tension between them. Slowly placing his hands on her shoulders, he squeezed them softly yet firmly. The tightness within her muscles released as he heard her breath exhale.

"We're going to be fine baby. I don't want you to worry about anything."

She turned around looking up into his eyes. A vulnerable stare that seemed endless. One that could see right through him, penetrating his deepest thoughts locked within.

"Tell me it's all okay, James," Karen said.

"What do you mean? We've got security cameras and an alarm system. No one is going to come back I…"

"That's not what I'm talking about," she shot back, cutting him off.

"Then what?"

"You can feel it, can't you?" she asked, now appearing nervous and afraid.

"Feel what? Please just talk to me."

"Ever since we got here," she stepped away, removing his hands from her shoulders. "There's something not right here. It's like a bad dream. Only this isn't a dream…at least, I don't think it is."

"Karen, you're not making any sense," James replied stepping closer to her.

She turned and looked out the window with her hands flat upon the countertop like she needed to hold herself from falling.

"I feel like I've been here before, James," she stated with a trembling tone, "I look out and can see the people in those fields. I can see their faces. The creases in their skin. The sweat stained clothes upon their backs. That look in their eyes. Each one like I know them. Like I've seen them before. But more than that…like I was one of them, suffering the same pain."

"Karen, please," James begged.

"And out there…out in those woods, that's where they died, James. So many," her voice quivered, "I can hear their screams."

"It's just stories, Karen," James replied wanting to believe his own words as much as he wanted to convince her.

"It's not though," she said, breaking down in tears as James drew her close, pressing her wet cheek to his chest.

"I think we might need to go talk to someone, baby," James said, "someone who can help you work through these thoughts and feelings."

Karen just stared off a moment as James held her tightly against his chest. He could feel her heart beating quickly. The cold sweat upon her.

"The Devil lives here, doesn't he?" Karen asked in a soft monotone voice as she raised her head looking him dead in the eye.

James had no response only the soft whisper of his own mind, telling him yes…yes, he does.

CHAPTER 13

James lay in bed quietly staring at the blinking red dot of the security camera feeling very uneasy. Karen was already fast asleep and even the sound of her breathing didn't quell the restlessness going through his bones. Quickly he got out of bed making sure to not disturb her as she seemed so peaceful. Something he did not want to interrupt as peace was now all too often missed from their daily lives.

Passing by the nightstand on Karen's side of the bed he made eyes with the small rag doll. Its presence, strange and almost disturbing, but seemingly benign, nonetheless. It was all she seemed to cling onto for comfort nowadays. He wished he had never found it in the first place or at least had just discarded it. *But hadn't he?* So much seemed to be a blur now as he was having trouble concentrating on just about anything lately. Regardless he still didn't understand how it had ended up on her nightstand. She claimed to have just found it sitting there, but he most assuredly had not been the one to put it there.

'Just let it go,' he told himself and quickly dismissed any more rumination on the subject as he stared into its black beady eyes. It was here and that was that. But there was still something about it he couldn't quite figure out. It seemed to watch him. To watch her too. But it was just a doll. *Wasn't it?* He thought about taking it right then and tossing it but how could he explain that to Karen. No, the doll would stay. It was just the night getting the best of him. Just like everything else seemed to be lately. His thoughts constantly wandering to dark places. He needed to relax. He needed a drink.

It got to be a regular routine to get up in the middle of the night and pour himself a glass of bourbon then retire to his office where the half dozen monitors would create the most boring television series he'd ever watched. Night after night he'd sit down and stare, not sure what he was looking for. He hadn't really thought about it. Things were relatively normal now but sometimes he could feel something. A thought that ran his blood cold. Not a dream. Not a memory. Just a feeling. A cold burning sensation. Hot and cold. Light and dark. A duality within a flicker of a moment. Something awakening within the empty corners of the house…or perhaps within himself.

Things always felt a little strange at this time of night, he thought. The witching hour some would call it. His mother never liked this time of night either. It was the time his father would be at his drunkest. The height of a twelve-hour binge of whiskey and cigarettes. He never drank beer. Just the hard stuff. Probably why as James had gotten older, he had developed a distaste for the stuff but oddly had seemed to be liking it more and more lately. A glass of bourbon had started to become something of a routine on these sleepless nights since they had moved in. But still, he couldn't see a bottle of bourbon without seeing his father's soulless eyes staring back at him.

Tonight, was as quiet as any other night since the break-in. Nothing exciting. Just another evening of tasting that sweet southern sting and slowly fading back to where he could maybe get a few hours of shut eye.

Since the break-in, the sleepless nights had gotten worse. He could hardly think of anything else besides who had been inside their home that night. Kids most likely, he thought. Teenagers thinking that the boogeyman still lived here and that if they showed their girlfriend what men they were, maybe would get laid. The thought made him smile as he remembered what it was like being a kid. Carefree and afraid of nothing. But it wasn't like that for him. He was afraid of plenty when he was a boy. Maybe that's why he felt he was the one that had something to prove that night all those years ago. The night he walked into this house when it was just ghosts and cobwebs and went into that bedroom to say the words and prove himself to his friends, but mostly to Emma. Just then the warm thought of her kiss against his cheek gave him goosebumps. He hadn't thought of her in so long. She was nothing more than a dream now. But like so many of these dreams they all seemed to be coming to the surface lately.

Staring into the black and white monitor of that empty room at the end of the hall he thought back on that night trying to remember other details, but all he got were flickers of half-truths and nightmares, reminiscent of watching a late-night television show with bad reception. The rest was just a jumble, like a scattered jigsaw puzzle with too many missing pieces. That's what it felt like. Just a jumble of memories. Too far gone to even know what was real or not anymore. But these were pieces he hadn't just put in a drawer and locked away long ago rather they were pieces that were erased…purposely, as to hide they ever existed in the first place.

A sudden movement from within the monitor caught his attention as his eyes darted to the right trying to see what had just happened. He was getting used to seeing the world through the eyes of a security camera, as the silence of each frame was easily disturbed by even the slightest intrusion. A bug, a moonlit shadow, a glitch in the frame. But this time it was something that ran his blood cold. Something that shouldn't have been there.

James stared at the monitor not understanding what he was seeing. It was as if the cameras peered back in time as he watched the faint outlines of objects move about the space. *Slaves.* Translucent figures floating across the screen. My god, he thought.

Not believing what he was seeing he scooted to the edge of his seat and looked closer. Their dark skin and stark white eyes moved about as if the world were as it was a hundred and fifty years ago. The furnishings were no longer their own. Along with every other room he could see time had been rewound. The dining room had a large table set with a feast attended by dozens of slaves, moving in and out of the room as if a party were about to be underway. Each face, cold and emotionless seeming to float across time.

The kitchen was busy with house slaves preparing various dishes. Pots and pans scattered about. Bread, bowls of soups and plates of meats all moving into the dining room. A feast was underway. The library was filled wall to wall with endless books. Each shelf overflowing with copies of fresh manuscripts. A fire roared within the living room as artifacts now lined the stone mantel and dead animal heads covered the walls. In another monitor, a young slave girl made her way upstairs. One hand sliding up the railing as she carried something unknown in the other…the doll.

James' eyes darted to the upstairs monitors. She was walking towards the room at the end of the hall. He could see the former master bedroom was no longer just a vacant spare room rather was filled with large furnishings and the walls covered in ornately framed paintings. A four-post bed sat by the window and there within it lay a man. A thin, sickly man looking right back at him. His eyes black as onyx staring into the camera as James felt his skin crawl and heart skip a beat. The figure did not move a muscle but rather peered into James' soul as if he could hear what he was thinking. His every thought and emotion carried into that room. The sickly man with wispy tendrils of white hair looked from beyond a place James didn't believe even existed. This wasn't happening, he thought. It couldn't be.

Pushing himself away from the screen, he felt the man's eyes follow him. Dark thoughts began racing through his mind. Familiar images he had seen before. Horrible, painful scenes that tore at his inner self in ways he couldn't believe. The air was taken from his chest. He felt faint and short of breath. The pain, so intense as if the acts themselves were happening within his own body. Torture, beyond measure. Bodies of slaves torn apart. Insides dissected. Hearts ripped from chests. Eyes staring into oblivion. He had seen it all before.
Yes…so long ago.

Just as he thought he could take no more and was ready to throw the monitor across the room, the images ceased as the sickly figure in the bed turned his attention away from James. His eyes now on the young slave girl entering the bedroom, but she wasn't alone. A tall luminescent woman stood by her side. Dark skin, long neck. Strong broad shoulders. A dress made of rags flowed from her body like a specter within the ethereal plane. Her movements like the others floated and sometimes skipped a beat as if frames were missing from time. But there was something different about her. Something powerful. Sudden jerky movements broke his stare as an almost ritualistic dance began. Her irregular actions startled him and seemed to affect the others in the house. The shadowy slaves began to crack and crumble before his eyes. A head twisted to its side. A hand bent backwards. Legs turned sideways as their bodies all seemed to move in a syncopated dance of the dead.

James watched as the tall dark woman began to shake violently. Hands raised to the sky. Her body moved in and out of the frame as if turned static. But it wasn't static. It was bugs. *Cicadas.* The small insects emerged from her mouth and filled the frame until there was nothing left but a black haze, and then in a sudden flash it was gone!

James sat dumbfounded as everything was back to normal. The spare room at the end of the hall, empty once again…but not completely. Someone was standing there. *Karen.* Her naked body covered in long deep gnashes as she clawed at herself screaming. Her body twisted and turned as the blood pooled at her feet. Something unnatural rested within her eyes. Even through the black and white monitor he could see it. A pain beyond anything he'd ever seen. She wreathed in torment.

"Karen!" James yelled as he jumped out of his seat and ran upstairs. "Karen baby I'm coming!"

He had never run so fast in his life. His heart pounded out of his chest and adrenaline surged through his body. The imagines of what he had just seen vibrated through his psyche, driving him mad.

What was happening to his life?

The madness swirled in his mind, throwing him off balance as he tripped and fell at the top of the stairs. Quickly getting up, he flew down the hallway, reaching out as if each second were his last.

Slamming the door open, James looked down upon his wife's body lying on the floor screaming as she dug her fingers into her skin, curling up large pieces of flesh beneath her nails. His stomach churned from the overwhelming smell of blood.

"Baby, please," James begged as he held his wife's naked blood-soaked body against his chest. "I can't lose you! Not you, too." His strength prevented her movement as she convulsed in his arms. Whatever God would do this please just take it away, he thought. He wept uncontrollably as if holding onto her for dear life and for the first time in a long time prayed for mercy upon their souls.

CHAPTER 14

Karen's body lay in the steamy bath as James knelt by her side gently running a rag across her chest. The water had turned a slight tinge of pink from the blood dripping from the long scratches across her body. He was still very shaken. His hand trembled as he laid the warm wet rag across her back and caressed her wet hair.

"You're okay, baby," he whispered as he examined the wounds further, now seeing the gashes were a bit deeper than he initially thought. "Might actually need to stitch you up here," he said barely able to speak without wanting to cry. The pain he felt for her was almost unbearable.

Her eyes just stared up at the ceiling, not seeming to feel a thing as he began to examine her further and clean the dirt from her nails. Within it pieces of skin that had been curled beneath the nail came out. The image made his stomach weak as he held back wanting to vomit right then and there.

"What were you doing?" James asked as he scrubbed the dirt and blood into the muddy pink water.

The dirt...where did the dirt come from?

Her nails. Her feet. They were covered.

"Karen, talk to me," James spoke softly as he continued gently caressing her body. "Where did you go?" he asked, not really wanting to know the truth. He had left her sound asleep and went downstairs. There's no way she could have left the house in that time. But there was no other answer.

Her silence gave way to more concern as his mind gave no reprise to the incident which made him feel even more out of control of the situation. Whatever situation it was. He really didn't know anymore. Nothing made sense. Nothing seemed real.

Lifting her head from the water, James leaned her forward and wiped the back of her neck and shoulders. Slowly wiping the dirt and cuts on her skin, revealed something he hadn't taken notice of before. The marks upon her back. Too far to have been reached by her own hands. He examined them closer as he attempted to make sense of their placement. Long fine lines of red, crossing as if she had been attacked by an animal.

"Baby, you have to talk to me. What happened in that room?" James asked, "please tell me where else were you tonight?" he asked again, only this time more insistent as she continued to stare off in some unseen distant void. But he knew she was in those woods. The distinct reddish hue of that Georgia clay from her feet told him that much. He didn't want to believe it for it felt too difficult to even comprehend why she would go out there in the first place. Unless she was sleepwalking. It was the only explanation.

Getting out the sutures from his medical bag James applied some antiseptic and began to go to work.

"This is gonna hurt a bit, but we need to close these up," he said, thinking he should have taken her to a hospital, but he was a doctor was he not. The bleeding was under control and as bad as it looked on the surface, she would be okay. Some topical anesthetic and a few stitches for the deeper wounds. She didn't need to be in some cold sterile hospital room anyway. She needed to be home.

But what is home? James thought, as he watched his wife's face not even flinch as he stitched up her back. One after another and she didn't move a muscle, it was like she wasn't even there. But it wasn't her body that he was worried about rather her mind. The body could heal quickly. But the mind, now that's another story. It was obvious the emotional stress of losing Elizabeth was more than she could handle. She was sleepwalking and the depression was sinking deeper into her. He couldn't handle it all. But even with all of this, he knew there was something else lingering beneath the surface.

James knew it but did not want to believe it. He tried to catalog an explanation for the incident but still couldn't understand what else could have done this. He knew the marks on her back were unreachable by her own hand. An animal? Something out in those woods. But why was she clawing her own body? A living nightmare as she perhaps was still not even awake when he had found her. She needed help, someone more capable than himself, he thought.

James could only stare silently down at the tub, feeling his own madness manifesting itself in ways he was not yet equipped to understand. The truth laying somewhere within that murky pink water.

Blood and earth. That's all we are.

***

Back in their bedroom, James sat at the edge of the bed watching his wife sleep. With each long deep breath, he could feel her sinking further and further away, wondering what distant place she might be. Maybe she was with Elizabeth, he thought. Imagining the two of them playing on some big green lawn on a beautiful summer's day made him almost smile. He wanted to be there with them. All of them back together again. Far away from this nightmare that was now their lives. Regardless, he just hoped she was at peace. If only for a moment, he thought. She had been through enough tonight.

No more nightmares. Just mercy. Please if there is a God have mercy.

Heading downstairs James went back to his office to take another look at the security footage of the last few hours. How could she have left the house without him knowing? He began scrubbing through the footage looking for anything to give him any semblance of what had happened. The images were like nightmares being rewound and re-lived. The timestamp read 2:30 AM as James watched himself get out of bed and head downstairs to his office. Within minutes Karen sat up. Not as if she woke up but as if something had woken her up. She looked to the right. James leaned in closer trying to decipher what he was seeing through the grainy footage. She was talking. Talking to who he wondered before realizing that the small rag doll sat alone on the nightstand directly in her line of sight. The interaction made him uneasy.

Another moment passed and she got out of bed, grabbed the doll, and headed out of the room. He scrubbed through the other monitors and could follow her path as she walked downstairs and out the back door. How had he not heard? The perimeter camera only caught her for a moment before she disappeared into the high grass of the western field.

Continuing to scrub through footage. He watched as the timestamp sped by. Now almost 3:00AM. She should have been coming back through that door and up to the spare bedroom at the end of the hall. But she wasn't. There was no sign of her ever coming back into the house. But also, no sign of the images he had seen before. No slaves, no feasts and paintings and fancy furniture as it once was. There was nothing but the house in its current state. Drab and lonely in comparison.

James leaned back in disbelief trying to figure out what had happened. Questioning even his own sanity. He switched to the image in the spare room where he had found her and rewound a bit. Playing it back he watched for her to return to the room…minutes passed and nothing. The room was as silent and empty as it ever was. And then suddenly static filled the screen. The image was gone.

"Come on!" James exclaimed, hitting the side of the monitor with his hand. The timestamp went on, but the static did not dissipate. "Not now," he said messing with a few of the wires when suddenly a bright flash filled the screen and there she was. The image was still very grainy and unclear, but he could see her, nonetheless.

But where was the tall African woman? The sickly man in the bed. The young girl with the doll? The slaves. Had he imagined it all? There was only Karen. He looked closer trying to gather some semblance of truth.

He watched closely through the static filled monitor as Karen wreathed in pain, clawing, and scratching her skin, screaming for someone to help her. It was hard to look at. Even harder the second time. He didn't want to see it, yet he felt he had to. Drawn to the grainy images, he felt sick to his stomach thinking of the pain she was going through.

Quickly he paused. There! Something else within the frame. *A hand.* Abstract, but a hand, nonetheless. He continued to scan through the grainy footage spotting another, then another. What at first, he thought only glitches in the static he could now see with his own eyes wasn't anything of the sort. There were countless human limbs within it, dark skinned hands reaching from some unseen world clawing at her body. Their presence, merely an absence of light, but all too real. Living shadows ravaging her body…but that wasn't all. There was something else there. *Someone.* The closer he looked the more he didn't want to believe. Someone was there in the room watching her suffer. He could almost feel its pleasure as the faint indication of a curled lip revealed itself from what could only be a mouth. A face within a dark corner staring out. It was the sickly old man he had seen lying in the bed, standing resolute and dressed in a dark suit topped with a black wide brimmed hat. He knew who it was but did not believe it. The man he saw in that same room almost thirty years before. The man that was now driving him to near insanity as he tried to ignore the reality staring him in the face.

"Samuel Black," James whispered under his breath. Whatever he wanted, he was getting closer now. Karen was slipping through his fingers and into a place he couldn't go. A place in between worlds.

A world you've seen before.

"Leave her alone," James uttered from quivering lips as he could feel his pulse rising the longer, he stared into the black and white monitor. The figure in the shadows locked in time. Watching her as she writhed in torment and pain. Her body frozen in madness.

"Leave her alone!" James yelled at the top of his lungs, ripping the monitor from the wall, and smashing it on the floor. Another then another until the room was nothing but broken glass, plastic and metal scattered everywhere. The feeling of pure rage flowed through him and only his father's cold blackened eyes stared back.

You're just like me James. You've always been me.

CHAPTER 15

It had been a week since the incident and Karen had spent most of her days in bed. It was obvious she wanted to be left alone, but she had finally recovered enough to leave the house. James knew he couldn't do this on his own and had made an appointment for her to see a psychiatrist who had been highly recommended.

Something was gone inside of her that he could not draw back and at last he felt helpless. She barely ate and could hardly get out of bed, if only to use the bathroom. A few times he even had to change the sheets as she had soiled herself right there without so much as a motion of acknowledgement that it had happened. It wasn't until he could smell the excrement that he even knew what had happened.

Concern grew to worry as the days grew shorter and the nights longer. So much so that James had permanently taken leave from the clinic to tend to Karen's recovery, although he couldn't predict how long that would even be.

Most days he found that the renovations of the house had taken on new meaning as almost a way of keeping himself sane rather than rebuilding a life. He stayed busy and tried not to think about the things that were out of his control. Only what he could fix. The hammer and nail in his hand. The sanding block, the tub of paint and brush. They were simple things and that is all he wanted in his life.

When not tending to his wife he focused his energy mainly on the library. Many nights falling asleep on the old sofa in front of the fireplace, later waking in the middle of the night with a book laid open on his chest and an empty glass of bourbon by his side. His eyes fixated upon the stone cherubim holding up the mantel. There was something about them as if they were alive, like two souls trapped within the house. The weight of that mantel piece forever upon their shoulders. He felt it too. Every bit of it as if it were upon him as well to keep it all together.

That afternoon, standing on the front porch, James watched in silence as summer gave way to the subtle delicacies of fall. The live oak lined drive remained green, unlike its deciduous counterparts whose burgundy leaves would have blanketed the ground this time of year. James could feel the change in the air as the temperatures began to drop and the sound of cicadas diminished as the annual breed died off as well as their periodical counterparts who would now be submerging back into the earth for another seventeen years. He would miss the sound of their call as it was always something he loved dearly since he was a boy. A soothing nighttime rhythm. Almost like a southern lullaby. Regardless, he was looking forward to the cooler fall temperatures as he continued the renovations.

Karen loved this time of year as well and he reminded her every day, attempting to brighten her spirits, even buying a small pumpkin, and setting it by her bedside.

She didn't seem to care much for anything and whatever had happened to her that night was buried so far beneath the surface its truth was never coming out.

He knew this was to be expected with the pain meds but sensed there was something more holding her back. The mind is a powerful thing, and he knew all too well the power it could hold over someone's recovery. He wished every day to take her place, to carry her burden and thoughts upon his shoulders, but could only watch as she lingered within some unseen purgatory, wrapping itself around her like a thin dark veil.

To balance her mind, he would read to her every night. Passages from her favorite book; The Secret Garden by Frances Hodgson Burnett. It was something her grandfather used to read to her as a little girl and since the day he met her she had kept a copy of a first edition gifted to her in his will by her bedside. Although it had been stored away since they moved to the house James thought it fitting to unbox it and open back up its old worn pages.

But there was something else he found in those old boxes. A shoebox. One that he had thought had been burned many years ago. *Size 9 Chuck Taylors. Black.* The box made him smile remembering all the adventures he had wearing that worn rubber and canvas. His favorite shoe. How could this even exist, he thought. Everything was burnt when he went to college. Purposely destroyed, leaving any memory of his childhood behind. Erased from existence, or so he thought.

Hesitating, he opened it up. It was nearly empty. A yo-yo. A short story written in sloppy cursive titled, 'The severed hand' by Scotty Baker. One of many Scotty had written. Why he had kept this one he didn't know. Scotty had a little knack for horror despite teachers thinking he had a screw loose. James laughed remembering the time Scotty brought the VHS copy of Halloween to Harold's tenth birthday party and scared him to the point he couldn't sleep alone in his room for a month. His mother never forgave Scotty when she found out.

Looking further in the box he pulled out a few baseball cards. *Hank Aaron.* No wonder he didn't throw this away. But then a few things filled his heart with a sharp pain. An old polaroid of the gang; Scotty, Harold and Emma…*Oh Emma.* Those green eyes still shown through that old, faded picture. These were the best and worst days of his life. When he and his friends would spend summers at the lake and late nights telling ghost stories by flashlight. He thought back about the days when the four of them were as thick as thieves. Before that night when they ran for their lives out into those woods. There was so much more he still couldn't see, and he didn't want to. But there was something else at the bottom of that box to remind him.

He reached down and picked up the old worn newspaper clipping. He didn't want to unfold it, but he did anyway. Slowly one corner at a time. Finally, the headline stared him back in the face.

LOCAL TEEN CHARGED WITH

RECENT DISAPPEARANCES

James could barely read the faded print. His eyes were bloodshot and tired and despite his curiosity he knew this was something he didn't want to see. The sickness rose in his stomach as a deeply sedated memory locked inside of him suddenly awakened. He slowly read the names of his missing friends who never came out of the woods that night. Emma Everly, Harold Able, Scotty Baker and Daniel Buckard. Good riddance he thought remembering Tommy's right-hand man. Daniel Buckard was a plague on society. He could still smell his foul breath and see those yellowed eyes standing behind Tommy like a puppet doing his masters bidding. The earth is better off without you, he thought. But his friends…they were gone too. They never came out of the woods that night. How had he forgotten so much.

James closed his eyes and took a deep breath, and there for a moment, could see Emma staring back at him with those green eyes. He could hear Scotty's voice telling a joke and Harold laughing at it. They were his best friends…They were his everything. He opened his eyes and read on…

LOCAL TEENS VANISH. SUSPECT APPREHENDED

James thought back to that fateful night remembering he and Tommy were the only ones that came out of those woods. Why them, he didn't know. But when the rest of the group never came home, questions were asked, and Tommy was the number one suspect. The investigation went on for years, but nothing ever came of it, and he never saw his friends again.

The authorities couldn't convict Tommy but something else did. Something drove him insane and James had heard that he ended up locked away at Shadyvale, a hospital for the mentally insane, about three hours outside of the city.

Just as he was about to close the box and never open it again, he saw one more thing that caught his eye, wrapped in a piece of ripped tee shirt. Hesitantly reaching in, he pulled out the small object and slowly unwrapped it. To his disbelief there it was. The small Italian style stiletto switch blade with the dark cherrywood handle. His hand began to shake as he stared at it remembering its familiar coldness pressed against his skin all those years ago. The initials TC carved right into the handle. *Tommy Clayton.* And with a quick flip of the switch, he could see the blood-stained metal blade staring back from the past.

He slammed the shoebox shut and pushed it back under the bed. His heart raced. The feelings of the past squeezing his chest like a vice. The air suddenly felt heavy and warm. Each breath, harder than the last.

He closed his eyes and began counting, *one two three four...* inside his head. Each breath taking him back down to where he needed to be. Feet on the ground, he thought. Karen needs you. Now more than ever.

***

Karen was still in bed, looking as distant as ever.

"Let's go take a walk," James suggested, needing to clear his mind, as hard as that may be sometimes. He sat on the bedside for a moment and waited for her to respond. But Karen just turned and looked up at him with those same distant eyes and just like a black hole he could see himself sinking within their deep dark reflection.

Sitting her up he helped her get dressed and grabbed a pair of sneakers. She could do everything herself but just seemed so weak as if she were to crack and crumble at any given moment. They walked slowly out of the bedroom together and carefully down the staircase.

Outside on the back patio the rather cool fall air drew upon their faces and James watched as he could almost see a smile curl up the corner of her lips.

"You always loved this time of year," James exclaimed following his wife's distant gaze as she stared out across the wavering field grass.

They walked the property for almost an hour like two teenagers on a first date. Hand in hand wandering with nothing more than the love that once grew between them. The feeling made him remember her as a young girl in college. The days when just holding her hand would send his heart pattering. When his palms would get sweaty, and he'd have to nervously wipe them on his jeans. Even now that feeling had not subsided but rather sustained itself through a life, he still would not have given up for anything.

Karen seemed entranced the closer they got to the forest's edge. Her endless gaze, peered into the shadowed spaces between the wall of sycamores and oaks. He wanted to know if she was okay. Wanted to know what she saw in those woods that continued to draw her back. Yet somewhere deep inside he knew… and so did his friends that never came back out that night. Whatever had happened in there was still buried so deep that he couldn't see what dark truth really lay within that shadowy forest wall.

As they made their way further and further from the house, the dark aura of the forest seemed to give James a growing discomfort. Starting in his gut and moving its way into the back of his throat. He couldn't place it, but it was there. As palatable as a bite of rancid meat. He stopped, unable to go any further.

Karen turned back to look at him when James jumped, seeing not the face of his wife but Emma. Her voice whispered inside his head and the smell of grape bubble gum that she used to chew wafted past his nostrils. Memories quickly rose, showing him the past. Little moments like the way she would bump into him pretending it to be an accident or laughing and telling jokes while playing Cat's cradle on her front porch.

He placed his hand in his pocket feeling the old polaroid as Emma just looked him in the eye, standing there, kissed by the late afternoon sun. He took a step forward wanting to reach out a hand, feeling like it would only pass through her skin like a ghost. Was it really her staring back at him? Smiling like she always did with her slightly crooked front two teeth and freckled cheeks running up onto the bridge of her nose.

"Emma?" James whispered under his breath, mesmerized by the shadow and light that seemed to dance around his friend. "Is it really you?"

James reached out a hand to touch her cheek, but she quickly drew back as he could now see the fear in her eyes.

"They're coming, Jimmy. They're almost here," she said turning and looking at the woods.

"Who is almost here?" he nervously asked.

"Don't you remember? You're the one who brought them here," she replied.

"Brought who?" James thought back but couldn't seem to come to grips as to what she was talking about.

"Them," Emma uttered with a terrified tongue as she pointed into the woods. "The Sullen Ones."

James turned and could see the eyes deep within the shadows of the forest staring back at him. Glowing orbs scattered about like fireflies.

Startled, he took a step back and was about to fall when her hand reached out and caught him. He turned and could now see his wife standing there once again.

James looked around, feeling his mind wanting to crack as the smell of Emma still lingered in the wind.

"James? What are you looking at?" Karen asked.

He glanced back at the forest's edge, and nothing was there except the shadows of trees under the amber sky, bleeding into the heavens. He stood frozen and just watched, almost dumbfounded, as everything felt all too familiar.

He intertwined his fingers within his wife's hand and drew her close, feeling as if he were going to lose her and his mind all at once. Then, glanced at his watch and realized they had to get going.

"Come on, we have an appointment. We're gonna be late," he said, trying to break himself out of the moment, crawling up his skin like a serpent wrapping its body around its prey.

"What do you mean?" she asked.

"Just come with me. We're gonna sit down and talk with someone...trust me."

"Who?"

"Just someone who can help."

She didn't move or utter any acknowledgement, only stared into his eyes like she was wanting some assurance that everything was going to be alright. He wished he could tell her everything was gonna be okay, but he just couldn't find the words. They were lost somewhere out in those woods, looking back at him reminding him the worst was yet to come.

CHAPTER 16

"Karen, my name is Doctor Edwards. I want you to just make yourself comfortable," the elderly white-haired doctor spoke in a slight Louisiana drawl as he crossed his leg and situated the yellow legal pad upon his thigh. The pen, a classic Watermen, began to scribble a few notes while James sat beside his wife with an uncomfortable stare.

"Just relax, baby," James said, putting his arm around her. Karen, who looked more afraid than anything sat there with her hands in her lap practically shaking.

"I don't need to be here," she added and turned to James with a look as if pleading to be released. "Let's go, James, please."

"Karen, this is a safe place. No one is here to harm you or make you feel uncomfortable. Your husband just has some concerns about your sleepwalking and some other things," Doctor Edwards exclaimed in a naturally calm tone.

Karen sat silently while the doctor gave her a long hard stare. James watched with growing curiosity as the lingering silence in the room began to feel awkward.

"Do you dream, Karen?" Doctor Edwards asked.

"Excuse me? I don't…I don't know what that has to do with anything," she replied with an obvious uninterested tone.

"Dreams are the windows to our souls. They bring us closer to knowing both ourselves and the unseen world around us," Doctor Edwards said as he re-situated himself in his large leather chair.

"When I was a boy, I had terrible, terrible dreams. Dreams that seemed to reach up out of that dark place and grab you by the leg when you least expected it, then pull ya back down into the darkness," the doctor said as he paused a moment looking to be reflecting back in time.

"Sounds terrible," Karen quietly added.

"Yes, it was. There'd be this fog rolled in from the swamps at night. Like a shadow they covered the lights that kept me safe…The stars, the moon, those little things that comfort you. Give ya hope," he continued, taking off his glass and rubbing the bridge of his nose. "Every time that fog rolled in, and those lights went out, I swear I had the most horrible dreams as if nothing could save me. No light could penetrate that veil cast over my bedroom. Even my mother couldn't help me. I was on my own. I felt so lonely, so scared."

"I know what you mean," Karen added as if she were a little more comfortable with the situation.

"But you know what I did. I studied everything I could about the night. The creatures, the night sky, the fog and everything else I could think to know. See, darkness isn't a scary thing, Karen. The not knowing is where the fear comes from. The unknown spaces we walk past, waiting for something to reach out and grab us. Take us back into that dark place. That cold dark place where we don't know what's looking back at us."

"It's not the same, though," she replied.

"Yes, it is…ya see, you don't know what's happening around you. Even what's happening within you. You've suffered greatly and that kind of loss creates a hole…A rip so to speak. And in that rip, a darkness can get inside. Makes that hole bigger, deeper, wider, until your body is itself just a void. A rip in time and space," Doctor Edwards said, giving Karen a deeply serious stare. "The soul needs a body, Karen. It is why we are here. Why we can live this human experience. As we are just spiritual beings locked within this vessel that allows us to feel pain, happiness, sadness, joy…all the things that make us who and what we are. But remember the bigger that rip gets, the more we lose ourselves. Become something else. The soul gets consumed…eaten by the emptiness that we allow to take over our spirit and eventually our bodies themselves."

"I just…I just want my daughter back. I want to feel her in my arms again. The way her hair smelled after a bath or how she smiled when she knew I was making her favorite dinner," Karen's eyes teared up as her voice trailed off.

"And what was that?" Doctor Edwards asked, handing her a tissue.

"What was what?" Karen replied as she wiped her eyes.

"Her favorite dinner?"

Karen sat for a moment as if the question did not even make sense. James watched as the memories collided within her mind.

"Homemade macaroni and cheese," Karen replied with a little smile peeking through.

"With the breadcrumbs on top?" Doctor Edwards asked with a childish grin.

"Of course," she replied with a genuine smile. One that James found deeply comforting.

"That's how my momma used to make it," Doctor Edwards said with a big, satisfied grin. "Ya see, all these things are good, Karen. Memories are such a valuable thing. A gift. Something we carry with us…always. The good and the bad. It's within that balance our humanity lay."

James squeezed Karen's leg, feeling the words touch all too deeply, as she finished wiping her tears.

"I want you to do something for me. I want you to think back. I want you to imagine Elizabeth in your mind. See every detail. Every hair. Every crease in her skin. Look into her eyes. Deep into the blackest part of those pupils. I want you to see yourself looking back in its reflection," Doctor Edwards stated while repositioning himself closer.

"Doctor, are you sure this is…" James asked as Doctor Edwards sternly cut him off, holding out a hand.

"Now, I want you to lean back and close your eyes. Listen to my voice Karen. Let it guide you, let it take you away."

And with that Karen closed her eyes and left this world.

***

Karen's screams echoed through the room as her body flailed violently. Doctor Edwards and James quickly attempted to hold her back from hurting herself.

"Wake her!" James yelled as Doctor Edwards calmly positioned himself near Karen's face attempting to guard himself from being hit.

"Karen, when I count to three you are going to wake up. Listen to my voice Karen, one..." Doctor Edwards said, as her eyes rolled back in her head. "Two..." he continued when suddenly a laughter rose from her lips. A sharp high-pitched laughter.

James quickly backed away, feeling his heart race as Karen's hand hit Doctor Edwards, knocking him onto the ground.

She turned her head towards James. There were no pupils, only the white foggy sclera giving a ghostly guise to her current state. Skin, paler than before as if all the blood had just run out of her body. Gray almost. The laughter rising. Then there was the voice.

"Oink oink little piggy...we're gonna get you, little colored boy. Gonna gut you like a pig!" Karen's voice rang out, not her own. It was Daniel Buckard.

James sat on the floor, his palms sweaty and pressed onto the ground bracing himself as if he were thirteen all over again wanting to run for his life.

"Gonna feel my blade soon, I've been waiting little piggy," the voice shifted.

Tommy.

James felt nauseous as Karen's voice warped between strange renditions of the familiar demons that tormented his childhood.

"Daddy, it's so dark in here, there's no lights. Hold my hand, please, don't let them take me again," it was now Elizabeth's voice.

Karen's eyes shifted and fluttered as James lay frozen in disbelief.

"Lizzy!" he yelled out when the tone deepened, and a strange female Cajun accent rose from her lips.

"We be seeing ya soon, Jimmy…we be seein' ya very soon. Best bring ya God wit ya. It be dark down here. Be so very dark."

Doctor Edwards' loud clap broke the moment as he yelled, "Three!"

Karen in a sudden jerk, snapped out of it. Her ghostly stark white orbs replaced with the familiar ocean blue James had fallen in love with.

She sat up gasping for air as James sat distantly still, while Doctor Edwards tended to her.

"Tell me how you feel, Karen…tell me where you are," Doctor Edwards spoke softly by her side.

"I'm…fine. I'm at your office," she said, still looking confused.

"That's right and nothing can hurt you here. Nothing at all," he whispered, "now tell me where you were. Can you remember, Karen?"

"I was with…my daughter. She was standing in the middle of a forest…a clearing within a forest. There was a large round circle on the ground. The moon was shining down on her. There was…green. Streaks of green light ran through her hair. I could see every tendril. She almost glowed, she…" her voice trailed off as she began to weep.

Doctor Edwards swiftly tended to her tears with a tissue as James got to his feet and sat beside her still looking very disturbed.

"What else was in that circle? The forest...what else did you see?" James urgently asked as Doctor Edwards looked up giving him a strange glare.

"I...I don't know," she replied, "the trees."

"What about the trees, Karen?"

"They had eyes, they were watching me," she said with a nervous glare.

"Karen, I want you to think back. Every detail. Every branch, every blade of grass," Doctor Edwards added, taking back control over the conversation.

"There was something else there, in the ground. Voices...they were coming from below."

She cringed, closing her eyes as if the memory suddenly began choking the air out of her. Grabbing her neck, she looked as if she were struggling to breathe.

"Here, Karen, here's some water. Drink this. Just relax," Doctor Edwards said, as he held up a water bottle.

Karen quickly took it and drank, some dribbling out onto her shirt.

"That's okay, that's okay, just drink. Clear your throat, clear your mind." He took the glass back. "Now take a deep breath."

She drew in a deep gasp of air as she looked over at James with terrified eyes. He knew what she had seen. He knew because he had seen it, too. All those years ago. The real memories inside were awakening and there was nothing he could do to stop them.

CHAPTER 17

It was dark by the time James and Karen pulled up to the house. Shutting off the engine James looked over, putting a hand on her thigh as she tried to get out of the car.

"Do you remember anything else? Anything that you might have forgot to tell Doctor Edwards?" James asked.

She turned back, saying nothing and gave James a long cold stare then got up and closed the door.

The air was stagnant and unsettled as he sat in the car and watched Karen head inside. Creedence Clearwater revival played on the radio in a low staticky tune. *Bad Moon Rising.* Fitting James thought. Very fitting.

The lyrics echoed within his mind as he stared blankly at the newly painted white columns of the house. They were still awe inspiring even in moments like this. It was like watching an old carcass coming back to life.

Necromancy.

The word popped into his mind and gave him a sudden uneasy feeling. He was helping it. Bringing back the undead.

***

As evening fell James sat beside Karen on the edge of the bed, finishing tending to her wounds. They were not healing as he had expected as they appeared as fresh as they had the previous night, almost looking infected. He ran his hand across her skin. She seemed to be sweating rather badly. A mild fever had begun to build as he started to worry.

"Take these," James insisted.

"What are they?" Karen asked holding the small round pills in her hand.

"Just antibiotics," James replied, "these cuts aren't healing up like I thought they would.

Karen took the pills with a glass of water on the nightstand and made herself comfortable for the night clutching the small rag doll to her chest.

The longer he lay there the more he hated seeing that doll staring back at him. The thing made him angry. He hated it now and wished it away more than anything.

Reaching out, he slowly pulled it from her grasp, trying not to wake her.

"You need to go," he whispered under his breath. Getting up out of bed he walked downstairs and went outside to the garbage can on the side of the house. The wind began to pick up as he stood there and held the doll over the smelly black container.

"Here," he said, "back to where you belong."

And with that threw the doll down into the can and turned away and headed back inside.

James lay his head back beside Karen. He could feel the sweat from her body. A gaunt heat radiated into his own being as the sickness was very evident. He would watch it closely. But for now, she needed rest, they both did. And with the doll gone he felt so much better.

***

It started as a tap. Rhythmic almost. Opening his eyes, James saw the glow of the alarm clock read 3:33 a.m. The bedroom, cast in a strange red glow, reminded him of some cheap motel room. The moonlight was all but vanquished by the night and some unnatural feeling of evil resting within the shadows.

He watched as the single cicada flapped its wings trying to get out of the window. It beat against the glass over and over. The sound almost lulling him back to sleep.

"How did you get in here?" he whispered under his breath as he got out of bed and opened the window.

"You're not supposed to be here. Didn't you get the memo," he added with a chuckle, watching it fly into the night towards the forest. The rest of the brood, having all begun their descent back into the ground for another long slumber. This one somehow was forgotten. Or maybe it didn't want to go back to that dark place in the ground it was meant to go at summers end. Perhaps it didn't want to leave quite yet. Hanging onto this life just a little while longer. Alone.

He stared out the window watching it vanish in the darkness, feeling the calming night air on his face. So many memories, but he couldn't quite understand what was real and what was a dream anymore. And that was just fine by him he thought.

Maybe some things are better left forgotten.

Getting back into bed, he now saw the empty space beside him and drew his hand across the warm sheets. The impression of Karen's body was still there. He could feel the heat against his palm as if her soul still lingered there within some other reality.

"Karen!" he called out, "Baby! You in the bathroom?"

The creak of the house awakened beneath him as he checked the bathroom, then headed out into the hallway.

You should have never come back boy. Never come back! But we're glad you did. Oh, we missed you.

The ravenous voices of Tommy and Daniel grew louder with each step. His fear rose as he could see the light on at the end of the hallway. Rather than relief, anger rose within him. He marched with his fists balled up.

Hitting the door open, he yelled out, "Karen, why are you in…"

There was no one there, rather sitting alone in the center of the room was the small rag doll staring up at him. James' stomach churned.

“How in the hell?”

The walls pulsed as his anger and fear seemed to rise with every second, he stood there staring down at that little ragged thing looking back at him. But there was something else, a small piece of paper tucked within. Reaching down he grabbed the note and slowly unfolded it.

Tick tack little Jimmy

Time to come home

Suddenly Emma's voice rang like a bell.

They're coming Jimmy, they're almost here!

He threw the doll across the room. It's small, ragged body lay limp on the floor staring back at him.

"To hell with you!"

He stuffed the note into his pocket and tried to gather his senses before heading downstairs to the kitchen. It was all some sort of joke she was playing on him. She was upset that he had thrown the doll away.

There was no light on in the kitchen. There was no light anywhere. The moon vanished as a dark shadow blanketed the house.

"Karen!" he called out again. Louder this time. He could feel the house almost laughing at him as his echo dissipated in the large foyer. Its renovations making it look like some half-beaten beast, in the midst of recovering from its defeat. He suddenly felt as if he were rebuilding a monster but quickly put the thought out of his mind as it all seemed like nonsense. There was an explanation. There always was. Then he saw the crack in the front door. The subtle evening breeze passed by his face like a hand attempting to get his attention.

He walked in haste towards the door and stood staring out into the night. It was pitch black. There was not a star in the sky nor a moon to guide them. The grounds looked like a desert of some forgotten sea. A black hole in which he knew his most beloved was out in.

"Karen!" he yelled at the top of his lungs, but there was no echo. There was nothing but the stagnant air as if the last breeze had just blown and the earth was dead…

It was all dead.

Heading out onto the back veranda he stood and listened. It was utterly silent without the song of the cicada to calm his nerves or the stars and moon to light his path.

He remembered Doctor Edwards' story and felt a similar veil of fear at the absence of the little things that comforted him in the night.

He took a few steps onto the hard dry ground. His bare feet against the earth beneath him. It felt good, he thought. The cold Georgia clay pressed against his toes.

He walked slowly…cautiously rather, wandering the grounds. The high field grass brushed up against his legs as he made his way across its dark sea. The place had a smell to it. A lingering rot that seemed to be even worse at night. It was a place where things came to die, yet now he could swear that he smelled the sweat and warmth of human bodies. The same bodies that worked these fields hundreds of years ago. Their souls forever trapped like butterflies in a dirty mason jar.

He knew it was all in his head. His own psyche attempting to tell him something. To warn him. But he would travel to the doorstep of hell to bring her back if he had to. She's all he had left.

"Karen!" he yelled out as the field grass dissipated and gave way to the forest's edge. "Karen please answer me!" He didn't want to believe she had wandered this far again. It was too dangerous, especially at night.

He peered into the shadows of the forest, standing upon its barrier like a child looking into his own nightmares. Each tree stood resolute, like a wall, but there was one place where the barrier broke and gave the subtle impression of a path. He couldn't believe he hadn't seen it before. Or didn't want to see it, rather. The limbs almost arching across its entrance as if creating a gateway to another world.

Welcome back, Jimmy.

Looking closer, he made out the impressions of bare feet heading into the darkness. Small footprints disappearing into the canopy of sycamores and oaks. He could not step any further. The voices of his past reminding him of the evil that existed within these woods.

His hands shook and his heart raced as he felt like a scared boy once again. He remembered running through here with his friends. Running for their lives after having jumped from the upstairs window. The thoughts of Tommy Clayton's knife upon his neck. He could almost feel the cold blade against his skin.

Taking a deep breath, he stepped across the shadowed threshold of southern oaks lining the outer forest. Each step further into the shadows made him want to run. He hadn't been here since he was a boy and had a feeling that everything about this forest was all wrong. It shouldn't be here. None of this should be here, he thought. Something bad is out there. But Karen…he reminded himself of Karen. She was out there somewhere. He had to find her. Every second could mean her life. So, into the forest he went.

He searched for hours. Deeper and deeper into the woods but there was no sign. Nothing but his own fear and anxiety getting the best of him as he seemed to just be going in circles. There was no clearing like the one he remembered as a child. It was just a dream he thought. Nothing was out here except trees. More and more trees. Nothing evil. Nothing supernatural, just a forest. But there was something in the back of his mind telling him it was already too late. Warning him that if he went any further the only thing he would find was his own demise.

Reaching into his pocket he pulled out the crumpled note he found with the doll and studied it like a detective looking at a piece of evidence. The writing was precise. Taking a closer look, he realized it wasn't even her handwriting and this wasn't any joke. It was a warning. But from who? He didn't know, yet somewhere inside he knew he did, and it turned his blood cold.

It felt like all of this was just a bad dream that he would wake up from and they'd all soon be back home in Los Angeles. Their daughter standing over him, telling him to wake up.

It was all just a bad dream Daddy.

CHAPTER 18

"You look like hell," the sheriff bluntly exclaimed as James sat in the kitchen chair by the window.

The sun, still rising over the horizon.

He could feel the long lean figure staring him down. A chiseled jaw and hardened heavily tanned face gave him a look a bit like Clint Eastwood in one of those westerns his father always watched. One of the only good memories James had of his father. The two of them sitting down together as some spaghetti western played on a lazy Sunday afternoon.

"I haven't slept," James replied running his hands over his face as he nursed a glass of bourbon.

"You had a few of those?" he asked.

"Does it matter?" James curtly replied.

"How about you tell me exactly what you remember from last night?"

James' mind began to churn as the events all seemed a blur. This past week was like a bad dream slipping through his fingers as the waning moments lingered on. But he knew he'd sound crazy if he told even a hint of the truth. Whatever truth that might have been. He didn't really know anymore.

"I told you. I was in bed…woke up in the middle of the night and she was gone," James replied matter-of-factly, feeling anger, sadness, and frustration all merge at once.

"And this was the first time she had been…" he searched for the word and glanced down at his notes. "Sleepwalking, correct?"

"There's been other incidents," James replied, watching the Sheriff jot down a note.

"And can you elaborate on that, please?"

"What do you want to know?"

"How long ago was the last sleepwalking incident?"

"About a week I'd say," James replied.

"Any reason to think she might not have been sleepwalking. Maybe she just left?" the sheriff asked.

James eyes looked up in a long cold glare instantly reacting to the Sheriffs brusque tone.

"And what would make you think she'd want to do that?" James shot back.

"Standard questions," he replied jotting down a quick note that seemed to un-nerve James. "I understand you had a security system installed after the recent break-in."

"Yeah, we took your advice," James replied rather nonchalantly.

"Any reason to believe these incidents had anything to do with one another?"

"Why would you even ask?" James replied.

The sheriff gave him a momentary stare as if trying to exude a silent authority to just answer the questions.

"Was there any reason to think that she might leave you? Was there any hint of infidelity…An affair?"

"What?!" James' eyes shot up, glaring daggers back at the sheriff as he felt the sudden urge to punch him. "Absolutely not."

The Sheriff's demeanor was rather cold, making this exchange feel more like an interrogation.

"I'm sure. But I'm just trying to get some clear facts here. People don't just leave without a reason. Especially don't just wander into the night and not come back. Sleepwalking or not," he said as he jotted down a few more notes. "And you'd mention earlier she had just started seeing a psychiatrist."

James didn't want to elaborate on that and wished he'd never said anything in the first place.

"She's not well, Sheriff. She hasn't been herself since our daughter passed."

"I'm sorry to hear that. I'm sure that makes all these moments so much harder to deal with," the sheriff's demeanor now somewhat sympathetic. His face almost seemed a bit more human as it looked like the thought was stuck in his head. "Can't imagine how a mother might deal with that. Any parent really. I'm sorry for your loss," he added.

"Thank you," James replied, as he sat silently staring down at his glass wondering what good any of this was going to do.

"Was she on any medication?" he asked.

“A small dosage of pain meds and antibiotics, but nothing out of the ordinary."

"Antibiotics? For what?"

James hesitated to answer, not knowing what further questions would persist.

"An infection."

The sheriff paused, seeming to ponder this line of questioning.

"So, no antidepressants or any mind-altering substances. Nothing prescribed by the psychiatrist?"

"No, this doctor specializes in a different kind of technique."

"And what is that?"

"Hypnosis."

The sheriff jotted down another note.

"Would you say you were seeing a positive effect?"

"I don't know, she only just had her first session."

"I see. What about being suicidal?"

A word that James didn't want to hear. A word that left a sour note lingering in the air.

"No. Sheriff with all due respect, I don't have anything to tell you other than what I already have," James replied, as if he hadn't the energy or patience left to say another word.

The Sheriff jotted down another quick note then put away his pad and pen and paused a moment with a sigh. "I'm sure there's a rational explanation for this."

The word rational rang in James' ear. There was nothing rational about this life anymore. Especially since they had moved into this house. Nothing made sense and normalcy was as distant a feeling as a dream itself.

"Well, let's see those security tapes then."

Entering the office, the Sheriff seemed to show no emotion or surprise whatsoever while stepping over bits and pieces of broken monitors and electronics. He just observed the mess for a moment, seeming to assess the situation before uttering any words.

"Want to explain this?" he asked, seeing James looking somewhat nervous.

"I know how this looks," he replied.

"You did this?"

A moment of hesitation and the look on the sheriff's face said it all. James knew how it looked. He knew no matter what he said at this point he wasn't going to get out of this one without some serious suspicion falling on him.

"It was just a moment. A moment that I regret," James exclaimed, reaching down and picking up a small piece of glass and setting it on his desk.

"I couldn't take it anymore. The things I saw were…"

He couldn't finish the sentence because he didn't know what he really saw anymore.

"What did you see that drove you to this point of destroying this equipment?" the sheriff inquired with arms folded.

"I…I don't know," James replied, as the black and white scenes flashed through his mind. *The Slaves. The tall African woman shaking violently. The cicadas. Arms reaching from some beyond grabbing Karen, tearing at her flesh. A wormhole back in time.* It all sounded like one of those Stephen

King novels Karen would get lost in. Nothing he could tell anyone without sounding like anything but a lunatic. So, he just said nothing and left it at that.

There was an awkward silence growing between the men. He could feel the Sheriff's mind spinning as was his own.

"When's the last time you slept, Doctor?" the sheriff replied.

"Honestly, couldn't tell ya," James shot back.

The Sheriff just nodded. His face looked as if he were an expert on not revealing emotion.

"How much property you got back there?"

"About fifty acres."

The Sheriff took a deep sigh and continued tapping his belt then quietly exited the room.

***

James led the Sheriff through the tall grass of the western field to the forest's edge under an early morning sun.

"You a God-fearing man, Doctor Elba?" the sheriff asked, lost in a long stare out into the woods.

"Maybe once, Sheriff," James replied.

"But not anymore?" the Sheriff asked, glancing over at James with suspicious eyes.

"No, I guess not," James nonchalantly replied.

"I think faith is important in a time like this myself. Something to hang onto…but also something to fear. Keep us accountable for our actions if you know what I mean."

"What are you saying, Sheriff?" James asked, feeling a rising tension between them.

"I'm saying I don't know what we're going to find in those woods. You sure you're ready to face those demons?"

The choice of words caused James to stop mid step as the Sheriff took a second to stop and turn back staring at him.

"She's alive, Sheriff," James stated as the moment seemed to grab at his soul.

"I'm sure she is," the Sheriff replied and turned back staring into the woods, his eyes lost within some deep thought. "If only these woods could talk."

The sheriff stepped within the shadow of the forest and James followed closely behind.

***

An hour later they were back at the house. The search had revealed nothing. The clearing James remembered still had not been found. Maybe it was never even there in the first place, he thought.

"Now is there anything else you want to tell me? Anything at all?" the sheriff asked probing for something more.

He could feel the note in his pocket like a weight pulling him down. He didn't want to share it for some reason. Whatever reason that was he didn't know. Maybe because it was crazy, and he didn't even know what it really meant. All he knew was she was gone and that was enough.

"No, Sheriff," James replied, feeling the suspicious glare piercing his wall of silence.

"I want you to call me if you think of anything else that might help us here," the sheriff said, handing James a business card. His eyes telling James he didn't trust him, and he knew there was more than he was seeing.

"Already got one, Sheriff," James replied handing it back.

"Of course." He tucked the card back into his breast pocket.

"You get some rest. I'll be in touch," the sheriff coldly stated as he turned and hopped into his cruiser leaving James sitting alone on the front porch.

He sat there feeling Karen's presence as if she were standing before him. Her smell, her voice, the sound of footsteps walking barefoot across the grass. His senses wanted to believe she was just inside and would be out with a tray of sweet tea at any moment. Or perhaps just coming back from a walk and he would see her heading down the drive beneath the shadows of southern oaks.

He looked up catching the sheriff's suspicious glare from the inside of the cruiser, no hint of emotion or any sense of empathy. A blank resolute mask that told him all too well that if something had really happened to his wife he would be to blame. No matter what the truth might be.

Inside, James put the kettle on the stove and waited. His fingers tapping the counter as the silence felt almost deafening. It had been quiet since losing Elizabeth but with Karen missing there was something beyond what he was ready to deal with resting around him.

James lowered his head, feeling the tears draw into his eye. It was as if they were his last ones. They had all fallen now and what was left within was something he didn't recognize. Sadness, anger, rage, madness. He didn't know which it was…not anymore.

The kettle whistled, startling James as he snapped out of his daze and poured himself a cup. He sat alone at the kitchen table, but his mind would not let him be. Everything seemed to be coming to a crescendo and he could barely hear his own thoughts, let alone understand what they meant.

Then he noticed the cup he had grabbed. The steam seeping into the air creating a ghostly haze in front of his face. The words number one Dad staring back at him. The pain felt all too real and, in an instant, threw the mug with all his force across the room shattering it against the wall. His hands clenched the sides of the table as if he were about to throw it as well when the phone suddenly rang.

Karen!

Lunging across the room, he grabbed the receiver and picked it up in haste.

"Karen?" he answered, nearly out of breath from the madness still pulsing through his mind.

There was no one there. Only breathing.

"Hello?" he continued, "Karen, is that you?"

Then it happened. James felt the sickness draw down his chest into his stomach. The laughter was unmistakable. The high-pitched squeal on the other end of that line. A laugh he hadn't heard in over twenty-five years.

"Who the hell is this?" James asked, but deep down he knew. He knew from the second it hit his ear who that was.

"Tommy?" James whispered into the receiver, "Is that you?"

"Oink oink little piggy. Oink oink oink oink oink…" he continued like a broken record as James dropped the phone to the ground. The sounds of a pig echoed from the receiver over and over until James could take no more and smashed the phone with the heel of his boot, sending bits of plastic all over the floor.

He knew Tommy had seen what was in those woods. Just like James, he saw it with his own eyes.

CHAPTER 19

Summer of 1980

James' ear lay pressed to the cold hard Georgia clay within the center of the clearing. The large chalk circle surrounded him like a barrier which none of his friends would cross. The surrounding birchwood stood resolute like watchers in the night as his friends stood witness on the perimeter with fearful angst. The moonlight was all but vanquished as the sickening greenish hue rose all around them. The voices below grew stronger with each passing moment. The vibrations sent chills over his body as the ground seemed to want to burst open and swallow him alive. But he couldn't move. He couldn't take his mind away from the voices calling to him from below. But within those twisted tongues he could hear a familiar voice…it was his mother. He could hear her as plain as day. The pain in her voice. The anguish and anger as she called out.

"Mom?" James called back. "Mom, is that you?"

"You brought them home my son. Now tell them all to come closer."

James stared down wondering if he were hallucinating. The ground, almost translucent. The source of the greenish glow emanating from within. The light pulsed as if beating with the same rhythm of his own heart.

"Jimmy!" Emma called out, "Jimmy. Come on! Harold's missing! We need to find him."

James could not peel his eyes away from what he was seeing. A dome. He was on top of a mirror-like dome. His own reflection staring back at him. But within his eyes he could see his father. The sinister grin overlapping his own. The dark circles appearing under his eyes, the heavy lines…and then the voice.

> "Tell them to come closer," James' father's voice now echoed from below.

"Harold!" Scotty called out, "guys, we have to find Harold!"

"Jimmy! We have to get out of here and find Harold!" Emma begged, jumping up and down on the edge of the circle.

"Here piggy piggy piggy!" Tommy's high-pitched voice suddenly rang out as he emerged from the forest into the clearing with a shiny silver blade to Harold's neck.

"Oink oink oink," Daniel echoed with his raspy undertone and laughter that sounded both sickly and terrifying.

James suddenly snapped out of it and looked up to see Tommy and Daniel.

"Guys!" Harold called out with tears in his eyes as Tommy held him close to his chest.

"We don't want your kind here. None of you's. We want none of you's darky's or anyone that thinks it's okay to be associating with that kind. All of you's as far as I'm concerned is a traitor to your kind," Tommy yelled out.

"Yeah, a bunch of traitors. All of ya's," Daniel repeated, laughing hysterically.

"Now which one gets it first?" Tommy asked as he pressed the blade harder to the side of Harold's neck.

"No! Let him go!" Emma yelled out.

"What'r ya gonna do about it, bitch!" Daniel called out, "you're actually kinda pretty, ya know. I think maybe I'd like to make you my girlfriend," he said, sticking his tongue out flicking it in the air like a snake.

"Don't touch her!" James yelled back as he stepped in front of Emma.

"You her boyfriend, colored boy?" Daniel asked. "Is that what you like girl? You like them colored boys?"

Emma withdrew into James' arms as Scotty stepped beside them.

"Just let him go and get the hell out of here!" Scotty called out.

Suddenly James lunged forward, grabbing Tommy by the wrist. The two fell to the ground as Emma grabbed Harold by the shirt and pulled him away. James held on strong to keep the knife from plunging into his chest while the two wrestled in the dirt out into the center of the chalk circle. Tommy struggled to regain control as James held the knife at bay.

"Get him, Tommy!" Daniel yelled out standing to the side watching the two roll around in the dust below.

"You're gonna get it!" Tommy yelled, "gonna gut you like a pig."

Tommy finally overtook James, flipping him on his back as the knife drew closer to his neck. James could not hold it away as Tommy's strength was overpowering him.

"Jimmy, no!" Emma yelled, trying to pull the knife away from Tommy before Daniel grabbed her and threw her onto the ground.

"Stay down, bitch!" Daniel yelled.

The knife drew closer. Harold and Scotty stood frozen as Daniel held a large stick ready to beat down whoever stepped into the fight.

"Now you're gonna die!" Tommy exclaimed with a smile full of stained crooked teeth.

James shook as the steel blade touched his skin on the left side of his neck. The metal was cold. His adrenaline rushed through his arms and fingertips enabling him to push the blade to the side just as Tommy attempted to plunge down upon him. The sharp edge running down the side of his neck rather than through it.

"Ahhhhhh!" James screamed as the blood dripped onto the ground.

A sudden jolt from below threw them off balance as James broke away, knocking the knife out of Tommy's hand.

"You're dead!" Tommy yelled out as James held the knife out before him. His trembling hand squeezing the dark cherry wood handle until he felt it could almost burst into a million pieces. The rage and anger rushed through him like he had never felt before.

"Leave us alone!" he yelled, "leave us all alone! You hear me you scumbag. You piece of trash!"

James got to his feet holding the knife out. A few swipes across the air making sure Tommy and Daniel knew he meant business. Emma stepped inside the circle and stood beside him as the rest of the group followed suit until another crack from below shook them all again.

"James, your neck," Emma exclaimed.

"I'm fine," he replied feeling the blood run down onto his shirt.

The two groups faced off in the middle of the clearing as the earth shook again. More and more with each drop of James blood dripping onto the ground.

"It's an earthquake!" Daniel yelled.

The ground continued to shake as everyone tried to stay together. The light rising before them began to grow brighter coalescing into a strange mist like substance filling the night air. A thick greenish hue surrounded them and spread itself out like tendrils of flames flickering in the night.

"Jimmy, what's happening?" Emma's voice trembled as she clung to his arm.

But James could not say a word. He couldn't say anything because the feeling he had inside was nothing that he'd ever felt before, as if every bad thought and nightmare had crawled out at once. He just stood frozen, staring into the light as he watched the green mist warping and changing before him…pulsing as if it were actually breathing.

The group struggled to stay together as the intensity of the light created a barrier between them, cutting each one off from the other. Only voices rose and fell while they listened to each other's screams. James reached for Emma's hand seeing only the faint outline of her face. Her terrified eyes searching frantically for him through the mist.

"Emma!" James yelled, reaching towards her. The tips of her fingers, just out of reach as they both were drawn apart into the dark green light.

James was alone now, separated from the group. The evil circled him as it held them all in some unseen world having risen from below. He could feel it as it drew his thoughts into its own. This light could speak. It had a voice. A living presence. But James knew it was not the living that spoke to him.

He felt his hands go numb. His mind began to warp and change as he realized he had done something terribly wrong. The anger of his father. The sadness of his mother. The hatred of Tommy and Daniel. The fear and the pain all rose within him at once. It wanted to take him…show him what it had done. Let him feel the pain. The pure terror of every life that had been taken within this very place.

His mother always told him that the Devil existed. 'If there was a God, there was a Devil,' she would say. 'You must stay vigilante. It can only harm you if you give it power. Remember what I told you to say.'

He thought back on that simple phrase she gave him to repeat when he had night terrors. Whether it be the boogeyman in his closet or the monster under the bed. He never believed the Devil was real though until this night. Until he had seen it with his own eyes. Standing before him was not the shadowed figure he had seen in the upstairs bedroom but something else altogether. The true form of the evil that rested within this land. Whatever Samuel Black had dug up in the woods all those years ago was still here. Awakened and hungry.

At first, they looked like men. *Slaves.* Each one draped in a long red sash. Eyes as black as Coal. They wavered in and out of reality, their forms shifting. There were thirteen in all standing on the outer edge of the circle. Each one looking down upon him, except they had no eyes to see. Rather in their place a deep black void as if another realm existed within their gaze. High defined cheeks bones shaped their elongated faces. No mouth, no nose. Tall slender faceless beings each covered in shimmering red cloth flowing to the ground like a river of blood.

"I resist you, Devil, in the name of God. I resist you, Devil, in the name of God. I resist you, Devil, in the name of God…" James repeated the phrase his mother had told him to say when the nightmares came. Again and again, he repeated it until he could repeat it no more.

CHAPTER 20

Slowing down to twenty-five, a small gas station on the right marked the beginning of what was a town that seemed to be on the edge of existence, west of Savannah off of highway 280.

James had been driving for hours and everything appeared to be just a blur as the motion of the car slowed down to a halt. The headache he had carried with him this entire trip grew to a crescendo as he surmised the only way to heal whatever pain grew inside his mind rested far beyond anything around him. No pills could touch the torment that he felt with every waking moment since Karen had vanished.

The small blade tucked into his pocket reminded him of the madness that grew inside. *Tommy's blade.* How he had it this entire time he could not understand nor fathom why he would have kept such a thing. The blade was a symbol of everything that he hated about his youth. The fear and the pain. The memories of the boy he once was. Scared beyond belief.

James parked next to one of the pumps that looked to be taken right out of nineteen sixty-nine. Its rounded rusted top and chipped paint made it look completely unsafe for the purpose of pumping combustible fuel.

Getting out of the car he was greeted by an elderly gentleman in coveralls and a red flannel with rolled up sleeves and a name patch with the name Carl stitched in.

"Pretty nice ride here," the attendant exclaimed looking up and down James' Audi sedan, "prefer the classics myself but these new automobiles just tickle my feathers sometimes with all the gadgets and such. Different world I suppose."

"You could say that," James replied, not in the mood for small talk.

"Just the fill?" Carl asked.

James gave a silent nod and started to remove the pump.

"I got that," Carl said taking the pump out of his hand. His large oil-stained fingers and arthritic knuckles made him look as though he'd been filling up tanks since that pump was spit shine new.

"Don't get this kind of service anymore. Thanks," James commented as the old man fumbled with the gas lever. He could hear the insides like they were about to fall out the bottom as the black numbers flipped back to zero and began their slow steady rise.

"Where ya headed?"

"Shadyvale," James replied seeing the old man's eyes change as if the word made him look at him a little differently.

"You been there before?" Carl asked with an overtly curious tone.

"No, first time."

"Well, make it your last," Carl replied as he took out a red handkerchief and wiped the sweat off his forehead.

"Why do you say that?" James asked.

"Those souls locked up there ain't right. None of em'," he replied.

"Well, some people just need a little help, I guess."

"And some need to be sent back to the fires of hell where they belong. People that have done unspeakable acts, yet we think they can be saved somehow."

"Isn't that what being a Christian is all about? Forgiveness?" James replied, surprised to hear the words out of his mouth as he knew he could never forgive the man that took away his own baby girl.

"Some things cannot be forgiven. Not in this world anyway," the old man commented.

"I agree with you but…I guess that means there really isn't any hope, is there?" James replied, feeling his own grief manifesting within the moment.

"Where you're going, there ain't no hope," Carl's eyes shifted. Widened a bit like a thought just popped into his head.
"Can I tell you a secret? Something this world don't tell you. Something no one wants you to know."

The old man's tone was now even more serious…reticent. He paused a moment, motioning for James to step closer, then whispered under his breath.

"The garden isn't what you think."

"Excuse me?" James replied.

"It wasn't God that cast out man, rather man that cast out God…you're in hell, son. You've always been, and you just didn't know it."

James stared quietly not knowing what to say as Carl hung up the gas nozzle and screwed the cap back on the Audi.

"That'll be thirty-five dollars."

CHAPTER 21

James drove slowly under the massive arch of the front entrance glancing at the bronze sign embedded in the stone column.

SHADYVALE

Psychiatric hospital

His thoughts ruminated to old gothic horror tales as the twisted wrought iron and ancient oaks seemed to have a personality of their own.

The decaying brick walls of the main building were covered in ivy. The grounds relatively well kept as a man raking a pile of leaves next to a large oak looked up staring at him as he passed. James just stared back feeling a rising tension in his gut. Something told him to just turn around and go home. There was nothing here he needed to see.

James waited a few moments sitting in the car, staring in the rear-view mirror trying to convince himself to stick with the plan. His eyes looked older now. His skin aged beyond his forty-one years upon this earth. The last six months were hard…he could do hard. But this was going too far. There were no other options, he thought. Whatever was in those woods he had forgotten but maybe Tommy hadn't. Maybe he could help save his wife…Somehow.

He stepped out of the car with weak knees but quietly regained his composure and strolled leisurely towards the entrance, like he could have been in a park on some overcast summer's day without a care in the world. Just another average joe enjoying life. But his life was far from average anymore.

Up ahead a large set of stone steps flanked by two angelic statues on either side awaited his arrival. As he passed, he paused noticing the fine details in each face. The archangel Michael with an unsheathed sword raised above his head ready to smite the unseen Devil. To the left was a stoic Virgin Mary covered in her headdress with outstretched hands as if saving the world with her touch. Both were heavily weathered, and the spotting and cracks gave each more of an ominous presence rather than the benevolent Christian symbols they were supposed to be. The eyes blank and lifeless. The faces cracked and riddled with years of weathering made him almost shiver as the thought that they both knew he didn't belong here suddenly crossed his mind…*or maybe he did.*

Inside, the echo of his own footsteps across a cracked marble floor reminded him of the first time he walked into his own house. Both places had a strange overwhelming feeling and this one was no less curious. The stark white walls, odd silence and strange smell would probably make anyone go insane. A world within a world he thought.

Protected from the outside but trapped within the presence of the walking dead.

A patient with a shaved head and white robe wandered up ahead into what looked like a main recreation area. Their head, down and shuffling along with no determined purpose as everything in their life was now a part of this place. One foot in front of the other, he thought. What more could you do here besides accept your own fate. Whatever life once lived was gone. He could almost see himself walking beside the man. Or perhaps sitting alone by a window staring out and wondering where life had taken such a turn. The voices of his past still haunting him. Some things never die, he thought.

"Excuse me sir," a voice rang out as James looked up. "How may I assist you today?" An elderly woman with a long nose and beady eyes looked back at him as if he were himself checking in to stay.

James leaned closer reading the small print on her name tag. "Hi, Betty. I'm here to see someone…" he hesitated, "last name is Clayton." The lump in his throat rose, making him feel as if he were about to vomit. "Tommy Clayton." That name emoted the same feeling in his gut just as it did back then.

"Hmm," she said giving James a little once over. "That man hasn't had a visitor in all the years I've been here, and I have to say it's been one too many. What makes today such an occasion?" she inquired looking suspect of the request.

"I just need to speak to him, that's all," James replied.

"Well. He doesn't speak much so the conversation might be a little dull I'm afraid."

"He seemed to be talking just fine last night."

"Excuse me?" she questioned with a squinty glare as if trying to size him up for his own room in the facility.

"Yeah, called me on the phone. Nearly scared the hell out of me."

"He what?" she repeated with a confused look. Her brow now fully furrowed sizing him up.

"Called me last night. Don't know how he got my number, but someone must have given it to him unless you let your patients have access to phone books."

"No, I'm sorry we don't, and I can guarantee it wasn't Tommy Clayton that called you last night."

"I think I'd know, ma'am," James bluntly replied.

"Well, then you should know Tommy cut his own tongue out over twenty years ago. Really ruined his singing voice," she added with a little chuckle.

James took a step back looking a little dizzy.

"Sir?" she said reaching out a hand ready to catch him from fainting. "Are you okay?"

It took a moment as James just stood there feeling the world turning upside down until he got a hold of himself and took a deep breath.

"Water?" she asked.

James just shook his head and composed himself steadying his body with both hands on the front desk.

"Just a little lightheaded from the drive, I think. Regardless I'd like to see him if it's all the same to you."

Betty gave a little sigh, turned out a clipboard and placed a pen by his hand.

"Sign in here. Leave your ID with me. You can get it back when you check out."

James nodded and signed, feeling her watch his every move as if everything he did was under suspicion.

"There you go," he said with a smile.

"Doctor Elba," she said taking note of the license emphasizing his title, now seeming to take a sudden shine to him.

"That's me," he replied flashing the pearly whites.

"Long way from California, aren't we, Doctor?"

"I live in the state now. Back home," he replied.

"Back huh, so you're a southern boy?"

"Yes ma'am. Born and bred. Came back to my hometown to start fresh," he said feeling this moment not a place for small talk.

"And where might that be?" she asked flirtatiously.

"Savannah," he replied.

"Well, that's good. Always preferred Charleston myself. The more sophisticated sister if ya ask me. Needless to say, the South needs more fine gentlemen like yourself. Now if you'd be so kind to empty out your pockets, please. Wallet, keys, bubble gum, whatever ya got, it goes in there," she stated holding out a small wire basket.

James dug through his pockets and tossed in a set of keys, wallet, some change and crumpled up receipt for a Dr. Pepper from the Piggly Wiggly.

"Very good," she said and headed out from behind the desk. Her one leg slightly dragging behind from a substantial limp.

"Keep your wits about you in here, Doctor. Ya never know when something can reach out and grab ya." She turned with a little smirk pinching his side, startling him as they passed beneath a security camera. "Here, you need this," she said and handed him a visitor's badge. "That way we know you're not one of the crazies."

A quick buzz released the lock on a large metal door as James walked closely behind, heading down a long hallway past a recreational area filled with a few couches and a couple television viewing areas. Each seemed to have seen better days. In the corner, a gaming area with pieces of board games scattered about. James watched closely as one woman sat playing what looked like a combination of checkers and chess by herself.

"How do you know, Mister Clayton?" she asked, throwing James a bit off guard as he quickly recalled the years of torment and hatred.

"We grew up together," he replied not wanting her to press the matter any further and still wasn't sure exactly what he thought he would get by coming here. A moment of clarity perhaps or just another dead-end road that would lead him back to where he began.

"When was this place built?" James asked, trying to change the subject as he looked around at the surroundings that seemed to not have been touched in decades.

"This is the newer building. Built in nineteen forty-seven after the land was donated by the church. The original building on the East end of the property still stands. Built in eighteen fifty and now mostly used for storage. We house one hundred and forty-four bodies and feel that Gods work is in our hands as these forgotten souls are guided back towards the light in his holy name."

James felt the statement odd as the facility felt more medieval rather than comforting and spiritual. By the looks of the water stains and cracked white tiles he could see that funding was rather inadequate and what care was here must have been far from God-like.

"Here we are," she said stopping at one of the many nondescript rooms running along the hallway. Just another white door with a small rectangular slit in the middle was all there was to be able to see inside.

Unlocking the door with what looked like an old skeleton key, she stood aside as James peered in like a child standing on the front steps of a haunted house.

"Mister Clayton, you have a visitor," she said, as James took a few steps inside.

Tommy was only a few years older than himself but looked as if he could have been twice his age. Just a bag of bones draped in a white gown sitting in a wheelchair alone in the corner of the room. His oddly shaped bald head leaned forward as if he hadn't the strength to keep it upright. Boney arthritic hands lay upon his lap and the thought that neither death nor prayer could have saved him from whatever state he was in seemed appropriate and well deserved.

The room was stark white with a single twin bed, desk and chair. Upon the desk was an array of books and a mess of papers.

"Mister Clayton has always loved to read and write. Since the incident with his tongue, we have found God has given him the gift of the pen."

"We all need something, don't we?" James added, now standing well within the room. His chest felt heavy. His heart rate, beginning to pick up. He suddenly wished he hadn't thrown out all his pills. His own panic attacks seemed rather mute in the light of recent events but now they felt all too real. Regardless, the man before him was just a shell of what he remembered, not the monster he had envisioned from his youth. It still didn't change the fact he was who he was, and James could see it in his eyes. The same evil locked inside there as had been all those years ago.

Reaching up, James touched the scar on his own neck. Even after all these years he could still feel that cold steel blade. He stepped a few paces in, maintaining his distance. His hand rested upon the desk giving him a little balance as the light-headedness passed.

"Mister Clayton loves his books," Betty said, then raised her voice addressing her patient in the corner. "Isn't that right, Mister Clayton?" The rhetoric left her lips but got no response. Not even a nod of the head.

Reading and writing?

He couldn't believe the Tommy he knew even had the ability to read a sentence let alone write one.

"If he wants to tell you something or you ask him a question, he's got this whiteboard here to communicate," she said pointing down to the small rectangular board and black felt pen hanging around his neck.

James looked down still not believing this man didn't have a tongue. There was no mistaking the voice he heard on the phone yesterday. He was sure of it.

Betty headed over and grabbed the back of Tommy's wheelchair and reached down, unlocking the wheel brake.

"Now, if you'd just follow me, I'll take you two down to the recreation area."

"Excuse me, ma'am, but I really just need a moment alone with Tommy if that's alright?" James insisted.

"Oh, I'm sorry, all visits must be supervised. Guests and patients need to be in the main rec area. Safety first," she added with a smile.

James stopped the chair with his foot as she tried to wheel past him. She looked up with a surprised glare.

"I'm sorry ma'am, I just…I don't how to say this. This has been a moment I've been anticipating for a long time and I…well I just need to have this time without all those other distractions, if you don't mind."

She gave him a long, hard stare.

"Well, I suppose if you are, in fact, a doctor. Maybe the rules can be bent. But just for a moment," she said putting the brake back on the wheelchair. "You have twenty minutes. I need to go get some paperwork filed and I'll be right back. If there's any trouble, an emergency or whatnot, you just ring this buzzer here and someone will be right over," she said pointing to the red button by the door.

"Thank you! Ma'am, I can't tell you how much this means to me."

She nodded, giving him another once over before closing the door behind her with a loud click.

Catching her eyes, staring back within the small rectangular window James suddenly felt claustrophobic as if the walls were about to cave in and wondered if this were really a good idea. Giving the handle a little pull, he realized he was locked in. The room was not that big and suddenly the situation felt very unnerving. There wasn't a window to look out of nor even a picture on the wall. Just the blank dingy white interior accented by the rather unappealing harsh overhead fluorescents. The buzz created a strange ambience within the space almost sounding like the summer cicadas' back home.

"Been a long time, Tommy," he said without further hesitation. He couldn't believe who he was speaking to or why he was even here. "My name's James Elba. But I know you know who I am…don't play dumb with me Tommy. You recognize me, don't you?"

Tommy just sat silent. His eyes lost in some distant space that no one in this world would ever see. The lines on his face, harsh and cruel. Time had taken no mercy on him over these years. He couldn't believe this was the same boy that used to terrorize him. Used to make his life hell.

"Mind if I sit?" He asked with some attempt to be polite but really could have cared less. He wanted to kill the man, even after all these years. Here he was at last, but sitting before him was nothing but a decrepit old man not able to move a muscle nor say even the slightest malicious insult. *Not much to say anymore Tommy. Devil got your tongue.*

As James sat quietly just feet away, he thought back on that fateful night. The memory becoming clearer. The last night he saw Tommy. The last night he saw anyone, when he stared down into that abyss. But what he truly saw he couldn't remember. Rather, could only

feel the crippling fear within his own mind, reaching out to grab them. He remembered being there in the circle. Just the two of them left standing. The madness rising within Tommy's eyes. But the rest was blank, like some piece of him was taken within that light. That sickly green glow. *The dark light.*

"You and I were the only ones that survived that night…You remember? We saw something…Something that changed us forever. But somehow, I've forgotten. I can't see any further into that memory. I don't know what I really saw but maybe you do? Maybe you can help me, Tommy. Do something good for a change."

Tommy just sat without so much as twitch to acknowledge he even heard a thing. James began to feel angry and leaned in closer.

"My wife is missing. Do you hear me? My wife is out in those woods somewhere Tommy and I need your help to get her back. Anything that might help. Tell me what's out there in those woods. You've seen it. You remember, I know you do. Help me, please!" James desperately exclaimed, placing the pen from the whiteboard in Tommy's hand.

He could swear the slightest impression of the corner of his lips curled. Tommy wanted to smile but couldn't. He wanted to laugh. To be cruel and loud as he always had. But could do nothing but sit and drool. The white crust building up on the corner of his mouth. Saliva hung off his lip and then dripped onto his lap. For anyone else James would have felt sorry but not Tommy Clayton. He didn't feel the briefest moment of empathy for the man.

"My wife Tommy! My wife. Do you hear me? Whatever took our friends all those years ago has taken her and I need her back! I can't lose her. Please I'm begging you. Tell me anything you remember," he asked, closing his eyes and clenching his fists, trying to quell the pain rising within. When he opened them, he could see the smile emerging on Tommy's face. It was unmistakable. James wanted to break him. To make him feel the same pain he had felt all those years ago growing up. He lunged forward grabbing him by the collar of his robe.

"Tell me what you saw! Tell me, God damn it! Write it. Draw it. Whatever you can do. I just need something. Please!" James yelled feeling more desperate than ever.

"Tick ta..." Tommy murmured as James quickly withdrew and regained his senses. He could, see indeed he had no tongue, just a mangle stump. His mouth hung open and looked as if he were almost smiling as he raised a gnarled hand and pointed to his desk.

James looked over at the desk. Piles of papers and books strewn about. He looked back at Tommy who just stared off. Lost once again in his own world as James quickly got up and searched through the madness and scribbled jargon. Page after page of nonsense. But there in the middle of it all was a small journal. Nondescript besides the familiar picture upon its cover. The darkest red he'd ever seen as if it were actually blood rather than ink.

James picked up the journal and stared down at the drawing of the cicada staring right back at him. He turned to Tommy as if to get some kind of direction, but he was nothing more than a living statue staring off into space once again.

James opened the journal and stood in wonder as the pages unfolded before him. The writing was harsh yet detailed and vast. One page even showing the circle in the forest as if it were a blueprint. The image, machine-like. Around its perimeter thirteen pillars. Symbols upon each. Strange lines intersected within. Page after page of something he couldn't comprehend. Words written in an unknown language, hieroglyphic almost, but between the pages themselves were drawings. Discordant scribbled works of what initially looked like nothing, but within it something emerged. Familiar faces stared back. Gaunt lifeless eyes sunken within an endless void, peering out from inside the nightmare. A twisted world revealing itself through the drawings of a madman.

The faceless ones.

A sliver of a memory emerged.

"Tick Ta..." Tommy's murmur suddenly rang out again. His breath wafted through the air, passing James' nostrils. A rotted stench filled thc room. "Tick Ta Ti ta," he repeated as James was sure what he was trying to say.

James took a step back as Tommy began to laugh. A sickened hysterical high-pitched laughter. One that he remembered so well but wished he had forever forgotten.

"Tick tack," James whispered under his breath seeing Tommy's eyes light up. "Tick tack, tick tack. Samuel Black is back...you remember, Tommy?" he asked as he listened to Tommy's laughter fill the room. His mouth gaped open revealing the stump of his severed tongue. Drool falling to the floor. Hands clapping. His head nodding back and forth, laughing hysterically.

The panic attack came on swiftly. James clenched his chest as he watched Tommy look back at him with rising satisfaction. The fear grew until he could take it no more and dropped to his knees. His heart pounded faster. He felt the world fading as he stared into the yellowed pupils of Tommy's eyes and watched them mysteriously turn black as night.

James froze as he could see his own reflection in the two black orbs staring down at him. The laughter rose into a high pitched crescendo. The familiar sound he knew as a boy.

Beyond that, any memory of what happened next was gone. James' head hit the floor. Tommy's journal fell to the ground and laid open beside him as a small trickle of blood dripped from the side of his head onto the cold white tiles.

***

James opened his eyes to the sounds of chaos and screams echoing through the room. His vision blurred as Betty stared down over him.

"Code Red!" her voice rang out in a panic as people rushed back and forth in the background. He still was getting his senses about him when he felt something upon his right hand like he had spilt maple syrup.

Lifting his hand, he looked at his finger covered in blood. Rubbing his thumb and forefinger together he stared at it a moment unsure of what he was really seeing. The smell of iron in the air made him want to vomit.

"Doctor Elba?!" Betty tried to get his attention as she examined the cut on his head. The pounding headache grew inside of him. "What happened?"

"I don't know," James answered, as he looked over at the body of Tommy slumped back in his chair, holding the familiar switch blade with the cherry wood handle in his hand. Thick dark red liquid ran from his slit throat down his chest and onto the floor like a river flowing back to the sea.

Oh my God!

James quickly pushed himself away from the body as the moment came to life. More people came and went in a rush.

"How did he get it!?" one of the orderlies asked, reaching over and picking up the switch blade.

"Don't touch it!" another yelled. As the panicked voices continued shouting at one another. The walls were covered in blood.

So much blood.

But it wasn't just blood. There were words within. Scrolled across the wall.

James could see the confusion as everyone tried to make sense of thc madness. But he knew. He knew what really lay within that room as he rested his hand upon the journal lying in a pool of Tommy's blood beside him. He quietly tucked it away into his waistband as no one seemed to be paying attention to him at the moment.

He stared with a longing to never want to see those words again. But here they were dripping down the dingy white walls. A phrase now all too familiar.

Tick Tack Samuel Black is Back

***

A young man sitting at the control desk in front of a series of monitors began to scroll through the video surveillance footage in the small security room. James, now flanked by a large security guard, watched as his heart raced not knowing what he was about to see.

Finally, there it was, the moment at hand. James could see himself have the panic attack and fall onto the floor. The tape suddenly went fuzzy as the next frames were nothing but static.

"Rewind that!" a deep voice spoke up from behind. A heavy-set man in a dark blue suit whom James assumed oversaw the facility.

"I'm sorry, sir," the young man replied as he scrubbed back through the footage. "Something happened to the camera here. Some sort of interference."

"Why the hell was he alone in that room?!" The man in the dark suit yelled, while Betty sat with tears in her eyes.

"It was just for a minute," she replied.

"Betty. I'm…" James tried to speak but was quickly cut off.

"Don't say a word. Just don't," the man exclaimed standing a moment in deep contemplation before turning to the security guard standing by. "Get him out of here."

"Excuse me," the guard replied looking confused.

"You heard me," he said and turned to James. "This never happened. Do you understand me? You were never here."

James sat dumbfounded a moment before standing and collecting his belongings.

"This facility can't take a mishandling of protocol like this. Not now when they're this close to shutting this entire place down. As far as we know, Tommy Clayton had hidden that knife in his mattress before he committed suicide." He then motioned for James to leave the room. "Don't ever come back here again doctor." And with that he turned his back as James gave a silent nod of acknowledgment and walked out of the room.

Sitting in his car, James stared down at his hands shaking uncontrollably, still seeing the dark red blood pooled on the white tile. Flashbacks of his daughter's fateful day exploded before his eyes.

Sitting back, he regained his composure and untucked the journal from his waistband, holding it out before him with a look of relief. The bloody cicada staring back at him reminding him of all that was evil within this world and within himself. He needed more answers. He needed someone who could see between the lines and translate this…someone who could see into the abyss from which this journal had come.

CHAPTER 22

The evening air was lit with a fiery ember of streetlamps as the moon rose across the eastern Atlantic and bled down the South channel of the Savannah River.

Heading along the cobblestone walkways passing Madison square, James looked upon the bronze eyes of William Jasper standing resolute holding his flag for all eternity. The ghosts of the past were everywhere here, he thought. Some that he felt he even brought himself as he pressed his hand on his satchel holding the blood-soaked journal as if making sure it was still there.

Glancing down at Margery's scribbled directions, he turned down a little narrow walkway off Charlton Street passing under the arches of a wrought iron gate, flanked by ancient brick walls, and accented by a few pieces of crude graffiti. It was darker here, he thought, heading down the long dimly lit alley before finding himself standing in a small, gated courtyard. The screech of the gate closing behind him echoed as he hesitantly approached the front door. A nondescript facade that appeared to be nothing more than an abandoned building, if not for the simple words scribed across the glass reading:

THE BLACK PALMETTO

"Natural healings and other oddities"

Gently opening the door, he entered releasing a smoky mixture of incense and must. The light was dim as if he had just stepped back into the eighteenth century. Much like the rest of Savannah, a piece of the past was preserved here. It was a part of what made this city timeless. The ghosts of the past locked within buildings and walkways that had seen the world move on, yet somehow had all stayed the same. A special place where candlelight and streetlamps still lit cobblestone walkways and a place like this could be hidden away in a little non-descript courtyard.

A small black chandelier hung overhead, lighting a space that was larger than it had seemed from the outside. An upstairs balcony wrapped itself around the room lined with books, floor to ceiling. In the back, a staircase spiraled down to the main floor filled with shelves covered in endless glass jars of all shapes, sizes and colors.

"Hello?" James called out, looking upon the empty front desk as he tried to peak behind the red velvet curtain hiding a mysterious fiery glow in the back room. He leaned over the desk to get a closer peak but could see nothing. Beneath his hands under the glass case there were more bits and pieces of things he did not understand. Names like Toads root and Alabaster powder, nightshade, essence of dark, tears of a raven. Rows and rows of various candles in all color's shapes and sizes. Snake skins, bird feathers, crystals and geodes, powders, and pills. The assortment was endless, and he wondered how much of this was just nonsense and asked himself if this was really the right place to be.

He had grown up around this sort of thing. Voodoo and the likes of its superstitions along with other strange religions and beliefs tucked away in the forgotten corners of the city, but it was never a part of his own life. His mother had become a Christian in later years, but she always held onto her past and the truth it held…a truth, that James was beginning to see was more and more real with each passing day.

"What on earth are you doing here doc?" Margery shouted, stepping out from a shadowy back corner of the room.

"I need you to see something," James curtly replied as he pulled out the blood-soaked journal and held it out before her.

"Doc, what on earth?"

"Your Grandmother, I need to speak to her. Is she here?"

"Yes, she is. But…is that blood, doc?" she asked, seeing the red stain on his shirt sleeve.

"It is."

"Your blood?" she questioned, seemingly more concerned with the situation.

"No, it's not."

"Then whose?"

James stared down at the blood on his shirt. He hadn't even thought about changing or about going home and showering. Something to take his mind off the horrific events that just transpired.

No, he only thought of here… of coming here and speaking with the one person he thought might be able to help him.

"Please just help me," James began to break down. His voice cracked, his emotions coming to a boiling point. "I really need to see if your grandmother can somehow translate this."

"Oh Doc, you're travelin' down a dark road. I hate to see ya like this," Margery uttered, now looking more concerned than ever. "I need you to promise me something though."

"What is that?" he replied.

"Promise me you'll come back, doc. Promise me wherever this takes you, you'll find your way home."

James never really thought much about himself. Whether he'd live or die. The thought honestly did not concern him, but he appreciated the warmth in Margery's voice.

"Bonjour," an old woman's voice echoed from behind the front desk, emerging between two red velvet curtains. It seemed that the shadow of the room kept her shrouded within some hidden veil as if her small frail body were, but a ghost draped in a purple shawl, covered in various beaded necklaces and bracelets. The sound, like a rattle snake slithering from the grass. Her eyes were covered by dark sunglasses. Her head wrapped in a scarlet gele making her appear taller than she was, which couldn't have been much over five feet. The heavy lines upon her face told volumes, looking to be nearly touching a century upon this earth.

"Hello," James replied stepping forward attempting to get a better look at the old woman.

"Mi'ma' This is da doctor I was tellin' you about," Margery said.

"Yes, so how can I help you?" she asked in a thick creole accent revealing her impatience with a tap of her hand on the glass countertop.

"My name is James Elba," he said, feeling unsure of what eyes lay behind those dark sunglasses."

"And my name is Miss Lolita, but my friends call me Lola."

"Pleased to meet you," he exclaimed feeling a moment of awkward silence.

"You seem rather troubled," she said, seeming to sense his discomfort.

"I'm just…not really sure what I'm doing here that's all."

"Like a child lost in the woods searching for a way home," she said in a tone that seemed to ease James' tension. "Be careful da witch don't snatch ya out of da darkness," she said with a quick jerk of her hand nearly grabbing his arm.

James jumped giving the old woman a little laugh.

"Relax, tis a safe place, dis da house of da black Palmetto."

James gathered his composure, feeling a bit childish as he glanced over at Margery who gave him a reassuring nod.

"What's ya seek is da truth, no? To see witin da serpent's eyes and know what it knows. For it sees all and knows what's ya fear and what's ya desire."

"I only want to find my wife. I don't know how but I think maybe this journal can help," he said, pushing the blood-stained manuscript across the counter. His palm lifted, revealing the cicada cast in the glow of the room's strange ambiance.

Miss Lolita adjusted her small round dark spectacles and took a closer look.

"My granddaughter has told me of your plight. Walk over da Devils' grave doctor and he will surely awaken," she said, slowly and methodically running her fingers over the imprint of the cicada as if her hands were eyes.

James seemed very uneasy looking as though he wanted to grab the book and run.

"Child, why don't you leave da good doctor and me for a bit. Lock up da front would ya," she said with a sudden severity within her tone.

Margery gave James one last concerned look, placing a hand on his shoulder. But it was more than concern, it was sadness…it was guilt.

"You take care now doc and remember what I said." She quickly left and locked the door behind her, leaving the room eerily silent.

"Where did ya find dis?" Miss Lolita asked.

James didn't know what to say really. His thoughts drowned in Tommy's blood still fresh upon the pages.

"Someone I know wrote it. I guess it found me you could say," James replied watching the old woman examine its intricate writings.

"Immortality and resurrection…Do ya know of da Cicada?" she asked.

"It's an insect," James replied.

"Ha!" Miss Lolita let out a bellowed chuckle. "An ancient polyvalent symbol once a delicacy by da ancient Greeks. Sacred to da

God Apollo," she retorted as if insulted by his simplistic claim. "Did ya know Aristotle was fond of eating cicadas? Taste like nutty popcorn," she added with a smile.

"I can't say that I did, no."

"A beautiful creature. Living deep within da earth only to emerge in periodical cycles to restart its life. Mating and dying. An endless cycle of eternal life." She flipped a page, drawing James' attention to the mysterious prose scribed upon the first page. "Dis language has not seen da light for many years. Like da cicada it has come to be reborn."

"Can you read it?" he asked impatiently.

She looked up, staring him in the eye. Somewhere behind those dark round spectacles he felt her digging within his mind. She slowly removed them and looked at him with one eye. The other white as a ghost as if the pupil had been erased from time. "Yes, yes I can, but look too deep into the abyss and ya might not like what be lookin' back," she replied as James was locked within her gaze, feeling like a scared boy once again.

"Tell me. Please," he begged, "I believe my wife's life depends on it."

She paused a moment and closed the journal. Then stood silently watching James like she wanted to mourn whatever was left of the young boy dying inside.

"What answers do you hope to find within deese pages?" she asked.

"I don't know, maybe nothing but maybe everything," James replied suddenly questioning his own sanity.

"You have seen dis before, haven't you?" she spoke softly as if reading his mind, "within your dreams...your darkest nightmares."

"I'm sorry but I don't know what you mean."

"Da mark is left upon you," she reached out and held a finger to his forehead. "There!" she exclaimed, digging into his skull. "A stain forever upon your soul."

"What are you talking about?" James nervously replied, feeling the greasy imprint she left upon his head.

"Who is your God, Mister Elba?" she asked.

"I don't understand?"

"But you will," she said as she picked up the journal and turned and headed behind the red curtain. Her crippled form disappearing into the shadows.

"Follow me."

CHAPTER 23

The small windowless room was lit in nothing but candlelight. Although he wasn't familiar with anything around him James felt the artifacts back here were darker somehow, even dangerous. Cracked human and animal skulls, bones, jars full of what could only be thick coagulated blood. Dead animals cut open with pieces of their organs missing and a wall of books that looked as though they had been written before the ages. Each one held up by the next like bodies lined within a morgue.

James stood nervously with nothing around him besides his own clothes to tell him he was still in the twentieth century. Something told him most people didn't see this part of the store.

"Buildings over two hundred years old. Wiring never seemed to work quite right back here. It was like this place was meant for darkness, so I just left it as it wanted to be," Miss Lolita said like a mother giving grace to her child.

They stepped further into the small room. An old wooden table sat in the center, stained with what could only presumed to be blood. He couldn't take his eyes off the chunks and pieces hacked and carved out of its top wondering what unfortunate lives bled out upon its surface.

"Quite a place ya got here," he muttered under his breath, feeling as though some unseen hand rested upon his shoulder.

"Dis is where da forsaken come for answers," she replied, her eyes scanning the wall of books. "I have traveled da world to gather texts of our forgotten ancestors. Da ones who drew da demon's breath, held da angels light and touched da word of God itself." She sighed, continuing to gaze row after row, finally coming upon an old burnt manuscript. "But sometimes it is within our own backyard, da darkest secrets lay."

James watched with apprehension as she pulled out the fragile manuscript. Its corners curled and flaking away. The cover and binding were heavily burnt and weathered with pages looking as though they could all crumble to dust at any moment.

"Sit." Miss Lolita gestured across the table as she took a seat. "Now please, if you would." She held out a hand motioning for James to hand her Tommy's journal.

She laid the two manuscripts out side by side, he could see they matched with an identical cicada on their covers. One crude by the hand of a madman, the other more eloquent…older and more refined. As she opened each to their first pages, there within the dim candlelight he saw in amazement they were both an exact match. Word for word.

"Da missing pages erased from time, for over one hundred and fifty years and now da words return home to once again see da light of a new moon," she said as she caressed its pages.

"What is this?" James asked.

The old woman looked up with a satisfied grin. "A grimoire of da darkest kind. Da original here, incomplete. I have held it for many years now. Passed down from my very ancestors. Translations of da Demon Stones written in days of darkness by a Haitian witch made a slave upon dis land…Nastassia," the name slipped off her tongue like a snake, "It was her and her alone dat could translate da ancient stones uncovered within da forest beyond da western fields."

"What do they say?" James asked like a child wanting to hear a ghost story around the campfire.

"Dark magic. Instructions for opening da gateway to an unseen space dat lives and breathes before our mortal eyes." She pushed Tommy's copy of the grimoire towards him. "Da spirit copy from da possessed you have found. Da hand who wrote it has walked within da dark light. Touched by da other side, its creator is forever connected to its power and da ones who live within. Da missing pages reborn."

James' eyes stared down at the identical copies of Tommy's writing and the old burnt manuscript in disbelief. His thoughts drifted back into the forest clearing remembering his friends. The blade against his throat. The blood, the screams…the light.

"Before you understand da future first you must understand da past. For it is here your fate has begun," she said drawing James' attention to the page before him.

He looked down with nervous apprehension building inside. He didn't want to see any of this. He'd gone his whole life pretending none of this stuff was real and now here it was. Standing before him as if it had always been a part of his forsaken life.

"Over one hundred and fifty years ago a nightmare was awakened upon your land. Da Sullen Ones whose words drew their breath from dis forgotten prose, grew from a dark light buried deep within da sour Georgia clay. They are da ones truly bound to da evil dat haunts you," she said as she drew his attention to an image of a circle with thirteen human figures around it.

James shifted in his seat, looking very uncomfortable.

"Da Sullen Ones are da original slave hands who first uncovered da ancient stones dat hold da dark light. Chosen by Samuel Black to bring human sacrifices before their demon counterparts. It is they who fed da creatures. They who had forsaken their very soul to live. But their lives would have been better lost than to be what they had become. For what they served forever changed them into something far from human. Mind rotted. Eyes no longer their own. An unquenchable taste for blood." She leaned closer as if to emphasize her words. "They had become da very demons in which they served." She turned the page revealing more unknown text. "But da Sullen Ones do not die Doctor Elba. Their souls forever bound to thirteen demon gods, trapped beneath da earth for millennium. Their prison marking da portal in which they first came unto dis Earth. A rip in space and time connecting dis world to da afterlife.

"You mean death," James exclaimed.

"Death is but a doorway. But to travel through it we must first shed da one thing we fear to lose…our very lives," she said looking deep into his eyes drawing his attention to the next page. A circle with thirteen hieroglyphic symbols around its perimeter and in its center, the cicada.

"What does it mean?" James asked like a curious child.

"Tis da lost circle of Solomon. Da key to da demon portal given to King Solomon by da faceless ones." She drew her finger around the perimeter, pointing to the glyphs. "Each is a name represented by a hieroglyph for which man cannot speak…a lock, drawn upon da tongue of da faceless demon who be locked inside a sacred stone, wreathing to emerge from its prison. Thirteen locks, guarding da way to da afterlife."

She drew his attention to the cicada within the center. "Its body but a vessel as it slumbers and is reborn throughout time, much like da demons themselves. Each one must be appeased with a sacrifice to unlock its piece of da portal and like da cicada leave its prison within da earth. But each sacrifice is never the same. Every one specific, for each demon has its own appetite."

"Who could do such a thing? Feed those creatures," James asked, looking somewhat terrified.

"A poisoned mind and a desperate soul…It was Samuel Black who attempted to unlock da portal with da blood of his own slaves and anyone else he believed could appease the demon guardians. Even his own wife, they say. Many lives were lost." She looked down as if something touched her soul. "My own ancestors amongst da ones who never came back from da forest beyond da western fields."

"I'm so sorry," James said, reaching out a hand.

"As fate would have it, it was da witch herself, his own slave, that stopped da madness and da mad man from completing what he set out to do.

"And what was that exactly?" James asked.

"To undo death doctor, for he believed to get his daughter back he could open da gates to da afterlife." She looked down at the pages as if gazing upon a child. Her hand delicately ran over every crease. "An innocent child taken too soon. Her death igniting a fire that still burns to this very day."

"How did she stop him?"

"She burnt da final translation of the thirteenth stone and killed her master in his own bed…in your very house doctor. Tis a tragic story of dark magic, resurrection…of death unbound."

James stared into the glow of one of the candles sitting across the room as if his eyes were lost within some place he didn't want to be.

"For over one hundred years the thirteenth translation has been erased from dis earth," she took a deep breath staring down at the page. "And now it has returned. Awakened from its dark slumber," she said turning to the last page, bringing the two manuscripts together. "Each an incomplete script, but combined whole."

James looked down seeing the strange words once lost to time.

"What language is this?" James asked.

"One dat man cannot comprehend. A devil's tongue whispering upon the darkness of mankind's dreams."

She ran her hand over the page with a gentle touch as if electricity pulsed through her very body.

"Your wife is da final sacrifice and Samuel Black already knew it to be. His shadowed hand upon her shoulder, guiding her to da dark light within da birchwood forest. But he has not da words to complete da ritual."

James sat quietly for a moment. His mind churning as a sudden thought brought him to the edge of his seat.

"What if I open the gate? You said yourself a place where death has no meaning…I can save them both! I can get my daughter back. What if she's there?" James uttered with a strange look in his eye, "If it's the afterlife this portal actually opens then death will have no real meaning. Once the gate is open, I can bring her back…I can bring them both back!"

Miss Lolita's eyes squinted into a sharp glare. "You can save nothing but your soul!" she shouted banging her hand upon the table." Keep dat Childs soul away from dis place, doctor. Do not sacrifice her eternal peace for da darkness dat lay within these pages."

"How could I not try?" James begged.

"What Samuel Black did not know was his daughter could never have been brought back to life. For dis gateway isn't to any heavenly realm such a soul would reside. Rather another place, a forsaken place where da dark light slumbers. Where only unnatural pieces of a soul rest."

"But if there's a chance," James pleaded.

"No chance!" she yelled back slamming her fist onto the table. "Keep dat Child's spirit away from dis madness."

Startled, James sat back and took a moment letting the thoughts settle within. His eyes becoming more terrified with every moment as the past awakened within him. "Then tell me, what is the dark light?"

"Tis da light dat emanates from da other realm. You've heard of heaven; you've heard of hell. But you've not heard of dis in Sunday school, I assure you. An energy…a dark magic risen from beyond da event horizon. Beyond da known universe itself. A thing dat needs to feed on dis earth. On da souls upon it. Its light, leaking into dis world since before mankind. You have seen it, and it has seen you." She reached out pressing a boney arthritic finger to his forehead. "Its mark forever left upon you."

He instinctively withdrew.

"You keep saying that but there's nothing there."

She smirked and leaned back in her seat.

"Sure, there is. You can't see what you can't see," she replied, "da same light dat touched da man who wrote dis has touched you. You just have forgotten doctor, but not for long."

The cryptic prose slithered within James' mind as he remembered laying within that circle in the forest. His eyes lost in its sickened glow, and within it, the faceless ones staring back at him.

Miss Lolita's face leaned over the flame of the candle sitting in the center of the table.

"There is one key yet to be unlocked for da portal to be opened and da dark light to emerge upon dis land like da sickness it is."

James shifted in his seat as the tension rose within his body. Miss Lolita turned the page, revealing a most disturbing sketch of the familiar beings. Eyes of sunken black voids. No nose, no mouth and high irregular cheek bones. "Da Faceless ones…thirteen demon rulers. Da true gatekeepers. Servants to da dark light, filling them with eternal life and da ability to travel da universe at will," she said in a soft sinister tone.

"I've seen them before," James said, now on the edge of his seat.

"And they you doctor. For you hold da final translation of da thirteenth stone. Locked inside, a demon whose eyes are already upon your wife…already upon you. Watching you with malice and rage from deep within da dark light."

James sat back. Confused. Alone. An innocent fear overtaking his gaze.

"You will follow da Sullen Ones. For only they know da way into da netherworld for which your wife resides. For she is da final sacrifice."

"How do I find them?" James asked, feeling his pulse rising.

"They will find you. For what you hold is what they so desperately desire as they are merely servants to their master and da demon circle," she said pushing the grimoire towards him.

James stared down at the pages. The images burned into his mind.

"A journey lays before you unlike any you've ever imagined. I will help you but first I must prepare. I will come to you when da time is right? Now please, you must leave the journal with me and go."

"What do you mean wait for when the time is right?"

"You know nothing of these creatures, doctor. You must be patient. As hard as it may be. There are eyes dat watch you even in dis moment," she said, looking around the room as if searching for something that was not ever there.

"This is madness," James whispered under his breath.

"No doctor, dis is da season. Da season of death…da season of sickness rising from da rotted fouls of da earth. Samuel Black will finish what he has begun for death did not find him upon that fateful night rather his own soul somehow was preserved through time only to be reborn with his eyes upon your most beloved as he guides her to something worse than death."

She closed both manuscripts and stared James deep in his eyes, placing a hand upon his forehead.

"Until now I thought it was forever buried. But you've carried da mark with you all these years and it is you who has come back home with da final sacrifice. For da path to da demon circle is death itself, and only within death shall you find your salvation."

CHAPTER 24

Night after night James sat on the back patio, alone with nothing but his thoughts, and stared out towards the forest wondering what might be out there staring back. The old woman's words spinning around inside his head made him want to scream. He felt helpless and alone but still would leave the porch light on like a lighthouse on a blackened sea waiting for Karen to somehow make it home. He had searched and searched until his mind could take it no more and even the clearing within the forest seemed to be gone as if he had just dreamt it all up. That forsaken circle lost within some shadow in between worlds.

The sheriff's visits became more frequent as his suspicions of James seemed to rise the longer Karen went missing. The drinking didn't help either as his own demise now seemed very self-evident. Slowly he felt himself becoming like his father. Alone, bitter, and angry at the world. A tortured soul. He just wanted it all to end as he could hardly look himself in the mirror anymore without seeing his father staring back at him.

Even the cryptic words of the old woman and the journal gave him no reprise from this pain as he couldn't make sense of anything and was tired of waiting for some answer or messenger that would never come. *Death is your salvation.* It was beginning to feel more and more true with each passing night. But he was alone. No one was coming for him. No one but his own demons he had created in the empty space where his wife and daughter once lay.

***

Upstairs, James got ready to try to sleep. The clouds had gathered and all but covered the last of the evening sun as he laid quietly staring at a picture of Karen and Elizabeth. The three of them as they once were. He couldn't understand how he could have lost so much and, in that moment, didn't know if he could go on living without them. He could see every action of his suicide. *Pills?* No, the .45 laid up in his closet would be quicker, he thought. Each had its own dilemma but each one nonetheless was not for him. He wasn't going to end his life. He could never give up as long as there was hope Karen was out there.

The moment he closed his eyes, the feeling of Karen's breath upon his neck tickled his skin. He laid quietly, feeling her by his side. Remembering the moments that now were nothing but distant memories.

He opened his eyes and stared at the empty place where she should have laid. Some voice inside him rose as he heard words within his mind, he hadn't spoken in quite some time. He could barely speak yet there it was coming back to him. He had nowhere else to turn.

"Lord," the name felt foreign and strange as it left his lips, "if you're really out there, then please hear my prayer. I need you now more than ever."

He felt a tear falling down his cheek as he stared at the empty cotton linens.

“She’s out there somewhere, and I need you to please help her find her way home.”

He wiped his tears as if embarrassed from himself.

He remembered back, early in their relationship. The conversations about how they'd grow old together and just stare out at a beautiful sunset off some large, covered porch and watch their lives fade away while sipping sweet tea. He could see her eyes still looking back at him. Just a nineteen-year-old girl talking about forever. He needed that forever. He wasn't going to live the rest of this life without her and wondered maybe if she was already dead. Her spirit lingering beside him. A ghost trapped within some netherworld for which there was no escape.

The idea made him feel ill. He didn't believe it. She was alive. He felt it. In every piece of his being, he felt her still within him. The smell of her hair. The softness and warmth of her skin. Her gentle touch and the way she would stare into his eyes and say a thousand words without saying anything at all.

"I love you," he said quietly as if he were speaking to her while being tormented by thoughts he could not control.

The sensation lingered and the silence overtook the room as the moment fell heavier upon him. Laying his head back on the pillow he just wished the nightmare to end.

A cold sweat ran down his back as he tossed and turned in the sheets half asleep but still growing more and more restless. The subtle breeze fluttered the white curtains, creating arms that seemed to reach out towards him.

Finally getting up he sat with his back to the wall wanting to scream. His hands dug into the sheets; his fists clenched the linens as if about to tear them to pieces. He just wanted relief. He just wanted to sleep but could only wait for the moment to pass as if something were there holding him. He could feel the past reach out and pull him back to some deep dark place. The pain crept into his side then ran up into his chest like a hand squeezing the life from his body.

Tick tack Samuel black is back...tick tack Samuel black is back. Again and again, repeated in his mind. He could hear voices like they were actually there. Scotty, Harold, and Emma. They were screaming. The screams were coming from outside. Echoes from the forest floated back like a nightmare risen from the dead. He had to sleep but felt the panic attack linger beneath the surface.

The screams of his friends grew more intense as the echo grew louder. Their cries for help rose within his mind to an indiscernible crescendo.

"Leave me alone!" he screamed holding his hands over his ears.

"Who is your God?" the voice replied, low and raspy. It wasn't just one, but many voices overlapping. The dialect familiar yet inhuman. He quickly turned to face whatever monster stood before him, but no one was there. And as suddenly as the madness had begun it all stopped and he was alone with only the sound of his still beating heart and the smell of burning wood wafting past his nostrils.

***

James listened closely as he stepped cautiously down each step. Grabbing a large heavy candlestick from the foyer, he readied it in his hand just in case, sensing the presence of someone in the other room. *Karen?*

In the living room James' eyes caught the flicking glow of flames rising within the large brick hearth.

"Fine evening be it, doctor," the old woman said, exhaling a puff of smoke from a large cigar twisting between her thumb and forefinger.

Startled, James turned to see Miss Lolita sitting in the chair with the small rag doll resting in her lap.

"Jesus!' James gasped grabbing his chest having dropped the candlestick to the ground.

"Jesus, got nothin' to do wit dis I'm afraid," she replied.

"What the hell are you doing in here? How did you get in?" James asked as he gathered his wits about him.

"Questions questions, no more questions, now is da time for answers. Can't be seein' in da dark when ya can barely see in da light ya know," she said.

James curiously looked down at the doll sitting in her lap.

"It has watched you since you arrived and bound itself to your beloved," she said. "It belonged to a young slave girl. A house servant who served her master well. Her name was Lila."

"I found it the day we moved in?" James replied. "My wife loved it for some reason. But I hate that thing. Why do you have it?"

"Nothing is what it seems, Doctor Elba. What we see tis not really what we see is it?"

Miss Lolita lifted the doll and examined it as if seeing an old friend. "Strange how such a small thing can hold something so big." She turned it over again and again, examining every stitch, finally staring it dead in its black beady eyes. Her demeanor suddenly changed as she whispered something in an unknown language, then in a quick snap of her wrist threw it into the flames.

"What are you doing!" James yelled, trying to retrieve the doll out of the fire.

"Leave it!" she yelled. "It's not what ya be thinkin' Doctor. Tis not da spirit of a little girl in dat doll. Dat child was there da night her master's demon was exercised and it was she who held his prison as death had become him. Samuel Black's very soul taken by da hand of da witch Nastassia. Aunt to da young child. Her doll but a vessel to store da rotted soul."

James watched as the flames wound itself around the old burlap turning it black as night. But there was something else. Something moving inside.

The sound rose from within. A high-pitched squeal pierced his senses. He covered his ears as he watched the doll moving violently about, whatever was inside was trying desperately to get out, pushing against the material as it became more engulfed within the flames.

"He has been watching you since you arrived in his home. You are but a guest, doctor. The true owner has never left. Rather waited…a long slumber, like da cicada itself. Buried within da earth awaiting to emerge when da time was right. He watched you through dat very doll as he whispered into your wife's ear, leading her into da birchwood forest."

James watched as the flame quickly drew itself up the body. Whatever once slumbered inside, pushed violently to get out as it was trapped inside screaming to be released. From within emerged the first cicada flying out of the flames. Then another and another until hundreds of cicadas flew from the doll's burnt body. Their wings, casting bits and pieces of hot embers throughout the room.

James covered his eyes trying to run, but stumbled over the end table and fell onto the ground. He rolled around, his shirt aflame. The cicadas swarmed him and covered his body as the flames enveloped his shirt.

He struggled to take it off as he pulled his arms out of the sleeves. "Damn you!" he yelled, "God damn you!"

He screamed as the cicadas continued an endless onslaught, swarming his body like vultures to rotted prey.

Looking over at Miss Lolita he could see her body covered from head to toe. Nothing but a black form of wings and legs moving about, yet she did not move a muscle, almost appearing like a spirit hovering in the air.

He tried to get up and run but the swarm had covered his eyes, blinding him. He could feel their legs and wings batting against his face, trying to crawl inside his mouth. He clawed and hit himself. Pulled bodies apart, smashed them to pieces. He was helpless. The swarm endless, the sound was deafening as he tried to cover his ears, but could not even touch them as a wall of cicada an inch thick blanketed his entire body. He tried to scream as they crawled inside his mouth, but they had choked the air from his lungs. He lay suffocating as the panic grew to an unnatural crescendo. Then suddenly, as if by some flip of a switch, it all ended and there was nothing around him but the air itself coupled by the gentle sounds of a crackling fire.

"Get up. It's unbecoming, doctor," Miss Lolita exclaimed as James screamed and continued hitting his body and face until he realized there was nothing there.

"What the hell?!" he exclaimed, still spitting and clawing his mouth.

"Dark magic," Miss Lolita replied watching James struggle to come back to reality. "Just breath, doctor. Give in to the madness and see what you are meant to see."

"Does this mean he's gone? Samuel Black." James asked, staring into the flames.

"Just because you burn something does not mean it is actually gone," Miss Lolita spoke, exhaling a large puff of smoke from her cigar. Her eyes gazed intently at what was left of the doll still smoldering in the fireplace. "Some say the ways of black magic to be the unnatural desires of mankind. Within da final translation lay the recipe for such desires. But go too far and you may not ever return to this world again," she said, taking another large puff from the cigar.

James felt his heart slowing as the room came back into focus. "This is crazy," he muttered, attempting to get to his feet.

"I have told you what you possess, yet you still doubt your own nightmares. Your eyes may deceive you, but your heart will not doctor. For you have brought back the complete translation of da demon stones and are now ready to travel into da dark light. Through its magic da only way to see your wife again."

"If this is real…where will it take me?" James asked as the nervous panic still lingered in his voice.

"The path unto darkness. True suffering unlike anything you've ever known. Only da Sullen Ones may lead you, but I have brought something to prepare you for this journey as best I can."

"I'll do anything to save her," James exclaimed.

"I know, doctor...I know."

CHAPTER 25

"Da forest is but a dream, Doctor Elba," the old woman exclaimed as she led James into the kitchen and prepared a pot of boiling water in the tea kettle.

"What you now see as a forest upon your land was not always as such. It was planted by unknown hands to hide what is within those woods and keep da evil it contains at bay. Layers upon layers insulating dis world from another. An outer range of sycamore and oak disguising an inner perimeter of birchwood. Mother nature's protective spirit. It is birchwood and a bit of dark magic dat keeps da circle hidden. Its inner layers buried within da spirit world."

James followed her gaze, cringing as he smelled the horrible rancid odor.

"You must prepare for da journey. Without it you shall never come home," she said as the kettle began to steam. Reaching into her pocket she pulled out a small glass jar looking like it had come out of the back room of her store.

"Not many have gone where you are about to go doctor. Here, Drink dis," she said as she poured the mysterious concoction into a small cup and held out the smoldering brew. "Like da cicada you too shall be born again. Within dis drink you shall have a power grow within you. Take it with you and remember your loved ones, doctor. It tis da only way you have a chance of coming back to da living."

James held the drink in his hands staring at the cup. One of Karen's favorite cups from a trip to Mexico when Elizabeth was only a baby. He could still see the small chip on the rim, when she had dropped it from the kitchen table. But Karen never could throw it away. James smiled as he drifted back there for only a moment. Then as the brew hit his lips, immediately brought him back to reality. The taste was horrible. Nausea quickly ran through his body.

"What is this?" he asked, wanting to vomit.

"Dead dreams, Doctor Elba. Drink and you shall see." She watched as he forced down the last drop.

"Very good…now come!" she exclaimed in a sharp demanding tone.

James followed a step behind as Miss Lolita headed upstairs and slowly made her way down the long hallway towards the spare room at the end.

"I don't want to go in there," James exclaimed.

"Want does not matter, doctor. Your fate lay where it lay."

They walked into the room and immediately James could feel the sickness in his stomach as he stared at a single red candle sitting in the center of the room…its flame creating strange shadows on the wall. He watched at a distance while Miss Lolita hummed a low melody and painted the familiar circle on the ground near the window. A small white circle surrounded by thirteen symbols and a cicada within its center.

"What are we doing here? We need to go to the forest. We don't have time for this."

“Many ways to travel in da afterlife doctor, but da demon circle has but one entrance now. One way in and one way out. A rip in time created by da witch Nastassia when she took da life of Samuel Black in dis very place.” She turned and looked at him with a curious grin. “Knock and you shall enter.” She tapped her finger upon the window. “Tick tack Doctor Elba…da Sullen Ones will show you da real nightmare which awaits you."

"But how?" James replied, stepping into the room as if finally accepting his fate.

"First remember…remember when you stood here as a boy speaking those simple words.

"That stupid children's rhyme to scare kids."

"A rhythm, doctor," she repeated tapping her finger on the window. "Tik tack doctor. A trifle to scare children yes, but buried within it a truth. A truth created by a young slave girl as she watched her master’s soul exercised from his dying body. But what you must know is like dat young girl, you too never left dis room."

"What the hell are you talking about?"

"You're still just da scared child standing here," Miss Lolita said with devilish eyes, "and your friends are waiting…" her voice trailed off as James began to feel the mysterious beverage.

"How do you know about my friends?"

"Because I hear their voices out there calling to you. Not just a bad dream I'm afraid, doctor. But a memory trapped in time. Da darkness is real, and it has seen you just as you have seen it."

"This can't be real," James stumbled as he felt the room begin to spin.

"Dis room is but a mirror to da other side. An entrance inadvertently created at da hands of a young slave girl and da blood of her master. Anytime you have seen da clearing within da forest. It began here doctor for here is where da nightmare awakened."

"What was in that drink?" he asked, feeling very uncomfortable with the situation. His heart rate, beginning to rise. His vision starting to leave tracers as he moved his head about, unable to keep a straight thought. Everything began to feel very strange.

"Listen to da sound of your heart. It is what reminds us we are wit da livin'. For where you be goin' there is no breath, so take it in deep now and watch da flame dance within da darkness," she said, directing his attention to the red candle. "A flame within da living world to guide you home. Its roots passing through time, burning since before mankind. A sacred place where da end and da beginning await."

The taste in James' mouth was rancid. The concoction felt like death.

"Lay your head witin da circle," she said guiding him down to the ground as he positioned himself accordingly.

"I want you to remember dis world can be tricky. Sometimes ya don't come back ya know," she spoke softly while lighting what appeared to be a large bundle of sage.

"What do you mean?" James asked as his eyes began to see strange orbs forming above him. The ceiling looking like a bloody sea lapping upon a shore.

"There is one way in and one way out. Find da way by feelin' your heart. Remember da living, doctor. Remember da breath in your lungs. Da kiss of your wife and da whisper of your daughter's words," she said, rhythmically tapping the window. *Tick Tak Tick tak*

James began to see images through the wavering air. The sounds of a storm rose in the distance. Screams came from within the walls. A pain was building as he could feel a sickness churning in his stomach.

"I'm gonna throw up," he called out.

"Just be still. Da journey has already begun."

Miss Lolita's voice became a song as the low rhythmic chant swept through his body. A pulse within him grew. He felt as though he were being pushed through the air…a thick heavy air. His body contracted and stomach tightened. He could feel every hair of his body standing on end. Each sensation heightened to near madness.

The old woman's voice became a distant echo as if she were a million miles away. His nails drew down the floorboards as his teeth gritted in pain. Insanity rose within him like nothing he'd ever felt. He wanted to die. He wanted it all to end as he watched the walls bleed…pooling onto the floor and moving towards him.

"I can't take it! Let me go! Let me go!" he screamed as the bloody face of his daughter appeared before him.

"Lizzy!" he called out.

"Come home, Daddy. We're waiting for you. Mommy and I are here."

"Baby!" he called back and reached out but found nothing but his own image staring back at him. His eyes were not his own. Blackened and full of hate. It was his father.

"There is no God to save you now, son," his father's voice called out, "go to the dark light."

"Father, please!" James begged as he held up his hands to shield the image of his father's face turning monstrous and old. The hallucinations were stronger than ever now!

"We are waiting for you," his father's voice transformed into a raspy low gargle of many voices. A legion of something not human. He'd heard it before. The same voices, speaking a strange unknown language.

The blood covered the entire floor as time seemed to rewind itself before his eyes. He could see the house as it once was. The ornate furnishings. The paintings. The statues. And the old man lying in the bed before him. *Samuel Black*. A sickly-looking man. A dying man. James could see his black soulless eyes staring back at him. The voice of his father ringing through his head.

"There is no God here, son."

CHAPTER 26

James' eyes floated in and out of consciousness as he stared up at the ceiling trying to hold back the overwhelming sensation to vomit. His head spun as his hands drew themselves across a dark red Persian rug. Against the wall beside the window sat a four-post bed, upon each post an angelic like being intricately carved within. Beside it, a dark wood dresser and chairs. A large mirror hung to his left and a fireplace which he couldn't remember ever even existed in this room was lit on the far wall, filled with a soft flickering flame. The crackle of the wood and the storm that beat against the thin pane glass window echoed through the luxurious space. Flashes of lightning and booms of deep thunder rolled through his bones, awakening his senses.

He sat up rubbing his head. A pounding headache dissipated with each second as the room came more into focus. His eyes were suddenly drawn upon a large painting hanging over the fireplace mantel. Its border was a gilded frame looking fit for a palace. The painting within, a family portrait, mother and daughter perhaps. On the bottom left a young girl in a white dress accented with a matching ribbon in her curly brunette hair. Her eyes unseen as a black stain covered what once was. Beside her, a middle-aged woman whose features were similar, and eyes hidden by the same black stain. Straight brunette hair hung over her left shoulder as James wondered what color pupils might have peered out from beneath that darkness…her beauty was undeniable.

The longer he stared at the painting the more the black stain upon it seemed to grow and warp. He rubbed his eyes as if he were hallucinating. The faces now almost fully encapsulated within its strange orifice, like some beast eating its way through time. He felt a sense of foreboding as the picture grew darker with each passing moment. He could feel their pain resting beneath its surface as it ate away at their flesh…at their souls. Screams rose from within. He turned away as the nausea within grew.

"It sees you, ya know," a girl's voice suddenly spoke from behind.

James quickly looked over to see a young African child dressed in rags standing before him. Her hands were holding a small, dingy washbasin and rag.

"It didn't always look like that. The Devil does not appear until he is awakened," she spoke softly as if afraid someone might hear her.

"Who are you?" James asked, taken aback. "How did you get in here?"

"Lila," she exclaimed as she turned and stared up at the painting with both love and fear within her deep brown eyes. "They were beautiful. They were kind." Her voice sounded sad as she turned back and dropped to her knees, beginning to scrub the floor.

"What happened to them?" James asked.

"A sickness took the young one," she said, looking as though she was holding back tears. "She was my friend…she taught me writing and how to speak proper. I learned many things that I was not supposed to know," she said, looking up at the little girl in the painting, "and her mother was just as kind." She wiped her tears. "He always blamed us for his daughter's death and blamed the madam as well. His cruelness grew with each day. He thought he could fix the pain in his heart when he took my people one by one out to those woods…to the bad place, Hades, some would call it. But as the fates would have it, what rested in those woods was something far darker than even the master could have imagined."

"What's out there? Please I have to know."

"Somethin' very old, somethin'…" she searched for the words as she stopped scrubbing a moment and looked up at the painting. "Hungry," she said quietly as if suddenly her own fears had risen within her. "It should never have been unburied. Aunt Nastassia told me it's like a nightmare…a nightmare that seeped into this world from another place. A darker place. But you can't see these monsters. They hide themselves within."

She stared at the empty bed with a nervous apprehension as if she wanted to suddenly get up and run out of the room.

"My master's mind was taken apart piece by piece until there was nothin' left but his own nightmares. But what he did not know was that he was the nightmare, and the nightmare was him."

James walked closer, examining the painting. Standing so close made him nervous as he watched the black stain warp and move within the canvas. It was almost living, he thought. Moving in a way like an oil stain spreading across the surface of water.

"What is it?" James nervously asked with subtle apprehension as he reached towards the canvas.

"Don't touch it!" she shouted, as James snapped his hand back.

"It's just a painting," he replied.

"It's nothing of the sort. It appeared the day they unburied that stone circle out in those woods. The darkness is alive within it. Just as it was alive within my master. There are places now that it can see and touch. This be one of those places…I wish they would burn it. But the master would not have it. Not at all."

James could hear the whispers of strange tongues coming from within the painting.

"I hear something," James said, leaning in for a closer listen.

"The voices of the ones who do not sleep. Their ancient tongues speak from within. But it is out there they rest. It is out there in the forest where their bodies lay locked within that prison, waiting to be awakened. The nightmare is here to stay I'm afraid. And once the master returns. I need to be ready. So, if you'll excuse me, I have work to do," she said standing beside the bed.

James could now see the bloody sheets covering its surface. A deep red stain soaked within the center. The smell of the blood was very apparent and came rushing past his senses. The rest of the room came more into focus as if seeing it for the first time…There was blood everywhere. The walls covered from floor to ceiling. He hadn't seen it before, but suddenly it was everywhere.

Lila got back down on her hands and knees and began scrubbing the floor. Softly at first then with a harsh rhythm as if she were imagining someone's face within the floorboards. She wrung the rag within the small wooden basin as James watched the red liquid drip down. Suddenly he was very uncomfortable. A rising anxiety built within as he watched the little girl continue to scrub the floor and wring the blood-soaked cloth.

"Ya have to get all the blood. Auntie says can't be none left. Nothin' left behind."

"What happened here?" James asked as he looked around the room as if a dozen eyes were suddenly upon him.

Lila stopped and stared down at the blood. Within her stare there was so much pain. So much longing for something he could not truly see, yet he knew it was there.

"Do ya know where it is that you go when you die mister?" she asked.

He stood silently for a moment, the question catching him off guard.

"I don't, I thought I did at one time, but now I'm not so sure."

He thought harder about the question as he stared down at the pool of blood upon the floor. It reminded him of something. He had seen this before. He looked deeper, now seeing his own reflection within it. His thoughts began to materialize as he suddenly remembered his little girl lying before him on that sidewalk. Her hopes and dreams, taken to the stars and her body left to rot.

He closed his eyes and began to weep. The feeling overtook him without warning.

"You have seen your past," she said as she stopped scrubbing a moment and turned and stared up at him with big brown eyes. "But look deeper and you shall see even darker dreams."

"My daughter is dead, and my wife…" the memories materialized quickly, "she's out there somewhere. In that forest," James uttered, as his mind flooded back with the memories of the life he once had. "Please help me find her. Please!"

"Dead is what is out there, mister. But dead don't matter in this place," she said as she stood up and walked to the window. Her eyes looked lost as she gazed deep into the storm-ridden night. "I don't go out there. Not never."

"But you can help me, can't you?" he begged.

"I watched each day as something grew out there in that darkness. Stood right here in this very spot by the window."

Tick tack tick tack. Her finger tapped the window.

"Always watching that horrible light pulsing off in the distance," she continued, her voice now trembled, and her gaze grew cold.

"The birchwood was not always there, it is the reason the darkness has been hidden. It was planted after my master's death and the stones buried once again. My auntie says it guards us from another world trying to reach into our own, but you cannot contain such things."

"What's really out there?" James asked, feeling a lump in his throat.

"You already know, do ya not?" she looked deeply into his eyes. "I can see it in ya. You've been there…you've seen for yourself." She turned and stared back out the window. "And it has seen you."

James followed her gaze as he could see a sickly glow within the forest. A greenish pulse painted the night sky above as voices rose within, speaking unknown tongues. Then as clear as day he could see something standing at the edge of the forest staring back at him. Tall dark figures. Their eyes illuminated in the night. The same color as the light in the forest. James took a step back, the fear rising within his eyes.

"The Sullen Ones serve the dark light. Thirteen slaves turned into devils to serve my master and feed the faceless ones."

She began to cry, looking more scared and alone than ever.

"My mother was taken by them and fed to the creatures. She too, is never coming back."

Her tears fell upon the floor mixing with the blood. James wanted to comfort her but felt frozen in time. His eyes locked within the sickly glow.

"They are waiting for you, mister."

James could only stare as fear pulsed through his veins. The Sullen Ones watched him from the forest's edge. Eyes glowing in the darkness.

"They can hear your thoughts," Lila said, "there is no dead anymore there is only that which awaits." She gestured to the forest's edge. "Time is short, Jimmy. Now please go, I have work to do."

"How do you know that name?"

"We know many things. Your name need not worry you. It is the only thing you have left, I'm afraid," she replied.

James could see the Sullen Ones still standing on the forests edge watching him…waiting.

"I'd be goin' now if I was you. You'll be awake soon, won't ya?" she said, giving him a strange grin and then went back to her scrubbing.

***

James walked slowly out of the room seeing a dozen silver sconces lining the hallway. A candlelit glow flickered all around him while paintings of stately men stared back with cold calculated eyes seeming to follow his every move. He cautiously walked down the hallway mesmerized at the new world before him. He could see that what was once his own master bedroom was now two smaller guest quarters containing elegant furnishings of mahogany and gold.

Standing at the top of the staircase he looked down taking in the grandeur of the space, resting his hand upon the dark mahogany railing. Its woodgrain polished to near perfection. The sparkle of candlelight lit the foyer as if stars were falling from the heavens above. A pathway lined with bright red velvet carpet, accented with gilded trim led him downstairs.

Stepping onto the staircase he walked slowly taking in every elegant detail of the grand foyer before him. Crystal shards gleaming with candlelight sent a magnificent sparkle across the perfectly polished marble floor. Everything was pristine as if it had seen but one day upon this earth. There was not a soul in sight, yet he felt as if something big were about to happen. A party or some gathering of some sorts. The smells coming from the kitchen were divine, like nothing he had ever smelled before.

The storm outside had seemed to dissipate and softly in the background there rose the sound of cicadas as if summer had returned and the night had been brought within the very walls before him. A soothing sound that made him never want to leave. He felt embraced within by some dark magic that he could not understand.

Very curious, he began to look around. The library off to his right was now full of books both old and new. The writing upon their gilded spines accented by the roaring fire within the arms of the two cherubim. Large elegant Persian rugs laid out across the floor encapsulated a place he had only imagined would be his sanctuary. And now here it was…just as he had always imagined it would be.

Across the other direction, the living room too was completely transformed. He took a few steps in as his eyes gazed upon the large heads of animals mounted to the walls. Dozens of trophied kills stared back at him as he walked over and gazed upon their faces frozen in time. Each one seemed trapped in a moment that it would never escape from. Their eyes were not right though, and he didn't like this room. The thought made him feel ill as he had never liked hunting and especially un-fond of the art of taxidermy. Why anyone would mount a live animal on their wall was beyond him. But here it was. The walls, covered in the remains of dead creatures. Both forest creatures and exotic animals that could only have been captured on some distant safari and brought back to this place where they would forever rest.

Everything else within the room was different as well. The furnishings elegant, the long red draperies covering the windows looked to be almost royal velvet. In between the cracks he could see the light of the moon was fading and the night turning into nothing but a void in time.

The fire within the large marble fireplace sent flickering shadows upon the walls. He watched as they danced before him. A fiery enchantment. Each movement, like some unseen ritual awakening the spirits around him.

Above the flames and mantlepiece hung a rather grand ornately framed painting. James cautiously approached, wondering where such a thing had come from. It was not his…none of this stuff was. But somehow, he felt deep inside this had always been his home.

Staring down upon him within the canvas were the eyes of Samuel Black. Just a man. The person he once was. Yet, still his eyes looked as black as night. A soullessness rested within them following him wherever he would go.

The eyes never lie, he thought as he studied the rather regal looking gentleman within the painting. Long white tendrils of wispy hair peeked out from the sides of a large black brimmed hat. His black suit and bowline tie pulled perfectly tight to his collar giving him an almost priest like sensibility. But still he didn't like the eyes…there was something in them. He couldn't place it, yet the feeling within ran cold as the lifeless portrait stared back at him.

James' thoughts began to dissipate in some palatial mist as the house seemed to be putting him to sleep. Anything before it and anything after just a distant dream. There was only now. The dark elegance holding him within some membrane of time.

He was getting tired. The flames were mesmerizing. The intoxicating smell of food wafted past his nostrils from the kitchen. A voice within his head began to rise. An unintelligible whisper reminded him that time was short...*don't go to sleep. Not here!* He had to hurry.

Opening the front door, a blast of cool air awakened his senses. He found himself staring down the long palatial drive lined with southern oaks and dripping Spanish moss accented by the light of a full moon. His eyes were lit up by streams of flickering candlelight lining each side of the drive. The southern oaks seemed more astute, the Spanish moss fluttered lightly in a distant breeze, making the scene as beautiful as anything he had ever laid eyes upon. The scene was majestic, like a dream. The flickering candlelight went as far as his eyes could see.

Walking away from the house he could see the exterior was bright with fresh white paint. The columns stood perfectly resolute without a crack or speck of dirt on them. The windows, crystal clear. The landscaping, immaculate. He stood a moment staring at his home as if he were seeing it for the first time.

Or the last.

James began to walk towards the forest. His thoughts ruminating on his wife and daughter and of everything that he'd ever lost. He had nothing left.

The eyes that were out in that forest watching him created the deepest sense of dread he'd ever felt, but he could not turn back. Whatever path his fate was upon, it was his to walk, guided by some unseen force, waiting in the shadows. A living nightmare that drew him closer with each breath as he stepped through the wavering field grass beneath the wake of a demon moon. The night air felt cold, and the darkness penetrated his soul as though wherever he was about to go, his own death lay upon the other side.

CHAPTER 27

The sound of cicadas gave no reprieve from the anxiety that bound up in James' stomach. A fear resting in the back of his mind grew with each step. The high field grass brushed up against his thighs, calming him almost. The forest's edge was just off in the distance and his fate stood upon its precipice. He wanted to go back. To be back in the house by the fire and forget whatever waited for him out here. But he knew there was only one way out.

He could see he was not alone. But there were not the many figures he had seen from the upstairs window. Rather just one man, only a few feet away, standing at least seven feet in height and with eyes that bled with pain and a red sash draped across his bare dark skin.

Blood. It looked like blood.

His body was darker than anyone he had ever seen, as if he were born of the night itself.

The Sullen Ones.

"Where is she?" James demanded but the man did not answer only turned and walked into the forest as if an invitation to follow.

James took a deep breath and walked closely behind. As he passed through the outer rim of oaks and sycamores, he could feel the change in the air. A suffocating sense of dread upon him.

He followed closely behind having a hard time keeping a visual as the man did not make a sound. Not the crunch of a leaf nor the snap of a twig. He was as silent as a ghost.

Maybe that's what he was, James thought. Maybe all of this was just madness. Memories and nightmares coalescing into a state from which he had no real sense of reality.

He felt himself drawn to the strange markings on the man's back. Scars from lashes that had raised the skin. But there was something different about it all. His body was almost transparent and wavered in and out of reality as he led him further into the forest labyrinth. There was no clear path anymore, but the man seemed to have a direct line he was heading.

He picked up the pace as they pushed onward. Deep down James knew what evil lay within these woods. He could feel glimpses of what he had forgotten so long ago and could almost hear the screams from the trees themselves. Then suddenly…

"Where are you, boy?" a voice rang out from the shadows. It was Daniel Buckard. His distinct brusque tone and gargled accent as if he had a mouthful of marbles.

James quickly turned his head, looking in that direction.

It couldn't be.

He was just hearing things. Of course, he was. Then Tommy's raspy high-pitched squeal called out like a siren.

"Come on boy! Squeak, squeak, squeak. Where are you, little piggy!"

James felt nauseous as the past came alive around him. He quickly darted his head back and forth trying to make sense of what was happening but could see no one but the shadows playing tricks on him. The whole world was under a veil. A nightmare that never ended. The voices got closer, but still he could not decipher which direction they came from.

"What is this?" he called out to his guide,"what's happening?"

The voices came in all directions and James could now see his guide seemed to have vanished before his eyes, leaving him alone with his dark past knocking at his door. Emma's sudden screams came from his left. Scotty's from the right. Harold from behind him. Their voices a rapturous crescendo, as something unseen, ravaged their bodies. The pain in their voices was almost unbearable until he fell to his knees and covered his ears. His palms pressed so hard against his ears, it felt as though he could crush his own skull. The panic attack was coming on quickly. His heart beat out of his chest. A cold sweat built on the back of his neck as his vision grew dimmer by the second.

"Just breathe," he told himself, taking in large breaths in rhythmic pulses. "Just breathe."

He tried not to let the panic get the best of him.

Not now...not when Karen is so close.

The screams began to dissipate. His heart rate slowed. His breath became more and more rhythmic. Then a touch upon his shoulder drew his attention. He looked over, thinking it was just a bug, but nothing was there. He listened quietly to his own heartbeat. The sound of his breath. His thoughts slowed like a freight train coming to its destination. And within that moment he could feel his mother beside him. Her hand upon his shoulder. Her breath tickling his ear.

"Mama?" James whispered under his breath, "are you here?"

There was no answer but somehow, he felt she was.

Gathering his senses, he could see a glow up ahead in the distance. Not a natural glow like a sunset. But a sickening one like a plague rising in a mist. A pulsing greenish hue.

Stepping from within the shadows, his guide once again stood before him, staring down as if he were just a lost child. As James got to his feet, he could feel the weakness in his knees and the electricity pulsing through his veins. He did not know what to say, rather just brushed himself off and stood as resolute as he could manage.

The Sullen One stared at him as though reading his deepest thoughts. James could see something more behind the man's eyes but whatever humanity was once there was too far buried to ever come back. There was sadness to it all. His pain and the pain of everything around him had risen to the surface and rested quietly within the man's eyes. The lives that were lost here were all too real.

James followed closely behind as his guide picked up the journey once again. The further they went the more he noticed changes happening around him. The smells, the sounds and even the trees themselves were different. The once dense forest of sycamores and southern oaks gave way to the familiar tall thin trunks spaced perfectly apart…the birchwood stood like watchers in the night. Their knotted eyes looked upon him as he walked further into his own nightmare. He wondered how he had ever gotten here before as a child. What dark magic led him and his friends that night? Up ahead, he could see a place he didn't believe even existed. This place was just a dream, but at last, he had returned to the heart of this forsaken forest.

The glow grew brighter the closer they got, until they walked out of the labyrinth of trees and stood within the clearing upon the edge of the chalk circle. No more than fifty feet in diameter, it was simpler than he remembered. Smaller. A place he had pushed so far down into his memory, it had become no more than a distant nightmare now come up to play.

So much time had passed since he had set foot upon this place. He was a man now but still it made him feel like a boy wanting to pull the covers over his head to hide from the boogeyman. The evil that slumbered here was real and no wishing it away would protect him from what he was about to see. Even the moonlight was afraid of this place as it had all but diminished overhead leaving nothing but a dark veil above.

He held himself up with an arm wrapped around one of the trees at the edge of the clearing, feeling a dizziness overtake his senses. The dark light pulsed from the ground in front of him. His vision slowly came into focus seeing the reddish hue of blood within the chalk circle marking the perimeter. The familiar thirteen hieroglyphs upon its outer edge and the large cicada drawn within its center.

Nothing grew there. Nothing but death.

The place where the slaves had dug too deep. The place he had stood so long ago.

As his eyes adjusted, he could see his guide, but this time he wasn't alone, rather there were others. Each identical, draped in a dark red sash standing on one of the thirteen glyphs with eyes as white as ghosts reflecting the greenish glow of the dark light rising from within the center of the circle.

A low hum began to grow…a rhythm. A pulse, moving through the air. The Sullen One's mouths did not move yet the chant came from inside their being, creating a buzz like the cicada itself. The sound grew louder as they began to clap and stomp in a strange sequence…rhythmic yet unsettling. The sounds nearly drove James mad…a ritual was at hand.

He could only watch in wonder at how any of this was even possible. Then in the midst of the madness there appeared within the center of the circle, a figure bathed in the glow of the dark light. Shadowy at first then as clear as day…a woman. Her body, naked, materializing as if out of thin air.

"Karen!" James yelled out.

She looked at him with cold calculated eyes and smiled as screams from within the earth itself echoed around him. The Sullen One's chant increased in pitch; louder and stronger as the tempo became disturbingly fast. Voices from below, rose and fell. His friends…Scotty, Harold and Emma…even the hideous sound of Daniel Buckard. Their torment, unbearable. He could only listen in horror as he watched a subtle smile curled upon Karen's lips.

He fought the nausea as the terror in his eyes revealed he was just a boy again and whatever evil stood before him knew exactly that.

The same boy he'd been all those years ago, standing in this very place where for the first time he knew the Devil actually existed.

The light began to coalesce into a thick fog separating the world around him and he soon found himself alone, desperately reaching out for his wife.

"Karen!" he yelled out.

The echo of his own voice was deadened by the power of the dark light as he crossed the threshold of the chalk circle. The world as he knew it was gone and an inner darkness welcomed him home.

CHAPTER 28

It was all black. James could see and feel nothing. His only sense was his hearing, which gave a haunting revelation of his current state of being, as ancient words echoed through his mind.

The voice of Miss Lolita spoke from beyond some distant space in time. He could hear her familiar dialect as she pronounced words that sounded as unnatural as they did, frightening…their inflections becoming more and more distant as he was drawn deeper into the darkness.

Images and sounds grew within the voids of his mind. He could hear the slaves that tilled the soil. Their breath, heavy and strong as they dug deeper into some place they never should have been. He could feel the pain in their hands. The ache in their backs. The torment and sadness pulsing through their minds.

The visions deepened as James saw the past as if it were right there, before him. The surrounding forest was not yet protected by the circle of birchwood. Only the vague outline of southern oaks and sycamores creating a rudimentary circle encapsulating the clearing that would one day devour his life and the lives of many others.

He could see the faces that unburied the first of the thirteen stones…the sound of a pickax striking the top of the first edifice. The vibration it made was sickly as if awakening the dead.

With that vibration, the darkness began to subside, giving way to a peculiar light as if he had come out on the other side of a long tunnel. He could see nothing but a bright glow, blinding his senses…and then suddenly within it, appeared a shape…a small house.

A postage stamp size front porch with three steps led up to a white door. An old screen clung to its side as it battered itself against its frame. The windows were cracked and covered in dirt. The paint peeling.

James' eyes were still adjusting to the light, coupled by a pulse, flowing through his veins like electricity. It was the same feeling as when the blood has been cut off from a limb, like a thousand pins and needles were suddenly in your skin. He tried to shake it off, but the feeling did not subside.

He took a step closer as the glow had almost completely dissipated and he was left standing before his childhood home. The one he never wanted to see again. The one he couldn't see again because it had been torn down many years ago. But here it stood like a ghost returned from the grave. The dark light seemed to flow within it. Pouring into the windows and under the front door. A sickly greenish hue whose density was closer to a floating river than the misty light that it was.

He stepped onto the front porch remembering the screams of his father. His mother's tears. He would sit there as a boy and dream about faraway places. Staring out at a sunset, that brought no reprieve from the pain.

He could hear the subtle sound of moonlight sonata playing from inside…the last song he had heard his mother play. It was a night he had forgotten for so long but was now back as if he had never left, only trapped in perpetual motion to forever return, and feel the darkness that grew within its memory.

He listened closely as he could hear something else within its melodic phrase. The notes giving way to voices from inside those walls; his wife…his mother…his Elizabeth. Their whispers telling him to come inside. They were all there, waiting to welcome him home.

James stared through the torn screen door. Inside looked just as he remembered. The front hallway led down towards the living room, his bedroom off to the right and his parents to the left.

Opening the door, it creaked on old rusty hinges, welcoming him inside. A subtle step onto the wooden floorboards and he was suddenly a boy all over again, standing at the head of the hallway after a day out with his friends wondering what he was coming home to. How drunk was his father? How dry were his mother's tears?

The melody of the piano became more out of tune with each step. Beneath its sound, only his own breath to remind him he was still alive.

The painting on the wall was the same one he remembered. A circus scene with animals and a clown standing in front of the big top.

One, his mother brought home from a flea market and put up with such joy.

See Jimmy. Look at all the balloons. One day we'll go see them in person.

Stepping further down the hallway, he caught the flicker coming from the living room. The old television set his father would sit in front of for hours on end after coming home from the mill. The old box that couldn't get more than three good channels. The sound of static filled the air as he got closer to the living room. His heart raced, feeling the anticipation of seeing his father sitting there.

James caught his breath but could not take another step. The memories of that monster and the look in his eyes practically paralyzed him. The sounds, as he yelled and tore the house apart. Broken dishes. Broken pieces of their lives. Broken hearts and minds. He destroyed everything.

A hatred built within as he felt the man inside grow. He wasn't a little boy anymore and his father couldn't hurt him. Not now. He stepped further down the hallway, clenching his fists, not realizing the pain shooting up through his arm. The melody of an out of tune piano floated past his ears as memories rose further and further to the surface.

Around the corner he looked and could see the old upright his mother had been given by the church sitting in the corner. The melody all but silenced as the static of the television overtook the air sending an odd static filled flicker throughout the room.

Everything was just as he remembered it. The wallpaper. The crooked bookshelf. The couch with the tear in the middle cushion and floral Afghan from his grandmother draped over the back. And there, still in the center of the room, deep within that thick brown carpet. The blood stain from the night his father beat his mother to death. Her head bled out onto the floor while James stood in the corner crying. Her bloodshot eyes staring back at him. Telling him it was going to be okay.

Everything would be okay.

A tear fell down his cheek as he remembered that moment.

Cold blooded murder.

He remembered everything. The smell of his father's sweat and the scent of iron in the air from his mother's blood. Such pain and sadness made his knees feel weak. The pain was almost too much to bear.

"Hi Jimmy," a child's voice suddenly echoed from across the room.

James' head darted over. His eyes deceived him, yet there he was. His younger self sitting and watching the static filled television.

"Are you who I think you are?" James nervously replied, recognizing the striped, green shirt he used to love to wear.

"Dinner's almost ready," the boy said, "Mama made meatloaf tonight."

James looked around the room searching for any semblance of an explanation.

"What is this?" James asked as he stepped closer to the boy.

"It's your nightmare, isn't it?" the boy replied, continuing to stare into the television. "You need to tell mama where you go at night. She gets worried ya know."

"Mama's dead," James replied.

The television suddenly went off and the room became deathly quiet.

"But didn't you bring her back?" the boy replied, still staring ahead at the blank television set. "You did as you were told, didn't you?"

"I don't know what you're talking about."

"You've grown up and forgotten but I haven't. I'm still here Jimmy. Maybe you can come back and play sometime. I get so lonely by myself."

He slowly turned, revealing two black orbs for eyes staring back at him.

"They're hungry Jimmy…so very hungry," the boy uttered in a soft sinister tone.

James closed his eyes and backed away.

"Stop!" he yelled, feeling the panic draw through his veins.

By the time he opened his eyes, his younger self was gone and before him sat his mother, alone at the piano as if she had always been there, playing the entire time.

"Mama?"

"I waited for you to come home that night. I knew you would," she said giving him a saddened smile then took her eyes back to the worn ivory keys before her.

"Mama, are you okay?" James asked, seeing the blood on the side of her head.

"He can't hurt me anymore, he can't hurt you either," she softly spoke, as the melody rose.

A feeling drew itself up his spine like a hand reaching under his skin. The subtle tone of the keys mesmerizing and almost speaking for themselves.

"Something found you that night my son…at that old rotten plantation standing alone in the bedroom," her voice saddened, "and when you came home you brought it with you. Something that you've carried with you all these years. But I tell you now, you could have never saved me," she said.

James couldn't take his eyes away from the side of her head, watching the blood slowly drip down onto the keys.

"What did I do?" James asked, feeling a nauseating sickness rise within.

"There is a darkness that permeates the layer between this world and the other. It will find what it must to survive…and it found you. Oh, my boy, it found you," she said, staring up at him with tears welling up inside. "You must return to the dark light now. For it has chosen you and you must finish what you have begun…they are outside waiting for you, my son."

James felt the melody grow cold and more out of tune as his mind spun through its own madness. He watched as his mother played the final notes. Her eyes turned away and stared back down at her fingers as they drifted across the keys. Slowly they played. The melody, sour and completely out of tune. Her hands became gnarled and barely able to play. Her skin aged rapidly, cracking, and turning shades of purple. Eyes rolled back in her head.

"Mama!" James called out as the room began to fall apart. The walls shook and fell around him, revealing the dark light emanating from the cracked and broken floorboards.

He quickly turned and ran down the hallway towards the front door. Pieces of the ceiling fell overhead, knocking him into the wall. The pain shot through his side as he pushed himself back to his feet and ran as fast as he could…just like that night in the forest, with Tommy and Daniel at their backs. They ran like the wind. Never stopping, never looking back. And now he was running towards something else. Something far darker than he could ever imagine.

CHAPTER 29

Outside the front door, James found himself back on the edge of the chalk circle within the clearing of the birchwood forest. He struggled to catch his breath, trying to make sense of the moment as his childhood home had all but vanished and his mind slowly ripped into pieces from a nightmare in which there seemed to be no escape.

"Emma is that you?" he asked, seeing her stark green eyes staring back at him from the center of the circle.
"Scotty…Harold…are you really here?"

"Are you?" she replied in an unfamiliar tone.

He watched them with subtle trepidation, feeling black magic running through his veins as the memory of that fateful night so long ago encompassed the darkness around him.

How he stood here he did not know. He surmised whatever concoction Miss Lolita had created, allowed him to travel in ways he did not yet understand. A part of him wanted to scream; a part of him wanted to run. The journey was all too real, as seeing his friends again was a feeling that both warmed his heart and chilled his soul.

"Ya'll…it's me…Jimmy," James called out, as his toes rocked back and forth upon the edge of the chalk circle.

The group stood in silence and did not say a word, making him feel even more uncomfortable.

"They're waiting for you Jimmy," Scotty uttered in a low, sullen tone. His voice was not quite the same as James remembered. The subtle undertone of fear subdued the cheerful character he had remembered him to be.

"Who's waiting for me?" James replied.

"You can't hide anymore Jimmy," Emma said, "now come closer and help us."

James' body wavered on the edge of the circle as if he were standing on a cliff.

"What's going to happen to me?" he asked.

"Don't be afraid Jimmy," Harold said with a serious undertone. The nervous boy James had remembered was replaced with something else…someone else. There seemed to be nothing left of the boy he once knew.

"Harold is that really you?" James asked, "you seem different, you all seem different."

"You see what you need to see. Your eyes are no longer your own," Scotty replied.

"I never should have left without ya'll that night," James sadly stated, feeling a wave of guilt and regret.

"You didn't leave us, you're still here, aren't you?" Harold said.

"I suppose I am, aren't I. But what happens now?"

"Step into the circle and you shall see," Emma answered.

James hesitated, looking at the group as if they were both friends and strangers all the same.

Taking a step into the circle, James crossed over the barrier feeling an unseen force flow through his body. The tingle within his arms and legs reminded him he was still alive as this place felt more and more like death the further he stepped.

He approached Emma first. James watched as her green eyes swirled in darkness. He looked closer and felt something untoward rested within them.

"Emma, what happened to you?" James asked, "what happened to all of you?"

"It found us, just like it found you Jimmy," Harold replied.

"I never meant for anyone to get hurt," James' voice trembled, as the feeling of something evil upon them grew with each moment. "The forest was the only way we could escape. Tommy and Daniel were right behind us."

"But there was something else," Emma replied.

"You saw something that night," Scotty said.

"Something you didn't share," Harold added.

"Until we saw it for ourselves," Emma finished, staring him dead in the eyes.

"I didn't want to scare any of you. I didn't know."

"But you did," Emma stated with a coldness that made him feel both guilty and afraid.

"We need to start digging now," Scotty said, looking up at the sky. "It's getting late."

"What are you talking about?" James asked.

James could now see each held a shovel in their hands. He hadn't even noticed before but there they were as if they'd been there the whole time.

"The entrance is here," Scotty said pointing at his feet, directly within the circles center.

"What entrance?" James asked.

"The Sullen Ones dug until their hands bled," Emma uttered in a low painful tone.

"They awakened them with each pick and shovel pounding into the ground," Harold added.

"They were buried for so long. But they don't ever die," Scotty said.

The three began digging into the hard clay surface.

"Ya'll stop! Please, just stop," James begged.

The group did not listen, only continued digging.

"Are you gonna help or not? It's you, they are waiting for Jimmy. Not us," Scotty said.

James reached down, grabbing a fourth shovel laying before him. With each strike into the ground the earth seemed to shake beneath their feet.

"Are you sure about this?" James asked.

"Just dig," Harold replied.

The group dug for what felt like hours as if they were digging their own graves. Each shovel full of dirt was like a hole growing within his own chest. The pain, getting deeper and deeper, every moment he stood in this forsaken space.

"Are we close?" James asked.

"We're almost there," Scotty replied.

Another moment, and the sounds of shovels hitting a hard iron surface rang in James' ear.

"What is that?" he asked.

"The entrance to their world," Scotty replied.

James kneeled and wiped away the dirt upon the surface of a black iron door, no bigger than the size of a small child. Pressed within it, the outline of a cicada.

"Help me," Scotty said, grabbing a handle on one side.

James grabbed the other side, and with all his might, the two of them pulled open the door on its old rusty hinges.

"That smell!" James exclaimed, covering his nose.

The steep, narrow, stone stairwell spiraled into darkness. Its breadth was no wider than the span of a man's shoulders. Nothing could be seen beyond the first few steps.

"What if I don't want to go?" James' voice trembled as if he were once again, just a scared little boy.

"But you already have," Emma replied.

James stared into the darkness, seeing his life swim before his eyes; the memories of his wife and daughter…his friends and family…everything that he had ever lost, awaited somewhere within that endless abyss, spiraling below him.

"Guys, what if I can change things?" James said. "What if whatever is down there, there's a way. There's a way I can save you all."

"There is nothing to save anymore," Emma painfully uttered, "a nightmare cannot die Jimmy…and I have the most wonderful nightmares to share with you."

"Emma please!" James exclaimed as he stood up and grabbed her by the shoulders, staring into her dead eyes.

"Remember the lake? Remember how we all used to play together and sit on that dock for hours, until the stars came out and our parents were worried sick about us…but we didn't care because we had each other. We knew no matter what, everything was going to be okay, as long as we were together."

"You left us Jimmy," Emma's voice was soft and cold, "now you must finish what you started."

"Why me? I don't understand. Why did Tommy and I survive that night and it took the rest of you? Why didn't it take us too?"

The group was silent. Their eyes staring at James as if he were just a stranger.

"You're all so different. I can feel a piece of you missing. Each of you," James stated.

"We are, what you remember us to be," Scotty replied.

"But I can't lose ya'll again," James' voice trembled in sadness.

"You must go now," Emma said, in a soft sullen tone.

Reaching out, he pulled her close, but felt nothing but death upon him.

"I love you; I love you all."

CHAPTER 30

At the bottom of the spiral stairwell, James found himself alone within a large, cavernous void. The walls were man-made of earth and stone. The ceiling, held up with rudimentary beams and the entire structure appeared to be on the verge of collapse. The only light came from the sickly greenish hue rising from the massive stone monoliths circling the central space no more than fifty feet across. It's perimeter, mirroring the chalk circle above. As he stared upon it, a feeling he could not describe penetrated the deepest parts of his soul.

Do not go within. Do not enter its gaze.

But he could not resist. Like a moth to a flame, he had to go. The first step made him feel sick. The next step, even more so. Step by step, he made his way towards its gaze until he was close enough to reach out and touch it.

He couldn't remember the last time he had eaten, but suddenly the hunger grew ravenous as did the anger inside for everything that he had ever lost in this world. His mother, his daughter…his wife. He could feel all the broken pieces of himself rise at once and stare back at him as he stood just outside the stone circle.

There were thirteen pillars towering over him at least twenty feet high. Carved, faceless beings with no eyes and high cheekbones, all looking inwards towards a central point as if something unseen were there, drawing their attention.

He stepped closer, now within their gaze, and examined the monoliths in more detail. What at first looked like granite he could see was not stone at all. The stone imagery at the top of each pillar was merely a capstone to an otherwise machine-like edifice. There was nothing crude and organic about it, rather, precisely formed cylinders with a glass-like surface, polished to a mirror finish. Each pillar held a figure unto itself, containing a single entity illuminated by greenish flames emanating from within. The glow was both sickly and unnatural as it revealed the tall faceless beings he had seen as a child, suspended in a clear gelatinous liquid.

Their skin was hard to decipher. Not man and not lizard, yet something in-between. It was unlike anything he had ever seen. Their faces were smooth and ageless, a mirror image of the capstone themselves…thin with high cheekbones and eyes that should have been but were nothing but black voids peering out of soulless bodies.

Beneath each figure, a metallic plaque shimmered in the greenish glow permeating the space. Upon it was inscribed a symbol…the same strange hieroglyphic symbol as was written around the chalk circle…it was their names just as Miss Lolita had described from the book.

Cautiously, James reached out and pressed his hand upon its surface. The energy flowed through him like electricity, but this was not anything he'd ever felt before. Every emotion seemed to awaken at once and flow through his mind like a river funneling into a vast sea. An ocean that was ready to boil over and flood the world.

He took a deep breath trying to get ahold of his nerves as a low hum echoed within his mind, like an engine idling. It pulsed with every memory of his past. He could see them all as clear as day. Each moment, like a projector of his life. But within each image there was something else…something that wasn't supposed to be there…standing in the background, watching.

It was them.

He quickly pulled his hand away and took a step back. His vision came into focus, suddenly realizing their gaze had been upon him since he was boy. The feeling was overwhelming but shadowed by the task that stood before him.

"Karen!" James yelled out over the machine-like drone that grew with each passing second, alongside his own fear. He did not try to hide himself as he knew there was no disguising his presence. Whatever they were, they knew he was here. He was exactly where they wanted him to be.

Staring up at the enormous figures, he could sense each one looking back. They knew everything about him, he thought. They were watching. Awakening. A twisted perversion of man floating before him. Just as Miss Lolita had told him, these were the ones that came before. The ones that slumbered in the sour earth. Here they were, locked within a prison, eating off the souls of mankind as their servants fed them with all they desired. Each one, needing the taste of human flesh.

He took a step back, suddenly seeing the tips of the bones protruding from the ground, scattered everywhere like an ancient graveyard. Hundreds of lives were lost within this hellish void, but Karen could not be one of them. He wanted to run but would not leave without his beloved.

"Karen! Where is she!?" James yelled at the sedated beings floating within their capsules, knowing that somehow, they could hear his pain.

His voice, which should have echoed in the vast space died as soon as it left his lips. Claustrophobia and panic began to set in. Trapped, he thought. He was trapped within another realm; no human should be here.

"Give me my wife!" James screamed out, gathering all his strength as he walked to the center of the demon circle.

He could feel their thoughts and hear their voices; twisted, high-pitched tongues maligned with an evil that he had never imagined possible. Their dialect weaved within the machine-like drone, echoing throughout the cavern. They spoke to each other about him. They wanted him to know she was theirs…and so was he.

"Do you see now, my love?" Karen's voice rang out from the shadows, as she emerged from the darkness surrounding the circle, and stepped into the glow of its inner horizon.

James looked up in disbelief and just stared a moment, his eyes still adjusting to the odd hue permeating the cavern.

"Karen? Is that you?" he said, reaching out to hold her hand.

"We can be a family," she said placing her hand in his, "it's time to come home, James."

He could see the wounds upon her were re-opened and the injuries were as fresh as when he had sutured them. Deep bloody ravines that made him want to weep, covered her pale and naked body.

"What did they do to you?" James asked, reaching out, running his hand down her body.

She stared up at him with pure bliss, smiled and gently touched his cheek with her cold clammy hand.

"Can't you see?" she replied as if hypnotized.

"We need to leave now!" James exclaimed, grabbing her by the wrist.

She pulled away and laughed at him. A laugh like he'd never heard before.

"What do ya know, doctor?" she said, revealing a Cajun dialect upon her tongue, "or should I call you pastor," she added with a hideous cackle.

He stood silently observing her every move, every crease on her body and every hair on her head. Then he could see it...her eyes. They weren't blue. They weren't anything at all but a lack of color and humanity within.

"You come into hell to see da Devil, and yet did ya not know that da Devil be in you," she said, moving closer, nearly kissing his lips. Her body smelled not of a familiar perfume but rather earth and rain mixed with the scent of blood. His senses went numb as he realized he was not standing with his wife at all.

"Who are you?" James asked, as his body felt suddenly numb.

"In da other place, you see your true self, do ya not?" she replied.

Her riddles were torturous as James felt as though he were held above a large abyss, waiting at any moment to fall further into nothingness.

"Where's my wife?" he asked.

"She is here, do you not see?" the woman responded calmly, as she ran her hands down her body…Karen's body. "Dis skin feels like silk. Untouched. Fresh. I have possessed her for some time now. She was easy to please. Promises of children dead and gone," she said reaching out trying to touch his cheek.

"You're her…you're Nastassia, the witch," James murmured under his breath, grabbing the sides of his head as if he were about to lose his mind.

"Some say witch, some do not say at all. I be da one who take you back. No longer your own, but can be sometin' more. Sometin' greater than what you have sacrificed. Even Samuel Black cannot see da true self he has become for he is but a spirit wandering dis place much like you. My servant, forever trapped seeking to bring back his daughter and da very wife he sacrificed…just as you shall be doctor. Yet you are more than he could ever be. You listen well, ever since you were a boy. The children you had brought pleased da masters well," she laughed. "It was your mother you wished to save as a child was it not? Da Devil whispering in your ear as you stood alone in dat bedroom staring out over da western fields."

James thought back upon that night, standing alone in the upstairs bedroom. The boogeyman standing in the corner, showing him things beyond his darkest imagination.

“It was Samuel Black who brought you here, just as you have brought others. Your mother is here with us, you can see her in da dark lights now if you look closely Jimmy…You can see them all.”

"You're crazy!" James exclaimed, staring into her dead eyes.

She just smiled a cold sinister grin and laughed as she raised her hands up to the sky.

"Da last sacrifice here, masta! I give you your forsaken soul!" she called out. Her voice was like fire upon James' ears as he began to feel faint.

A low rumbling grew below him. The walls began to shake. A deep moaning rose from within the pillars. The creatures within suddenly came to life, their bodies, twitching as a small glowing orb grew within the center of the circle.

She called out in foreign tongues. With each syllable it felt like a knife was drug across his mind. Her voice turning into familiar inflections of his past.

Tommy and Daniel.

"Gonna gut you like a pig boy!" she exclaimed as she laughed, seeming to enjoy his torment. Emma’s, Scotty’s and Harold’s voices then emerged simultaneously. "Jimmy! Save us, please!" Their screams were captured within her vocal cords as if they were held inside her belly.

"Please make it stop!" James begged.

"You want to awaken and be at home? Rewind time to have your wife and daughter back in your arms?" the witch asked, giving James a contemptuous sneer.

"I would give anything…anything!"

"I'm afraid you already have, doctor," she replied, plunging a cold steel blade into his heart with a sly grin. "Tell Miss Lolita her debt is now paid."

James gasped for air, grabbing the blade and falling to his knees. He looked up in despair as Nastassia stared down upon him with a sinister smile.

"It was Lila who tried to save your beloved, whispering in her ear. My precious little niece trapped within da rag doll, warning your wife to stay away from da forest. But I must thank you, for da night you threw it away was da night I was free to take your wife with me into da forest. Her possessed soul no longer stopped by that child whose heart could never be blackened."

"That's impossible…Miss Lolita, told me what the doll was…it was Samuel Black…it was…" he felt faint, unable to speak anymore.

"Nothing be what it seem and Miss Lolita, played her part well, burning da last remnants of da one thing saving your wife. Lila's soul taken back upon da wings of da cicada. Never to be meddlesome here again."

James stared into her eyes feeling his world tearing itself apart.

"It was never your wife who was da final sacrifice, t'was always you…since you were just a boy, it has been you. But your soul was not ready. Da pain had not yet turned you from God. Had not destroyed your faith and taken your only loved ones. A soul, not yet ripe, is a soul not ready for sacrifice. But now that your beloved is ours, you have nothing else to lose and da final demon can be appeased with your forsaken soul…da gateway will be opened!"

James could see the creatures pounding inside the translucent pillars, their bodies writhing to break free. Long skinny limbs draped in rotten flesh. High pitched screams pierced his mind as he fought to hold on to his sanity.

"Miss Lolita stands within da room overlooking da western fields speaking da final translation from da missing pages you have brought back. Your body lays there, but your soul is here upon da precipice of worlds, ready to be taken into da shadows…a journey into da darkest afterlife is upon you." Nastassia's voice screamed out like a banshee as the glow within the center of the circle became something nearly indescribable. A dark green, glowing orb expanded the space like a child being born unto its mother. Foreign twisted tongues sliced James' mind as he peered through the light into another place…another realm where man did not belong, and the faceless ones walked again.

CHAPTER 31

The morning air drew its breath across James' tired expression as he opened his eyes and grabbed his chest. Gasping for air, he took a deep breath and calmed his nerves, still feeling the pierce of the cold steel blade in his chest.

Rolling over, he drew his palm across the empty sheets trying to remember how he had gotten to bed. A funny taste in his mouth ignited a wakeful panic, remembering Miss Lolita and he conversating down in the living room. After that, it was all a blur. The empty feeling rose within as his eyes fluttered, taking in the sunlight scattered across the white linens. He felt the oddity of the morning as memories weaved themselves in and out of his consciousness like burning flames.

Stepping out of bed onto the cold hardwood floor, he gathered his thoughts, dismissing everything he felt was off about his surroundings and the forgotten moments that lingered beneath the surface. Everything except the ornately framed painting that hung on the wall as if it had always been there.

A familiar-looking portrait of Karen and Elizabeth reminded him of the family he had lost. But he had not put this here and had no memory of it ever being commissioned. There was a familiarity within the canvas, though. The way the two were posed and the way the eyes followed him no matter where he moved. He had seen this before but could not remember where.

Stepping closer, he looked at the small black stain forming in the bottom right corner. It looked like an oil spot. The longer he stared the more it seemed to grow and move up towards the girls' faces. He scratched at it but could feel it was a part of the painting itself. The moment was all together unsettling as a sense of deja vu came over him…at least until the smell of coffee drew his attention elsewhere.

James headed downstairs and into the kitchen. He stood confused, staring at the coffee pot which was now full, percolating its last few drops. He knew he hadn't set any timer, yet here it was as fresh as could be. Picking up the pot he held it with curiosity, staring at it as if it were some kind of magic.

"Morning, babe," Karen's voice rang out.

James dropped the pot of coffee and it burst onto the tile floor, sending hot brown liquid and shards of broken glass everywhere.

"Oh god," Karen added, running over to grab a towel. "I'm so sorry. I didn't mean to scare you."

"Karen?" James asked, looking down at her with a startled apprehension.

"A little jumpy this morning, are we?" she asked, getting up and giving him a kiss on the cheek. "Don't worry, I'll make another pot."

James stood dumbfounded as she threw the dirty rag in the sink and grabbed the coffee tin from the cupboard.

"What are you…?" James' voice trailed off as he didn't know what to say.

"What am I what?" Karen replied with a little chuckle. "Ya know you're acting very strange this morning. Did you have trouble sleeping again?

"I'm okay…I just need to sit down I think," he replied taking a seat at the small kitchen table by the window. Outside was overcast but beautiful. The wind was blowing the field grass in large sways as the sound of cicadas rose off in the distance.

"What month is it?" James asked, as Karen gave him an odd look.

"Honey, this summer heat must be really getting to you."

"It's summer still?" he replied.

She gave him a curious glare as she knelt and swept up the broken glass.

"Here, let me help," James offered, jumping up and grabbing a rag to sop up the dirty brown liquid.

He hesitated to speak. His throat felt dry as if he hadn't had water in a week. "Karen…where have you been?" he asked, finally regaining a bit of composer.

"What are you talking about?" she replied.

"I mean where have you been? You've been gone for almost a week now. Haven't you?"

She just looked at him and smiled. "I don't know what you've been doing but maybe we should go see someone. I think maybe your dosage on those pills is off or something."

"I stopped taking the pills, remember?"

"Well, something's off because you're talking like a crazy person." The sound of her voice was both comforting and maddening as James stared dumbfounded.

"Maybe I just need a moment," he said, getting up and heading to the sink.

Karen stepped beside him and emptied the shards of broken glass into the garbage as he wrung out the dirty rag. She stood just inches away and he could smell the familiar scent of her lavender perfume. Leaning in, he placed a hand on her cheek as if it were the first time and kissed her soft pursed lips. Pulling back, a smile suddenly appeared that he hadn't felt in a long time.

"You're in a good mood," she said.

"The best," James replied.

"Well, why don't you go get Lizzy and tell her to come get some breakfast."

"I'm sorry, what?"

"Your daughter whose been sleeping all morning. Can't hardly get her out of that room anymore. She's practically a teenager."

James slowly backed away and headed out of the kitchen trying to hide the look of disbelief on his face.

"Where's her room?" James asked, as Karen just laughed and shook her head.

"Ha ha, very funny," she replied.

Each step up the stairs James felt his heart flutter. *What was happening?*

He quickly picked up the pace down the hallway. The door at the end, now painted pink, stood slightly ajar. This place…it wasn't the same, but he felt a familiar fear to say the least, like he'd stood here before, staring at that door as if his own death lay upon the other side.

Cracking open the door, James looked down upon Elizabeth playing with something. Her back facing him. He couldn't see her face, but he could smell her… like sunlight captured in a raindrop upon a rose pedal…it was her. It was his angel, sitting alone by the window overlooking the western fields. A dark feeling suddenly rose inside of him.

"Lizzy?" James said as he knelt on the ground.

Slowly she turned and gave him a big smile.

"Hi Daddy," she said and turned back, going about playing.

"Baby, Daddy missed you so much. So, so much," he said with tears falling down his face.

"I missed you too Daddy," she playfully replied.

"Come here, please. Let me see you," he said holding out his hands. As she turned, he could see the familiar rag doll. It gave him a jolt as he grabbed his chest.

"What's wrong, Daddy?"

"Oh nothing…just startled me that's all.

"Lila isn't scary, Daddy," she said with a little laugh.

"Lila, huh? Where did you get that?" James asked.

"I found her outside by the forest," she replied.

"What are you two doing in here?" Karen's voice suddenly chimed in.

"Just playing mommy," Elizabeth muttered and went back to her doll.

James silently stared back not understanding what was happening. He rubbed his head, feeling a headache rising as his eyes began to water.

"Listen, you two. Daddy's gonna go take a quick drive and when I get back, we're gonna have the best night. Sound good?"

"Okay, but dinner's gonna be special tonight so don't be late," Karen replied with a strange smile.

James smiled back and gave them both a kiss as he headed out of the room trying to run from the rising consternation growing from within.

***

Parking the car on Charlton Street, James sat a moment wondering how any of this was even possible. The memories were vague, yet painfully vivid as he could still feel the blade in his chest. The vision of the demon circle slipping back into the depths of his subconscious.

Passing under the wrought iron gate and down the back alley, he could see the boarded-up windows and front door of what was once 'The Black Palmetto'. He stood a moment retracing his steps, wondering if this was the right place. It had to be…except there was nothing here but his own vacant memories of something that should have been.

A corner of the window was exposed from the graffiti covered plywood and James knelt to get a better look through the dusty window. Inside was nothing but empty shelves and cobwebs. The place looked as though it had been abandoned for years. Not a soul in sight. Just the ghosts of the past, looking out at the stranger passing by and a familiar voice whispering in his ear.

"Promise me you'll come back, doc. Promise me wherever this takes you, you'll find your way home."

He didn't understand how this was possible but somehow didn't even care. He had his wife and daughter back. Whatever else happened didn't matter. Nothing mattered anymore…he was home.

***

That evening, Karen set the table as James finished up the steaks on the grill. He could hardly contain the bliss he felt, watching his daughter play in the field. The sun setting over the tops of the trees gave the place a glow that warmed his heart. It was almost normal…like he'd always dreamt.

"Come on, Lizzy! Time to eat," James called out.

Back inside, James headed through the kitchen where a pot of baked beans simmered, and collard greens lay resting in an iron skillet.

Things always tasted better in that old skillet.

One of the only things he had left of his mother, besides her bible…and moonlight sonata. But those memories seemed as distant as ever, washed away by some magic surrounding him. A wonderful feeling, he hoped, would never go away.

"They're ready!" James yelled out as he set the steaks down on the dining room table. At first, he didn't notice but then stopped and counted the place settings.

"Karen?!" he called out, looking around the table at the thirteen wine glasses. "Are we having a party?"

James stood a moment not sure what he was looking at. The place settings around the long dining room table, coupled by beautiful crystal wine glasses and a rather large spherical crystal centerpiece were surprising to say the least.

He didn't remember Karen saying anything about guests nor did he remember her having any place settings of this sort at all. He looked closer at the centerpiece, seeing his own warped reflection staring back at him. Within it, the faintest glimmer of a greenish glow.

"I was saving that for a special occasion," Karen proudly stated as she entered the room holding a couple bottles of red wine.

"Karen, what is this?" James asked, standing dumbfounded beside the table.

"They're all so excited to meet you, James," Karen replied continuing to arrange and situate pieces on the table.

"Who's excited?" he asked, feeling a strange churning in his stomach.

The smile on her face changed to an almost seductive glare as she ran her hands down his body.

"I've been waiting for this for so long. Just relax…you'll see."

"I didn't make enough food, Karen. I didn't know we were having a party. There's ten other people coming over?"

"Thirteen and this isn't for us. This is just for them," she replied, "they haven't eaten in such a long time."

"What are you talking about? Are you feeling okay?" James asked, now very worried about the situation, suddenly realizing the steaks he had just grilled and set on the table were completely raw.

"Of course, I am. Of course. I've never felt better in my life," she said as a knock on the door echoed out from the foyer.

"Oh, I think they're here!" Karen exclaimed, "go greet them. They have already waited for so long."

James stood nervous and confused staring down at the table. The subtle greenish glow within the crystal center piece was growing brighter with every passing second, beating to the sound of his own heart.

The knock came again. Only this time louder.

Bang bang bang!

It rang through the house.

James headed towards the front with a sudden fear growing in his gut. A sickness all too familiar.

The banging continued. Harder now.

"I'm coming!" James yelled out.

Opening the door, he was greeted not by dinner guests but rather by the sheriff and a mob of deputies behind him.

"Hello, Sheriff, uhh…are you here for the dinner party?" James asked.

"The what?" the sheriff replied giving him a strange glare.

"My wife. She said we were having guests over."

The sheriff stood silent a moment staring at him as if he were crazy.

"Doctor James Elba," the sheriff firmly and official stated, "you are under arrest for the murder of Karen Elba."

He grabbed James' wrist and slapped handcuffs on him.

"You have the right to remain silent. You have the right to an attorney, if you cannot afford an attorney, one will be appointed to you..."

"Wait, wait, wait! What the hell are you doing?!" James yelled out struggling to release his wrists from the cuffs. "You've got everything wrong. My wife is here. She's in the kitchen making dinner. My daughter, she's out back."

"Your daughter?" the sheriff replied with a questionable glare.

"Yes, my daughter. We're having a dinner party!" James exclaimed, feeling a dizziness come upon him.

"I bet you are," the sheriff replied as the other deputies barged into the home.

"Hey, you can't go in there!" James yelled out. "Sheriff what is this? Karen! Karen, come out here and see the sheriff so he doesn't think I'm crazy!"

The sheriff just stood silently holding James in the doorway as the deputies entered.

"Sheriff, you need to come take a look at this," the voice of one of the deputies rang out from the dining room.

The sheriff grabbed James and pulled him inside, walking into the dining room where the smell became almost unbearable. The stench of rotted meat permeated every corner of the room.

"Oh my God," another deputy replied as they watched the maggots crawl out of the rotted meat. A feast was prepared; meat, fruits, cheeses and wine were spread out in an elaborate setting. All rotted and covered in mold, flies, and maggots.

"What the hell is this?" the Sheriff asked as he jerked James' wrists towards him.

But James could hardly think to answer. His eyes, shocked and mesmerized, were drawn to the place settings. Each glass overflowed with red wine. Each plate piled high with rotted meat.

"You're one sick son of a bitch…" the sheriff exclaimed but couldn't even finish his sentence as he looked as though he were about to vomit.

"I didn't kill my wife!" James yelled out, struggling to break free.

"One thing you did tell the truth about. Your wife was out in those woods like you said. But you should have dug that grave a little deeper, doctor."

James felt his blood run cold as his knees buckled and pulse raced, feeling as though he were going to have a panic attack. The sheriff and two deputies held him up and took him away.

Passing through the foyer James' heart skipped a beat seeing the dust and cobwebs covering nearly every square inch. He couldn't believe his eyes. Dirt and debris littered the space as if it had not been touched in decades.

Outside, he sat in the back of the squad car looking out at the old plantation. There was no fresh paint and no renovations or landscaping to be seen. It was as if he had never done a thing. Everything was still as rotted as the day they had moved in.

James closed his eyes, praying for something to save him. To wake him up from this nightmare and have his wife back in his arms, with the fresh air on his face and a hard day's work on his back. But there was nothing but the sound of the deputies scouring the lot and talking amongst themselves.

He could see the stretcher and body bag being placed into the ambulance. It was her. It was his Karen. The feeling in his stomach told him exactly what this was as the sheriff looked back at him with a cold calculated hatred. His eyes asked the question, how could you do it? He didn't know but as the sound of moonlight sonata rose in his mind, suddenly he realized he did. His mother's face stared back at him within the reflection of smudged glass and in an instant, he remembered everything.

CHAPTER 32

Clouds gathered above the old brick edifice standing resolute in the middle of the country. There was not a soul in sight to hear the screams or bear witness to the lost lives confined inside.

James walked the grounds aimlessly on a daily basis as he was allotted one hour to feel the sun on his face and wind upon his back. Shadyvale had become his home. His life was now more a dream than a nightmare as the routine sedated his emotions.

Kneeling, he dug his hands into the dark brown soil in the garden where he had taken ownership of tending its many vegetables growing under the hot Georgia sun. He watered, he planted, he spoke to them all as if they were his friends…the only friends he had left. Memories were like a distant dream, each day slipping into some forgotten place where he kept them locked away.

"Times up, James," the sound of an orderly's voice rose from behind him. He hated the thought of leaving his garden, but he had gotten used to it. The routine was his savior. No more surprises, no more pain. He had lost everything and now there was nothing left.

James got up, brushed his knees off and headed back towards the old brick building. The structure itself, he thought of as a watchful elder as the two shared secrets and passed the time together. Just like himself, he knew this building was more than it seemed.

Back inside, the smells of the cafeteria wafted past his nose…meatloaf day, he thought. The other patients moved about in their own worlds. He wasn't friends with anyone really. Everyone seemed to keep to themselves, and he preferred it that way. He had all the company he needed in his garden and the rest of his time he was left to his own thoughts. He even started a journal and wrote in the evenings when the mood struck him.

"Doctor Edwards is waiting for you, James," the orderly said, gesturing for him to hang a left and head towards the open door just down the hall.

His first days here, he was harsh and disobedient to the staff, but he had nothing left in him to fight or argue about. It had been almost a year within this place, and everything became as it was. Nothing more than a waking dream…everything seemed almost normal.

James sat down and made himself comfortable in the cracked black leather chair he had gotten used to sitting in every Wednesday at noon. Across from him an old man with thinning white hair and small round spectacles perched on the end of his nose, sat and waited. He watched James with a pensive apprehension, a notepad in his lap and a pen at the ready.

"Good to see you, James," Doctor Edwards said with a genuine smile and thick Louisiana drawl as he pushed a cup of water across the coffee table.

"Thank you," he replied, taking a sip before resting his hands upon his standard issued slacks and giving his button-down white shirt a quick tug to pull out the wrinkles. "When did you get the glasses?"

"Excuse me?" Doctor Edwards asked.

"The glasses…I don't remember you having them the first time we met," James replied.

"The first time?"

"Yes, when I had brought my wife in to see you. You had your practice in Savannah then. Remember?"

Doctor Edwards just nodded and jotted down a few notes.

"As we have spoken about this before, your wife has never been a patient of mine and I've never had a practice in Savannah."

"Sure, she has…you must just not remember," James replied.

"Of course. That must be it," he said and continued writing a few more notes. "So, you look good." Giving James a quick once over. "How you feeling today?"

"I feel fine," James replied.

"And how's the garden?"

"Garden is doing well. We've got some carrots and peas almost ready to harvest."

"Carrots and peas. Very good. My grandmother used to grow the same…that and okra. Nothin' like a little fried okra if ya know what I mean," Doctor Edwards said with a big smile, digressing for a moment. "Well now, let's get to the point here. I think we've made a lot of progress over these past months wouldn't you say?"

James nodded silently.

"Let's talk about your sleep first. How is that going?"

"I sleep fine, doctor. Thank you."

Doctor Edwards nodded, jotting a note down on his pad.

"How about the voices?"

“What about them?”

“Do you still hear your daughter and wife? Your friends? Do they speak to you from the other side as you say?”

James avoided the question and just looked around the room as if searching for an answer.

Doctor Edwards shifted in his seat getting comfortable as his eyes grew more serious.

"Well, I’m happy to see through our hypnosis sessions you’ve been able to remember some things…and you've been writing and drawing in the evenings quite a bit, I hear."

"Yes, I guess I have."

Doctor Edwards held up a picture…a crude sketch of a monolithic circle. "A demon circle, I believe you've called it. An ancient stone circle buried within the forest behind your home."

James looked across at the drawing and then away as if unable to see his own nightmare. "Not stone."

"Excuse me?" Doctor Edwards inquired.

"Stone. It wasn't stone. It was…” James thought a moment, “glass-like. Almost like something you'd see in a lab…and inside was THEM…the demons."

Doctor Edwards jotted down a few notes.

"And you think these demons…thirteen of them as you have stated, were…" he looked down, flipping back through some notes, "guardians of an ancient portal which contained a special light. The dark light, as you called it. And what exactly was this light?"

"I couldn't really tell you…death perhaps. But more than that. More than you or I could ever comprehend," James replied seeming somewhat shaken by the thought.

"And please clarify again where this portal was supposed to take you?"

"Where is heaven, where is hell? You tell me," he replied, rubbing his head as he felt a headache growing.

Doctor Edwards flipped a page in his notes and shifted in his seat as if also shifting his train of thought.

"We've never gotten past the root of what happened when you were a boy. As a child your mother was killed at the hands of your father, was she not?"

James nodded.

"A cold-blooded murder in which you believed could be reversed by unlocking the power of these ancient monoliths. That's why you killed your friends in those woods that night, isn't it? Their bodies were recently found not far from where you had buried your wife."

James shifted in his seat, looking very uncomfortable.

"Just like you killed Tommy Clayton…a patient here in this very facility and one of the kids that was with you that night."

James looked up. His eyes, stone cold. "I didn't kill anyone."

"And those pills that you took. They were never for panic attacks. I have your medical records right here James." He flipped the page in his manila folder, running his finger down the margin. "Right here…Chlorpromazine. One of the earliest known treatments for schizophrenia, and as you've stated, you had stopped taking your dosage just before your daughter's death, only weeks before you moved back to Savannah with your wife. That's when you began to remember your past. A past which you so clearly had pushed into the darkest corners of your mind."

James shifted in his seat unable to look Doctor Edwards in the eye.

"When you were just a boy the doctors knew something was wrong with you after your mother's death. They helped you hide the memories for all those years with the medication. Hide the pain and dark visions you had. It was never panic attacks, James. It was your mind waking up to a reality that you had created and one that you had experienced firsthand as a child trying to cope with the reality of things you had absolutely no control over. But once you stopped taking the pills, the memories came back. Everything came back, didn't it?"

James took a moment before speaking as if his own thoughts betrayed him. "The blood stain on the floor had been there for a week. She had been beaten to death by my father. Over what I couldn't tell you…and moonlight sonata…that's the last thing I remember her playing," James softly replied as he stared down at his pants, hearing the subtle melody rising in his ear.

"I can only imagine the impact that had on you."

James just looked away.

“I saw the Devil that night.” James' hand began to tremble as he whispered under his breath. "Tick tack Samuel Black is back."

"These words still haunt you, don't they? Because they were real to you, weren't they, James? They still are."

"Nothing can hurt me anymore," James replied as Doctor Edwards looked at his notes, briefly jotting an additional thought.

"It's important that we face these facts, James. You had stopped taking your medication and the old memories came trickling back, which is how you remembered there was a way to save your daughter. The same way you tried to save your mother all those years ago. You came back home to finish what you had started. All in hopes of bringing to life some legend that could open a portal to an afterlife in which they were still alive.”

“I wouldn’t hurt anyone. Don’t you believe me?”

“I believe you can’t see the difference between reality and a fantasy in which you have concocted to deal with the loss of your loved ones. You're sick James, and whatever anger your father had within him is also in you. Your life has been nothing but torment and pain. An illusion in which you've perpetrated to accept a lie."

James seemed angry but before he could reply, looked up as if he had just heard something. The subtle inflection of Miss Lolita’s Cajun accent echoing through his mind. Her words, like a distant prayer. Unintelligible phrases repeating like a broken record.

“What is it, James?” Doctor Edwards inquired.

"I thought I heard something, a woman’s voice."

“Whose?” Doctor Edwards asked jotting down a note.

"I don't know, maybe nothing, I just…" James' voice trailed off as he stared at the small red candle sitting in the middle of the table. The flame, dancing in the dim lighting of the office, created strange shadows on the wall.

There is one way in and one way out. Find da way by feelin' your heart. Remember da living. Remember da breath in your lungs. Da kiss of your wife...da whisper of your daughter's words.

"Has that always been there?" James asked, reaching out and holding his hand over the flame.

"Yes James, yes it has," Doctor Edwards replied with concern as he watched him move his hand closer.

"There is one way in and one way out," he muttered under his breath as he watched the flame turn a strange shade of green. His palm, nearly touching its tip.

"James, please!" Doctor Edwards exclaimed.

He quickly withdrew his hand, staring at the candle with growing trepidation as he rocked back and forth unable to comprehend his own thoughts. The distant voice of Miss Lolita still echoing inside his head. "What did you give me?"

Doctor Edwards glanced down at the cup of water on the coffee table, "It's only water James. What do you think I would have given you?" Doctor Edwards replied.

James licked his lips tasting something odd, as he drew a suspicious gaze at the cup with the small chip in the rim.

"You're fine James, it's just nerves…everyone you have ever loved is gone. It's time you start healing and accepting a truth you've been hiding from all these years…it's time to let go."

James shifted in his seat and drew his hand to his chest, feeling a sharp pain suddenly rise within. Despite the feeling, his gaze was calm as he turned and looked out the window. The sun hung low on the horizon creating a beautiful blanket across the well-manicured grounds. He was lost in the moment. Some distant place far away from that room. Far away from anything that could ever harm him. Elizabeth was there. So was Karen…his friends…his mother. The subtle melody of moonlight sonata whispering its secrets as it guided him to the dark light where they all waited for him to come home.

For da path to da demon circle is death itself, and only within death shall you find your salvation.

ACKNOWLEDGMENTS

You know who you are…you have been a part of my life through the ups and downs. Through thick and thin. Those that I see often and those I haven't seen in years. You're all a part of my heart and I thank you for your love and support.

www.harryjvaughn3.com

Printed in the USA
CPSIA information can be obtained
at www.ICGtesting.com
LVHW041127061124
795842LV00016B/295/J

9 798987 287514